CODE NAME:
WILLIAM TELL

CODE NAME: WILLIAM TELL

COLONEL DON WILSON

WestBow Press

Copyright © 2013 Donald Lee Wilson.

All rights reserved. No part of this book may be used or reproduced by any means, graphic, electronic, or mechanical, including photocopying, recording, taping or by any information storage retrieval system without the written permission of the publisher except in the case of brief quotations embodied in critical articles and reviews.

WestBow Press books may be ordered through booksellers or by contacting:

WestBow Press
A Division of Thomas Nelson
1663 Liberty Drive
Bloomington, IN 47403
www.westbowpress.com
1-(866) 928-1240

This story is fiction. It is emphasized that the agencies and events depicted herein which are characterized as having a security classification and as being unknown to the public are also fiction. Any similarity to actual people, entities or events is purely coincidental.

Because of the dynamic nature of the Internet, any web addresses or links contained in this book may have changed since publication and may no longer be valid. The views expressed in this work are solely those of the author and do not necessarily reflect the views of the publisher, and the publisher hereby disclaims any responsibility for them.

Certain stock imagery © Thinkstock.
Any people depicted in stock imagery provided by Thinkstock are models, and such images are being used for illustrative purposes only.

ISBN: 978-1-4497-8409-6 (e)
ISBN: 978-1-4497-8410-2 (sc)
ISBN: 978-1-4497-8411-9 (hc)

Library of Congress Control Number: 2013902294

Printed in the United States of America

WestBow Press rev. date: 2/7/2013

DEDICATION

To the most distinguished citizens of all, better men than I: the many brave young men and women who sacrificed their lives on foreign soil because their elected countrymen, older and wiser, for whatever reasons, asked them to lay their lives on the line. To honor old friends, no longer with us, I have used some of their names in this story because each in their own way had a hand in shaping my life.

ACKNOWLEDGMENTS

I wish to thank to my daughter Jan and my son Mark for their advice. A special appreciation and thanks to Peggi Shapiro for her review and editing of my very rough draft.

TABLE OF CONTENTS

	Introduction xi
CHAPTER 1	The Quest 1
CHAPTER 2	The Discovery 7
CHAPTER 3	The Boy. 21
CHAPTER 4	The Opportunity 37
CHAPTER 5	The Man 59
CHAPTER 6	The Leader 79
CHAPTER 7	The Recruitment 99
CHAPTER 8	The Test 129
CHAPTER 9	The Reunion 167
CHAPTER 10	The Revelation 189
CHAPTER 11	The Baton Pass 195
CHAPTER 12	The Bite. 213
CHAPTER 13	The Deception 237

INTRODUCTION

Looking back over an army career spanning twenty-three years and two wars, I feel justified in espousing a particular point of view concerning the use of armed force. Just as one does not enter into a parlor game without the prospect of winning and, if forced by family pressure to play anyway, participates lethargically without inspiration, performing below one's potential, so the soldier's efforts under similar conditions lack the absolutely vital ingredients of dedication and commitment. A commanding officer once told his men prior to a proficiency test that, without enthusiasm for one's work, a soldier is dead from the neck up and soon will be dead—*period*. Therefore, in the service we emphasize and promote *esprit de corps*. That, coupled with just cause and good leadership, *is* an awesome combination.

Few leaders choose a military career because they love a good fight. I have never known a leader who didn't regret the tragic loss of blood. I've seen commanders shedding tears over casualty reports. Through the centuries, the profession of arms has attracted the brilliant, the loyal, the stupid and the egotistical looking for a measure of immortality by carving a niche in history through generalship. And there are those few who are simply intrigued, fascinated and, yes, stimulated by the study of armed conflict. History tells us of men with the warrior's spirit, like Stonewall Jackson who just before a major engagement turned to an aide and described his feelings at the moment as "delicious excitement." General Robert E. Lee is said to have commented when surveying the bloody battle's aftermath, "It is well that war is so horrible—we would grow too fond of it." In today's America, there are few responsible men who would fight for the glory of it. The professional soldiers I have known and lived among consider themselves a deterrent to war and regard the military as an honorable vocation, a way to serve their country which offers constant challenge, agreeing with an acknowledged warrior, General George S. Patton: "Compared to war all other forms of human endeavor pale to insignificance." However, while the study of war is both fascinating and necessary for preparedness, the actual fighting should be avoided where possible. But, if unavoidable, have "Plan B" ready. And we must never forget that wars have started because *one* side believed the *other* would not fight, or it would be a conflict of short duration. Wars always cost more than expected.

The history of our nation's military shines with stirring chapters in the application of righteous might to preserve and protect our Constitution and the American way of life. Conversely, there were occasions when the best intentions to continue this noble heritage were perverted and overtaken by disaster, with its bitter aftermath of disillusion. As a people, we are not very good students of history; we keep repeating the same mistakes at dreadful cost. Fresh in the memory of our adult population, but being ignored in our schools, is our recent involvement in Southeast Asia. Here, in effect, we patted the South Vietnamese on the head and said, "Step aside, boy. We'll handle this." The end result recalls to mind a seemingly-appropriate epitaph by Rudyard Kipling, "Here lies an Englishman who tried to hustle the east."

Evil exists to provide the necessary conflict in this life which shapes the character of us all, as individuals and as nations. In this respect, life is a game, a test. Looking back over our recent conflicts, one may fairly ask, "Why is being good so costly?" Let it not be written that in human and economic terms America was bankrupted by war, or that America was destroyed by leaders who, by engaging in war, became an evil in themselves by seeking power or a loftier place in history.

Considering that since the end of World War II we have been dealing with an unreasonable and dogged adversary who plays by only one rule, the end justifies the means, any rational person would have to agree that over the years our government has done a reasonable job countering communist aggression—Vietnam being the exception. We have done this by side-stepping the United Nation's superpower's veto. There is no last word in diplomacy; we have done well when we have exercised it and poorly when we have not. Despite a public clamoring for the president to do something, many times the precise thing to do is nothing. Over the years, effective covert action has stalled Soviet aggression and contributed in no small way to force Soviet thinking inward to solve growing domestic problems and to finally begin restructuring their society and warming the chill of the Cold War.

Deeply engrained in the American character is to treat winners as heroes and defeats as events to be forgotten. Yes, we have been playing to win. Our experience in Vietnam told the world we would not make it easy to spread Soviet communism over the globe. As we consider the radical change from the Soviet Union to the Russian Federation, our winning the many covert battles has won a better future, even for citizens of Russia. However, because of our suspicion of Russian leadership and the threat of radical Islamic terrorism, the free world must fight fire with fire without fanfare and in such a way that it will appear we are doing nothing.

Although fictitious, this is a story of *possible* continuing efforts which could have secretly aided in bringing us to where we are today in our relations with Russia. It also suggests that we continue to search for effective ways beyond the usual to prevent escalation of incidents into a general conflagration; or *worse*, to prevent our standing by and watching the evil in this world close in around us until it's too late and we stand alone. It is not a question of *if* we are to play the game we *must*, so let us play to win by using our imaginations to conceive methods which achieve our noble goals with the least expenditure of our precious human and material resources. This is a story of leaders who tried to do just that. This is a story of winners.

CHAPTER 1

THE QUEST

THE POST-KOREAN WAR ERA

The heavy responsibility of office had taken its toll. A haggard and exhausted president old before his time was grateful for this short period of peace and quiet resulting from a cancelled appointment. These were trying times and, thoughtfully, his aides allowed him this hour to relax. Furthermore, he asked not to be disturbed. Frustrated and demoralized by Soviet pressures around the world, and sick at heart over the lost opportunity in Hungary and his failure to take decisive action which might have prevented the construction of the infamous Berlin wall, he search for answers. Making a conscious effort to release his tensions, he rose from his desk, walked to the far end of the oval office and seated himself before the warmth of the fire. Gazing into the flames, he imagined that over the millennia man has learned to control fire for his own advancement, but unless something was done soon, the entire world could be ablaze. He'd feel gratified, in spite of his mistakes in office, if by the end of his term he could make amends somehow; if from his missed opportunities could be born something innovative in foreign affairs; at the very least a step forward. Leaning back in his chair and closing his eyes he allowed his imagination free rein.

Heretofore, aggression anywhere in the world had been appeased, ignored or met with force; whatever these responses, they were wrong. Historically, appeasement meant eventual war, and looking the other away was worse than taking the wrong action; at least our allies could say we tried. War, on the other hand, was the result of failure; failure of diplomacy, failure of intelligence, failure to prepare, failure to act decisively when appropriate action became apparent, failure to call a bluff and failure to prevent open conflict which resulted in the decimation of a generation of high-principled young men. *Failure,* oh how the president loathed that word!

Why is it we do the right thing only as a last resort? Since our birth as a nation, our diplomats have not been as successful as our soldiers—we win wars but keep losing the peace. Why does delay change what is unthinkable to what is necessary?

Foreign policy is the president's realm, with the advice and consent of congress. Ah, there's the predicament. If the president consults congress, surely lengthy debate will ensue, prohibiting timely action, causing the loss of the initiative. Is not the conduct of war the responsibility of the president, as commander-in-chief? Although never formally declared a war by congress, is not the Cold War a de facto war? Have not the Soviets accomplished the same objectives in the Cold War which have been achieved hitherto by armed conflict? Cannot the Cold War be waged literally under the cloak of foreign policy? By their actions, the Soviets have already answered that question in the affirmative.

The world situation has become one of stubborn confrontation and perilous brinksmanship in which a miscalculation can initiate a mindless holocaust. However, successful resistance on an underground level to Soviet methods of subversion might not lead to war, if their failures appear to be accidental or just bad luck, but instead force negotiation and dialog as the only acceptable alternative. Once lines of communication are opened, understanding will follow and eventually effective incentives can be offered the Soviets which will be clearly in the interests of both societies. Thus, the veil of suspicion which clouds minds and creativity on both sides will, in time, fall away and we can deal with one another as partners in peace. That is the distant objective but, as the first step, we must divert the Soviets away from the destructive course of world domination and toward the conference table by quiet and effective resistance to their current methods and to eliminate, if need be, the old guard purveyors of subversion as they ply their trade against unsuspecting target countries.

As commander-in-chief, he was the most powerful man in the world yet, ironically, he felt helpless—impotent. He headed the armed forces, a sleeping giant whose very existence prevented conventional warfare, but commitment of which, in a cold war situation, could ignite a hot war. The "big stick" should be brandished as a symbol of our national resolve and held in readiness, but clearly it is too big for commitment in the Cold War.

The president thought, "So, what next?" and propped his feet on a footstool, his mind settling on what he considered a key point. To the consternation of every previous president, government had grown unwieldy. Well-intentioned campaign promises are hard to keep once the president becomes mired in the bureaucratic bogs, political bargaining, compromise, special interests, and highly stacked in-boxes of civil servants who avoid close scrutiny by not rocking the boat. Yes, we have a civil service system which perpetuates mediocrity, where no one is responsible, so a very visible president often becomes the scapegoat. Our bureaucracy is partly to blame for our citizen's suspicion of big government. If the president is to be blamed, let it be for something he has done or for actions over which he has direct control. Good government is that which has the confidence of the people, no less than a good president is a man the people respect.

The very nature of democratic government makes it impossible to seize the moment and act quickly. An astute business tycoon would never burden himself with such bulk and organizational layering—grossly inefficient. The more he pondered, the more a separation seemed in order, a separation of a few talented people from the cumbersome herd. It would be a smaller stick which can be used in a limited preventive role at the discretion of the commander-in-chief unilaterally. He began thinking, not in terms of government entities, but in terms of people. He imagined two boxers in the ring; a lightweight and a heavyweight—in this case a *super*heavyweight. The lightweight was trim and fit with lightning-fast reflexes, moving in and out throwing quick blows and avoiding punches. Like the intransigent bureaucracy, the heavyweight was slow, flatfooted, an easy target, unable to strike quickly or react with the speed required to seize and hold the initiative. The analogy was clear. A lightweight was needed whose manager would be the President of the United States. But who would be his trainer—the Central Intelligence Agency? The CIA is and has been a known adversary to our enemies; its covert operations provide vital intelligence. Could he use the CIA to shield, unknowingly, a covert effort by the highest authority—the president?

The president felt like a carpenter with no hammer; he knew what must be done but hadn't the tool to do it. What would be the instrument of such a covert effort? He'd need a small, tightly-controlled organization which, once unleashed, would have the freedom to act independently, quickly and decisively on mission-type orders to thwart enemy plans globally. Its effectiveness would depend upon timely action and anonymity. Yes, he would manage this lightweight strategy deciding who and where his boxer would fight. The president's new foreign policy tool would need military skills and resources, but, to be efficient, he must coordinate its intended action with other government entities without their knowing of its existence. These would be State Department, the CIA, and the FBI; and there's the congress, which cannot be left totally in the dark. How could he get all these organizations into the act and remain clandestine and effective? There was another problem: how to convince congress to appropriate funds to run such an organization and still maintain secrecy. Nothing remains a secret in Washington for very long, but this will have to; so the circle of secrecy will have to be very small and remain so—no empire building. Funding, hmm, a glimmer of light flashed in the president's mind; if the tool was small enough, could he bury it in a larger toolbox which was already funded? The more he thrashed out the possibilities, the stronger his sense of being close to the answer. It all came back to people; operatives had to be America's best, neither "gung ho" nor ultraconservative, but courageous and responsible men who, within the framework of the mission, could do that which was necessary, including the taking of lives.

In a nutshell, there was consensus among his advisers that in every recent brushfire there had been a critical point, early in the game, when timely action against communist operatives could have defused the situation before it reached crisis proportions. The covert nature of communists' activity worldwide seemed to be an open invitation to challenge them on their own underground level. Communist agents had to remain in the target country stirring up trouble to further their sinister ends. To stop them in their tracks would require precise intelligence, short reaction time, specific missions, quality people with freedom of action, a swift strike, a quick withdrawal and secrecy. The keys to future long term success of this foreign policy tool would be minimum exposure to the enemy, in terms of time and numbers, with maximum negative impact on his subversive operations.

The president opened his eyes and, dropping his feet to the floor, sat erect in his chair. Now he knew what he wanted, it was time to forge the tool. Although he held high hopes for his brainchild, he had no idea that of all the hours of all the days of his turbulent presidency, this hour, granted him by providence, would prove the most productive and would have a far-reaching impact on his own and future presidencies.

CHAPTER 2

THE DISCOVERY

TWENTY-FIVE YEARS LATER.

My name is Coward, a less than appropriate name for a professional soldier, but a name to which in my twenty-three years of active duty, let me hasten to point out, I failed to exemplify. I made it easier on my friends, encouraging the use of a nickname acquired in my youth while a cub reporter: "Scoop." Drafted into the army by World War II, I stayed on and made a career of it. Since my retirement, I've made a name for myself by writing military history from the perspective of the common soldier, tipping the balance more toward individuals than do conventional historians. Therefore, my readers have come to call me the soldier's historian. Unfortunately, some of our past leaders have leaned toward the notion that the military is a weapon, tin soldiers with all the heart, intelligence and sensitivity of smoking pistols to be sent into the meat grinder of war without compunction. By design, my rendition of history, while accurate, is directed toward changing that attitude. So this is my slant, my angle, my literary niche. In this light, as this story unfolds, my particular interest in it will become clear.

While engaged in research on the recent military history of the United States, for what I hoped would be the monumental work of my life, my effort was sidetracked at first and then virtually halted by an overpowering fascination with the exploits of one rather elusive individual. He kept appearing and reappearing with distracting frequency and having an incredible influence on events. I came to regard this soldier with admiration, a heroic figure who personified the very spirit of the citizen-soldier-patriot. This feeling grew stronger with each new exposure in my research. Busy as I was, I didn't welcome this distraction, and it soon became disturbingly clear that this hindrance had grown into an obsession and my work would proceed no further along the lines I intended until light was cast upon this shadowy figure. Acceding to the inevitable and seeing my kind of angle in the story, I dropped everything to focus my research solely on this mysterious man.

I first stumbled upon him while studying reports from Military Assistance Advisory Groups (MAAG) in several different countries. These reports referred to trouble, problem areas and threats to the mission which worried the writer at the time. However, expecting a solution to be detailed in subsequent reports, it just didn't happen. These concerns seemed to evaporate without any action by the advisors. Alerted to this sort of situation, I began to look for similar instances in other countries, and the same pattern emerged: serious concerns over matters jeopardizing the mission and then the unexplained lack of follow-up action, as if there hadn't been a problem in the first place. One reporting officer went so far as to confess that he was mystified by it all, but connected an accidental meeting of an old friend—a fellow officer on a short visit—with the time period when the threat ceased to exist.

I dismissed the coincidence as pretty thin, until it happened again in reports from an altogether different country and the same name was mentioned as the mystery officer by another of his acquaintances. When this avenue of approach in my studies dried up, I didn't know if my man had ceased to function or if the advisor's reports had been purged of all references to him. Despite having nothing further to go on, somehow I couldn't help suspecting the latter.

Because the concept of a mystery man was so unlike the army, I was puzzled. For one thing, I could not imagine one man being involved in so many hazardous operations over so many years and still surviving. Secondly, his motivation was suspect; no ordinary soldier (although he would prove far from ordinary) would exhibit the drive and resourcefulness for so long a period without some kind of lucrative pay-off. Yet, he was no mercenary, but on the active rolls of the United States Army. Thirdly, the circumstances of each episode uncovered indicated that here was a man who could and did, on occasion, operate independently of any known military organization or entity, apparently on his own initiative. Despite appearances, the effect of his actions, with rare exceptions, was in the best interests of the army and the country.

Attempting to dig deeper, I had to be content with accounts of conventional military historians, who wrote more of missions, organizations and tactics than of individuals, and that which was inferred by reading between the lines of official reports, individual accounts and personal journals. Becoming vaguely familiar with the man from the few oblique references to him, I began to recognize situations which were typical of his style despite the fact no name was mentioned. I began seeing him everywhere in my searching; or was I hallucinating or simply making more of this apparition than I should? This had to stop. My value as a historian, an impartial observer and interpreter of events, had become diminished by my obsession with this phantom. I would not do my work properly until I was satisfied that the whole story of this fascinating man had been written. What I had learned up to this point was only an appetizer, and the trail was fast disappearing back into military secrecy. If I could examine his service record for only a few minutes, perhaps my suspicions would be confirmed—it was worth a try.

That night I scarcely slept. Questions kept occurring to me in my slumber, and I committed them to paper lest I lose them in my sleep. Eventually, the morning dawned as gray and foggy as my picture of the man I sought. Driving to the Pentagon by way of the George Washington Parkway, I felt like a child on a treasure hunt, filled with the excitement of curiosity and anticipation but, nonetheless, a man with a mission.

When I arrived at the office of the Adjutant General, a receptionist handed me a form to fill out. Paperwork! After filling in the boxes pertaining to me and my work, I came to the heart of the form; "Specific Action Requested." I printed carefully: Request the service record of Bowman, Hunter William. Rank: Unknown (Officer); Branch: Armor. Signing in the box provided, I returned the form to the receptionist. She looked at the form carefully and then at me.

"Mr. Coward, haven't I read one of your history books in school?" Scanning her name tag, I replied,

"That's quite possible, Miss Hines. Two of my textbooks are used by school districts around the country."

"I thought so. I'm honored to meet you. I give you credit for my interest in history. You really make it come alive for me."

"Well thank you, I appreciate the compliment." Examining the form once again, her face twisted a little as she apologized,

"I'm sorry, sir, but personnel records are not included in the Freedom of Information Act because of the personal nature of their content. That's to protect the privacy of the individual and to keep requests such as yours at bay." She sensed my disappointment and added quickly,

"But that's no help to you, is it? This has happened before, so I think you can get what you need by contacting the Office of Military History or perhaps Armor Branch. They have access to personnel records and might be able to answer any specific questions you have."

"Thank you. I had hoped to have more information before prevailing on my friendship with the Chief of Military History, but I'll start there."

I arranged an appointment with my long-time friend and colleague Brigadier General Albert J. Betancourt, the army's historian and collaborator on one of my books. He had held that post longer than any of his predecessors, and, although I often wondered why, I was thankful for the long-term association which made my job easier. And, come to think of it, I never heard him complain about being stuck in what most officers consider a backwater of army assignments. But this too was part of the amazing story which was about to unfold.

Awaiting the appointment date, I studied the pieces of the puzzle, trying to clarify my picture of Bowman. But it was no use. The trail was lost, and there was only one way to pick it up again; I hoped the army would cooperate. When phoning for the appointment, I told the General who it was I wanted to discuss, but he showed no surprise and made no promises. In fact, he seemed a bit tight-lipped on the matter.

I arrived on time and was greeted in the outer office by General Betancourt himself,

"Good morning, Scoop. Good to see again."

"You're looking very fit, Court."

"Thank you and congratulations on your new book. That has to be the best account of Operation CAT CLAW I've read. Good work."

"Coming from you, Court, that's a real compliment, but without your help, the story could not have been told. You're appropriately mentioned in the acknowledgements, of course, as my technical advisor."

"So I noticed, my friend. Thank you again." The General turned to his secretary; "Hold all my calls, please, Miss Bishop."

He ushered me into his private office, locking the door behind us, and asked me to sit down. He seemed a bit uncomfortable as he poured a cup of coffee, seemingly to give himself time to formulate his next words. Then, with startling abruptness, he looked me straight in the eye and asked,

"Now, what do you know about Hunter Bowman?" It appeared that small talk was unnecessary, and the General assumed a very business-like attitude as he repeated accusingly, "What do you *know* about Hunter Bowman?" Dismayed by his tone, I replied,

"Well, Court, only enough to be intrigued and fascinated. I understand a Top Secret clearance does not entitle me access to Top Secret material unless I have a legitimate need to know. Hunter Bowman has been named twice in routine reports, classified Confidential, in connection with certain critical situations. That, together with the unexplained remedies of these adverse situations, caused me to suspect the whole story had been buried. Furthermore, he, or someone very much like him, keeps resurfacing again and again in my research at critical points, taking action having a significant bearing on the outcome of a given situation. The official record offers no explanation. But my study of him has been impeded by his virtual disappearance; he seems to have been covered by a cloak of secrecy."

There was a long silence. The General reached for a tissue and began to clean his glasses, absorbed in deliberate thought. He had no authority to release the Top Secret information Scoop sought, and yet refusal would only reveal he was on the right track. He could only hope that being refused, Scoop would let the matter drop. Finally,

"Scoop, knowing the reason for your request, I agreed to see you out of respect for your work and our years of friendship. I also knew when you called I could not help you this time. Believe me when I say there's nothing more I am permitted to say on the subject. Is there anything else?"

"No sir, only Bowman. Court, what you've just done, of course, has only sharpened my curiosity. You've already told me enough to prove he is not a figment of my imagination—he does exist and my suspicions are confirmed. If you persist in shutting me out, I must tell you for the sake of our friendship that I will continue to dig—tunnel through until I see him in the light of truth."

"Scoop, leave it alone! You've no idea what you're tampering with—abandon this search before you do something we'll *both* be sorry for."

"Court, you of all people know what it means to a writer to track a lead, to realize you're onto something and closing in. As an historian you must know what you're asking me to do. If I dropped this investigation now, it will gnaw at my gut forever."

"I'm sorry Scoop, but it must end here." I thought for a moment, hesitating to use my trump card, but if there was no other way,

"General, you and I both know that as the army's historian you deal in just that, history, and you would not classify anything so highly. Therefore, you leave me no choice but to go over your head to the Chief of Staff and the Secretary of the Army."

"That's just what I mean about a move we'll both regret."

"Why?"

"Because neither of those men have a need to know and, as such, know nothing about Bowman's activities."

"Good grief, then who does, if not the top two men in the army?"

"Stop, I've said too much already."

"Sir, believe me, I'm obsessed with this man. Even if I'm not permitted to write a word, I still must know. If you won't tell me, one way or another he will be the subject of my continued research and investigation!" The General held up his hands to shut me off.

"Scoop, we're through for today. Give me a few days—I need to talk to some people; but promise me you'll keep a lid on it until I get back to you."

"A few days, fair enough."

"Mind you, I can promise nothing, and if it goes against you, I'll expect you to obey a direct order to find another… obsession."

I left the Pentagon and returned to what I hoped would be the peace of my townhouse, but in view of the General's stance on the subject of Bowman, only more questions were being generated. Learning that Bowman's activities were unknown to both the Chief of Staff and the Secretary of the Army was puzzling indeed. How could this be? What possible duty could take him so far afield of the army chain of command? Another thing disturbed me; if the top civilian and military men in the army knew nothing, why would General Betancourt, who was not in the chain of command, know anything at all about it? Aside from secrecy, this seemed very strange. I reexamined my notes, desperate to find a clue in light of my new but meager information. What was going on? What had I blindly stumbled upon? I began to smell the faint odor of conspiracy which might account for the top brass being out of the picture, if in fact they were not involved. No questions were being answered, but new ones kept coming at an alarming rate. What had I gotten myself into? For the first time I felt a sense of danger and foreboding. Nevertheless, the desire to know Hunter William Bowman overrode any other emotion, and I decided to see it through to whatever its conclusion.

On a dark and stormy evening two days and two sleepless nights later, the phone rang, shattering the peace and serenity of my study and, in my emotional state, startled me,

I recognized General Betancourt's voice. "Scoop, I'm coming to pick you up in twenty minutes. Be ready."

My mind began buzzing with expectancy. Where would he be taking me in this weather and at this late hour? There were more questions, but I shook them off in deference to a trusted friendship with a colleague I respected and admired. The staff car arrived and I joined the General in the back seat.

"Good evening, Scoop. Sorry to call so late, but you wanted to go over my head and my boss told me he'd see you tonight. I'm not at liberty to discuss this situation at the moment, so let's let it go at that." With that, we accelerated down the dark, wet street with no announced destination.

"Are you working on anything pressing, Scoop?"

"No sir, I haven't been able to work at all since we last talked."

As we traveled, I realized I had been expecting to go to the Pentagon, so I was mildly surprised when we turned across the Potomac into the city, and flabbergasted when we arrived at 1600 Pennsylvania Avenue and the gate guard let us pass. Why were we at the White House? The General answered the silent question which rested between us without my asking it, as we drove up the driveway,

"You see, your probing has struck a nerve at the very top." The president's military aide met us at the door and informed us,

"The president is ill and has asked that you join him upstairs at his bedside. Follow me please." As we entered the room, the president was in bed talking to a visitor, a full Admiral, but as we entered he smiled and spoke most amicably,

"Here they are now. Good evening, Court. And this must be my favorite historian…how are you, Mr. Coward?"

"I'm a little overwhelmed, Mr. President." He grinned and with a knowing look said, "Yes, I imagine you are." He reached for a book on his nightstand, "I'm nearly finished with your latest book. Reading your work I sometimes forget its history; you are quite the storyteller."

"Thank you, Mr. President."

"Sorry about being laid up; nothing contagious, just the doctor's orders. You have already met our illustrious Chairman of the Joint Chiefs, I believe."

"Yes Sir. I've had the pleasure. How are you Admiral?" The Admiral merely nodded; it was plain to see this was the president's interview.

"Mr. Coward—I'm told you like to be called Scoop?"

"All my friends do, and I'd be privileged to count you a friend, sir."

"Well said, and thank you, Scoop. I asked you here tonight to clear up any doubts about the ultimate authority in this situation you've unearthed." His eyes sparkled as his choice of words accentuated the mystery. "I suppose it was to be expected sooner or later, but we cannot assume that others suspect anything, nevertheless, I must turn off the tap here and now to prevent you from unwittingly leaking damaging information. You really amaze me, Scoop. We have taken great pains to conceal Bowman's activities. His name could not have been mentioned enough in official reports to conclude he was anyone out of the ordinary. How is it you attached so much importance to him?"

"I owe my interest to a prodigious volume of research, sir. You're right, he wasn't mentioned often by name, but I've come to know him well enough to recognize his imprint on certain situations, his style and the kind of situation he would be called upon to tackle. I feel a look at his past assignments would confirm my suspicions. That's why I asked for the General's help." The president shook his head as he spoke,

"Excellent detective work, I must say, but as the old saw goes, I've got good news and bad news for you. The good news is this: your eminence as a first-rate historian and your security clearance have influenced me to permit you access to TOP SECRET information which, and here's the bad news, I'm sorry to tell you it is not for publication now or for the foreseeable future, and hopefully not in your lifetime. You see, we know that if we were to stonewall this story, a professional of your caliber might discover enough on your own to publish something on Bowman. That would be a serious blow to national security. So here's the deal. In exchange for your solemn oath not to reveal what you know, witnessed by those in this room, I agree to satisfy your professional curiosity. I can do no more."

"I understand, Mr. President, and I'll take that oath."

"Good, you are at the top of your field, a specialist in your brand of personalized military history. I would not expect another to stumble upon this situation in the manner you did, but just in case, perhaps we should remove from the record even a few more references to Bowman. We would appreciate your help, Scoop, in pinpointing exactly where in your research your suspicions began."

"I'd be happy to help, sir."

"Splendid, I have authorized General Betancourt to brief you fully at the proper place and time. As a writer, I suppose you'll want to take notes, but they must be left with the General for safekeeping. They will be returned to you if and when the information is declassified." He paused, looking around the room at each of us. "Now, if you gentlemen will excuse me, it's time I heeded my doctor's advice and got some rest. Goodnight, and thanks for obliging me at this late hour."

General Betancourt had asked me to be in his office the next morning at 1030 hours. I arrived on time. Closing and locking the door to his private office he began speaking immediately,

"It's hard to know where to begin. The secret professional life of Hunter William Bowman is the stuff of legends, privy only to a few responsible men with a need to know. I dare say that someday when his story can be told, his name will shine in the schoolrooms and libraries of our country as few other heroes. However, his saga must include a second man, the dark side of a tale of good and evil, a sinister adversary so removed from human decency he can be labeled amoral and vicious, an unleashed Lucifer. But I'm getting ahead of my story. Scoop, I don't use the word legendary frivolously, but to give you a hint of what you've got ahold of here, I'll tell you something astounding, even to me. Bowman is the only man in our nation's history to wear an Oak Leaf Cluster on his Congressional Medal of Honor."

"Two?" I had a mental picture of twin medals hanging from a blue star spangled ribbons around the neck of a faceless Bowman.

"Yes, Scoop. Do you realize that makes him the greatest hero in our history, but his countrymen, the general public and the school kids of our nation, have never heard of him?"

"Incredible. But why is this fact a secret, Court?"

"If we are to continue this conversation, I must ask you to come this way." I followed Him across the office to a closet. He opened the door and twisted the hanger rod backwards; the entire closet interior swung inward revealing a short passageway to another heavier door. He opened it by inserting a special security access card into a slot in the wall, activating a face scanner, to reveal a large interior conference room with heavy drapery all around and a long table seating twelve. The General closed the big door behind us and motioned me to be seated at the conference table.

"I know what you must be thinking, Scoop." anticipated the General. "Why would the Chief of Military History need an elaborate secure room? Am I right?"

"Exactly, Court." I replied with what must have been a puzzled look.

"The answer will become apparent as we move along, but I must say that my personal burden of secrecy is lightened somewhat by being able to share it with someone outside the privy circle, which by the way, you are about to enter. However, your burden will be perhaps heavier because you, as a writer, will be unable to repeat what you know to anyone. You are the last link in the chain of secrecy. And knowing you as I do, you'll not be the weakest."

"I'm fully aware of that responsibility, sir."

"Good. I don't have much time so I'll keep this first session brief. But here, at least, we can talk freely. As you know, the Congressional Medal of Honor (CMH) is accompanied by a citation detailing the act for which the medal was awarded. His first award is public knowledge, but it is vitally important to our national security to keep the details of the second from our adversaries. Even so, the president did not want to overlook the deed. You see, the second CMH was presented to Bowman while he was working for a super-secret joint services organization attached directly to the Chairman of the Joint Chiefs of Staff, called MOPS."

"Mops?"

"Yes, Scoop; that's an acronym for Military Operatives to Prevent Subversion."

"That strikes me as a paradox; violent political action."

"Well, it is, and it has to be. It takes a very special soldier to acquit himself well in circumstances where political considerations are paramount. We discovered through bitter experience the devastating effect on moral that letting politicians dabble in war has on professional soldiers schooled in its efficient prosecution. A soldier cannot be asked to lay down his life with no prospect of winning unless in direct defense of home and family. So MOPS was designed and created to perform political services of a military nature with the least expenditure in lives and money. It eventually proved to be the best solution to the hitherto knotty problems of unorthodox political action and worldwide terrorism. The concept, as it turned out, became an efficient team of highly professional political and military experts operating only beyond our borders and only at the discretion of the President. Thereby, unknown to most, a great number of messy situations were cleaned up by using MOPS—pun intended."

"Intriguing, but where does Bowman come into the picture?"

"He was recruited a while after receiving his first CMH, about 1964; MOPS was just two years old at the time. We were aware that winning the CMH is sometimes a matter of circumstance and luck, but indeed, his subsequent service record was impressive. Bill Bowman was blessed with an important quality. One didn't need to know him long to realize he was a man to be trusted. There was no phony façade to cast suspicion on his motives. Bill was Bill—he'd rather die than violate a trust. Because MOPS operations required a boldness of action in a relatively short time-frame, his ability to gain quickly one's confidence made him indispensable.

"MOPS' planning staff, though small, had one expert each, recruited from the State Department, CIA, FBI, Army, Navy and Air Force. MOPS' action arm was tailored to each mission; a task team, and Bowman became one of our four Task Team Commanders (TTC). One of our planning staff, noting Bowman's full name, gave him the code name WILLIAM TELL and dubbed his missions as OPERATIONS ARROW, ARROW II, ARROW III...and so on."

Looking at his watch, the General apologized for cutting my orientation short and told me we'd resume the briefing after his trip. I told him I'd like to learn more details about Bowman, man and boy, his family background and schooling.

"The best person to help you there is Colonel Matthew Fleming, Chief of Armor Branch and Bowman's best friend and colleague for many years. I'll arrange for you two to get together. A word of caution, however; their friendship notwithstanding, Colonel Fleming knows nothing of MOPS, so stick to the personal stuff. Call me in a week's time and I'll have a complete briefing set up for you covering the past twenty-five years, including some of WILLIAM TELL's more interesting missions."

CHAPTER 3

THE BOY

The sign over the door read, Chief, Armor Branch, and in the doorway stood a tall slender Colonel, smiling. I extended my hand. "Colonel Fleming, my name is Coward. It's good of you to see me, sir. General Betancourt said you might be able to help me with a pet project I'm working on."

"Of course, having studied your work, Mr. Coward, I can see that Bill Bowman might be just your kind of subject."

"Let's drop the formality; my friends call me Scoop."

"OK, Scoop. The General told me to roll out the red carpet and, since you're properly cleared, I can cooperate fully. Won't you come in?"

"Thank you, sir. I feel at home already."

"I can't think of a better topic over which to become better acquainted than Bill Bowman. Believe me it warms the heart of this old 'tanker' to recall the years of our friendship. I've been reminiscing constantly since the General's call, and it has served to remind me what a genuine pleasure our association has been.

You see, in my eyes Bill is a man who didn't just grow older but grew up, matured from a raw kid into the finest, most unselfish man I've ever known."

"That's high praise indeed; no warts at all?"

"Oh, he made mistakes to be sure and big ones too. No, don't think for a moment he wasn't human. It's his very humanity that made him such a fine man. Bill is the best friend I have in this world. We entered the service together and for a while our careers paralleled. We used to sit and talk for hours at a time. We confided to each other our innermost feelings, like brothers. I know as much about his boyhood as if I'd lived it with him."

"Could we begin with what you know of his early life?"

"Sure. Bill had an unusual childhood. In 1931, as an infant 'navy brat,' he was taken abroad by his parents. For the first six years of his life, he traveled to Japan, China and the Philippines before returning to San Diego, California. Later, his vague memories would make him feel at home during his duties in the Far East. For the next four years, until the Japanese attack on Pearl Harbor, he was raised near naval bases in San Diego and Alameda. Since his father knew no better way, he chose not to raise a boy, but to build a man the navy way, applying the principles of basic military training to raising his son—strict discipline. As a result, Bill grew up with great respect for his parents and the military service, and developed a self-discipline and patience rare in a lad of his age; attributes some adults never acquire. Bill learned and enjoyed living within clearly marked boundaries of behavior.

"Bill later viewed the army as a mere extension of home and was comfortable with the structured life where he could focus his attention and see tangible results. An expensive college education seemed out of reach to Bill because all his life, his parents, whose attitudes were shaped by the 'great depression,' had harped on the careful management of their finances. Bill simply chose, what to him, was an attractive way to get ahead without burdening his parents."

"That brings another question to mind, Colonel. Why would a 'navy brat' choose the army?"

"When I asked Bill about that he told me there were long gaps in his relationship with his father because of frequent sea duty that had caused some friction between them. Each time his father returned he found Bill bigger physically, and more independent, used to having his own way and budgeting his own time. In his father's absence, Bill was always earning money somehow: delivering prescriptions for a drug store, mowing lawns and at one point working two newspaper routes. Hence, his father's attempts to reestablish his strict control created discorded, resentment and friction. Bill understood the conflict and, looking to the future, vowed there would be none between himself and the son he hoped to have one day, so the service which seemed to offer the least family separation was the army. Bill's experience taught him that the greatest gift a father could give his children was time together.

"But Bill wasn't much of a student, which was a great disappointment to his father. After trying with limited success to motivate Bill to improve scholastically, his father, in frustration, resorted to belittling him, which had a lasting and detrimental influence on the teenager's fragile self-esteem. You see, Bill's vision for the future was a career in the service; whatever the service wanted him to do, he reasoned, they would train him to do. So what was all this fuss over better grades in subjects in which he had no interest? He simply wanted to graduate from high school so he could get started with his new life."

"Understanding all this, Colonel, was he some kind of dunce academically?

"On the contrary, given the interest, he pursued the subject with the fervor of a true scholar. To better understand Bill's academic motivation, you should know about his war room."

"Did you say *War Room?*"

"Yes, you heard me right; a war room that would be the envy of any news service of the day. Bill became so wrapped up in the conduct of WWII that his teachers were helpless to compete for his time. Shortly after Pearl Harbor, Bill converted a basement alcove into a virtual war room in which he spent most of his spare hours. At any given time, you could get a current briefing on the progress of the war, in any of its far flung theaters of operation. In those years, the National Geographic Society published quality maps of the theaters of war: China-Burma-India (CBI), The Southwest Pacific, Central Pacific, North Africa and Mediterranean, and European Theater of Operation (ETO). He posted his maps daily according to radio and newspaper reports. Each defeat and victory was faithfully recorded, marked with miniature flag pins of all the warring powers."

"World War II was total war, at home and abroad. On the 'home front' mothers and wives hung a blue star in the window for each son, daughter or husband in the service; these were changed to gold for those killed in action. The irritations and inconveniences of rationed gasoline, food and clothing were accepted as doing one's part for the war effort. People listened attentively to their radios; during a broadcast it was considered bad manners to carry on a conversation. Families gathered nightly to hear their favorite commentator with the latest war 'communiques.' Patriotism ran so high that movie audiences rose to their feet at the sight of Old Glory on the screen. They applauded President Roosevelt (pronounced Rose-velt) when he appeared in a newsreel. Periodic scrap metal, newspaper and rubber collection drives became routine in every neighborhood. This was the patriotic atmosphere in which young Bill grew up.

"Bill's mother belonged to the Book of the Month Club and, of course, books about the war were very popular. By the time he read one, he eagerly awaited the arrival of the next selection. Many were written by eminent war correspondents of the day,

Edward R. Murrow, Richard Tregaskis, Quentin Reynolds and Ernie Pyle. Near the end and after the war he read with interest and a passion he could not muster for schoolwork, the accounts of the great leaders of the war including Winston Churchill's five volume history of WWII. At the greatest moment of our history as a nation, when all our citizens collectively rolled up their sleeves and struggled for total victory over a universally hated enemy, this impressionable boy had seen the best of examples indelibly etched in his conscious and subconscious mind; the sacrifices and triumphs of the greatest nation on earth in its finest hour. Bill's deep insight into WWII taught him lessons never to be forgotten and was prolog to the rest of his very active life in the service of his country.

"Young Bill had only two real interests in school; history and geography. This was primarily due to one teacher who had a gift for teaching young people the relevance of events in a colorful and interesting way. Had all his teachers been as talented, Bill's scholastic record may have been a different story, but here is why I bring up Miss Holt. During the study of the Declaration of Independence, he was made to understand the full meaning of the framer's pledge, '…our lives, our fortunes, and our sacred honor.' As a service man he could pledge no less.

"Still, he won no laurels in school, and his dad's degrading comments and jokes only made matters worse. Bill's shaky self-esteem was further jolted by another unfortunate incident, which could have devastated the boy had it not been for his fixation on a service career. One day at school, he was just beginning to enjoy his lunch hour when his English teacher, another antagonist for whom his only quality work had been book reports on subjects of his own choosing, called him into a small office, sat him down and without explanation proceeded to administer a written examination. Few questions pertained to the subject of English and Bill became so irritated that he answered the many true-false and multiple-choice questions without first reading them. Later, he caught a glimpse of the graded test on the teacher's desk and couldn't help chuckling over the high score. However, he was unaware he had taken an I.Q. test which, although invalid, showed him to have below average intelligence. Attitudes toward him changed overnight and his teachers, counselor and parents gave up on him. So, the pressure was off, but he didn't know why until he saw his high school transcript; there it was: I.Q. 93."

The Colonel leaned back in his chair, took a deep breath, stretching as he did, and clasping his hands behind his head, continued. "To this high school graduate the road ahead was clear. Despite considerable self-doubt, he made his way to the local army recruiter and humbly, with hat in hand so to speak, expressed hope that he was good enough to get in. It was peacetime, 1949, between wars, and the recruiters latched on to any warm body who showed a willingness to listen. Bill wanted to be a paratrooper and draw that hazardous duty pay he'd heard about. After signing the papers, Bill was sent to the main recruiting station in San Francisco, the big city, and the army paid his way.

"The adventure had begun. He was given government meal tickets, set up in a hotel for the night and instructed to return at 0800 for his physical and preliminary written examinations. Bill, to his surprise, breezed through it all. It was on the train to Fort Ord, California, that I met Bill Bowman. During our processing, I had seen him, but we had not spoken until we were seated together on the train. I must admit that he and I were different kinds of people, and at first I didn't think we'd hit it off. I was cocky, looking at the world as if it owed me something and proud of my lofty high-school grades. Bill was the opposite; introverted, humble, sure that he'd have to work hard for whatever he got. But the longer I knew him, the better I liked him. Eventually, he came out of his shell but never lost his deep sense of purpose. He had a depth of character I was unable to fathom at the time. His growth in confidence during the next few years would be a joy to witness. The army was Bill's natural habitat."

I could see warmth in Colonel Flemings face and manner reflecting an obvious affection and admiration for Bill Bowman. It was clear that Colonel Fleming deeply appreciated the change in his own attitudes, brought about by knowing Bill so early in their careers. The Colonel continued his story.

"Our first days at Ford Ord were hectic and fast paced, learning to respond to orders instantly without question and taking batteries of examinations so the army could determine individually, our aptitudes—what on earth we were good for. Bill and I found it both stimulating and fun. At the end of a long day of processing, we were waiting to march back to our company barracks when our leather-faced Sergeant commanded, 'At ease! Now listen up you recruits!' One-hundred-and-seventy-two burr-heads turned toward the veteran NONCOM. 'The following named recruits front and center: Atkins, Clark, Fleming and Bowman.' Gesturing to a spot immediately in front of him, he bellowed, 'Right here, on the double! The rest of you, fall-in company formation, over there!' Then turning to the puzzled four of us, he said, 'Stand at ease. The processing officer wants to talk to you four. Can you find your way back to the company?' We nodded assent.

'What? I didn't *hear* you!'

'Yes, Sergeant!' we replied at an acceptable decibel level.

'OK, report to your barracks when you finish here. He then marched the company off, leaving us standing there. Bill wondered how he could have screwed up and was lost in thought when, suddenly, Clark sounded off, 'Attention!' A Captain stood on the porch, 'At ease, men; follow me.' He led us into his office and sat us down. He began looking at some file folders on his desk, one by one. All of us shifted nervously in our seats. The Captain noticed our uneasiness. 'Relax men, smoke if you like.' Atkins reached for a smoke but thought better of it. We just sat there wondering. Finally, the Captain dropped the last folder and smiled, 'Congratulations!' You four men have the highest scores in your company.' Bill's mouth fell open and remained slack in utter dismay. He closed it again as the Captain continued, 'There were other high scores, of course, but none high enough to qualify for one more test.' Clark groaned aloud. We all thought, not another test! The Captain continued, 'This test is optional—you don't have to take it. It's the Officer Candidate test; if you pass it, you will be eligible for OCS.' Bill couldn't believe his ears, this was a wonderful, positive lift for his sagging self-esteem and did wonders for his confidence. 'The age limit for entry to OCS is 27, so you don't have to take the test right away, but my advice is to take it now because you men are on a roll—by now you are very familiar with the style of our written tests, so it's a good time to qualify if you want to pursue the opportunity or hold it open for the future. Think about it tonight and if you want to take the test notify your First Sergeant and be here at 0800 tomorrow. The test is in four parts, so you'll be here all morning. Remember, you needn't go to Officer Candidate School, but you might as well qualify now. You might change your mind later. Good luck and I hope to see you here tomorrow.'

We rose, saluted and filed out of the office. Reaching the street, Bill uncharacteristically leaped high, his fist pumping the air, yelling at the top of his voice which brought several faces to the windows, including a grinning processing officer who commented, 'He's got a good command voice.'

"Clark looked a Bill, 'You crazy or something? I'm not volunteering for anything, especially OCS.' Bill looked at the three of us and said,

"You guys just don't know—you don't know what this means to me." Atkins chimed in, "No more tests for me. I've had it." Bill looked at him in astonishment,

"You mean you'd pass up a chance to be an officer?" Atkins just shook his head, "Not for me."

I reached around and put my hand on Bill's shoulder,
"It looks like it's you and me, ole buddy."

It was as if Bill had been reborn. He had a chance to prove himself to everyone, but especially to himself. One week in the army had transformed this young insecure boy into a young man with a solid goal, new hope, a chance to turn a boyhood dream into reality. Most other men in this situation would be content to revel in their good fortune, but, pondering his buddies' reactions to the OCS test, Bill thought they were very short sighted and began to look at his friends in the light of evaluation and learned something about leadership in the process. As Bill came to know the guys better, he concluded that Clark seemed to avoid responsibility, preferring to be one of the boys. Oh, he was a good soldier, a hard worker showing some initiative, but lacked ambition and never asserted himself in situations demanding leadership. There were also men who were simply overwhelmed by the new life, but later adjusted and eventually became good NONCOMs. Atkins, on the other hand, who reconsidered and took the OCS test, was a personality kid. OCS was a game he played well. Bill envied him. He had traits Bill found lacking in himself: confidence, personality, high intelligence and the ability to project these traits when under the watchful eyes of the instructors. Bill saw a bright future for Atkins who eventually graduated in the top 10 of a class of 126 Officer Candidates. But, as Bill learned, Atkins wanted only the privileges of rank, not the responsibility. Once the OCS game was behind him and he was assigned to the 'real army,' he neglected his duties, becoming a disciplinary problem for his commanders; eventually he left the army under a cloud. Bill now looked at any organization as *people* and realized that even bad organizational structure could be overcome by good people."

Colonel Fleming took a moment to light his pipe and then picked up his story. "The door of opportunity had swung open for Bill, and he chose to dash through it before it slammed shut in his face. His dad had retired from the navy as a Warrant Officer, but Bill had a chance for a commission and, who knows, some day he could retire as a Captain, or a Major! That would make his dad proud. But enough dreaming, there was still the exam to pass just to qualify. And qualify he did, but by the skin of his teeth; after all, he was not a scholar in the usual sense, and there were few points for a superior knowledge of WWII. However, the recall of what he *did* know was excellent, his ability to solve problems of logic, his excellent vocabulary and his ability to express himself well in writing won the day. He could now apply for OCS.

Thereafter, Bill was a marked man. He was given many opportunities to demonstrate leadership potential under the close scrutiny of his unit cadre. His Company Commander called for his officer's and NCO's recommendations before endorsing Bill's application for OCS. Each was positive.

Bill qualified as expert with every weapon and became a model trainee. Appointed trainee Squad Leader, his confidence soared, but occasional mistakes served to keep his feet on the ground and his head on straight. His concern for the welfare of his men brought the respect and affection of his peers, who bore no animosity toward him; a fact duly noted by the cadre. The brilliant success he had not attained in school had been his in basic training. The fact that his qualification tests placed him in the top two percent of his peers had not escaped him, but he did not allow himself to dwell on it. After all, there was a long road ahead and, while it was fun and challenging, he'd better not count on past laurels if he was to continue to excel.

Predictably, Bill was the unanimous selection as the company's outstanding trainee at graduation, whereupon he formally applied for OCS. But before he'd be accepted, there was one more formidable obstacle to overcome: a selection board of officers, before which many a young hopeful had stumbled. His training record was spotless and his OCS test score meant nothing, because the board knew only that he qualified. His Company

Commander's glowing recommendation counted heavily in his favor, and written statements had been taken from cadre who knew him well, all of whom seemed certain of his future success. Now there remained a personal interview with the selection board of three commissioned officers, all with combat experience, whose job it was to find weaknesses in character which might prove disastrous when leading men in the heat of battle."

I will continue to relate Colonel Fleming's remarks from my notes in my own words.

Bill appeared sharp and self-assured as he stood at attention in front of the board and reported in a strong and clear voice,

"Sir, Private Bowman reporting to the President of the Board, as directed."

"Be seated, Private Bowman." There was no table or desk between them. The room was softly lighted, furnished casually and had a carpet, the likes of which he had not seen since leaving home. The senior officer present was a Major, and the other two were Captains. All wore Class A uniforms adorned with decorations; a quick glance revealed a Distinguished Service Cross, the nation's second highest award for valor, and two Silver Stars between them.

"Private Bowman, let me introduce the board. I'm Major Buck, Captain Greenbaum and Captain Gallucci. We want you to feel relaxed and comfortable. Please don't feel pressured in any way because this is an unstructured interview. We ask most of the questions but if any occur to you, please just ask. We hope to get to know you better so we can add our comments to those of your commander and cadre prior to forwarding your application to the approving authority. Do you have any questions before we start?"

"No sir." Bill felt his confidence slipping a bit, a little intimidated as he awaited the first question.

"OK, I'll begin with the obvious question. Why do you want to be an officer?" Bill was quite comfortable with this one.

"Sir, I grew up in a navy family. My father, my uncles and my grandfather were all navy men. Being raised in the military tradition, it never occurred to me to pursue any other life. I feel that becoming an officer permits me to better myself while increasing my value to the army. Aside from that, a commission would be a dream come true." Captain Greenbaum smiled,

"Where are you from, Hunter? Do you mind if I call you Hunter?"

"No sir. Thank you. But I feel more comfortable with Bill. I'm from Richmond, California, an oil refining town north of the Oakland-Berkeley area of the east bay."

"OK Bill, tell us about your parents."

"Well sir, my father retired from the navy two years ago. I don't think I fully appreciated my strict upbringing until now. I can see how it's made my adjustment to army life easier. In some ways, my dad was tougher on me than the army has been. On the other hand, my mother was more understanding, protective and supportive of my efforts to get out and make new friends; you know—a mother. It was she who enrolled me in vacation Bible School and the Scout movement. Because my father was at sea during most of WWII, my mother had to be father as well. I guess that's why I chose the army, hoping that if I had a son someday, we'd be closer than I was to my dad."

Captain Gallucci spoke up,

"Have you ever been in any serious trouble, Bill?"

"Yes sir." Surprised, Captain Gallucci asked,

"Oh? Would you explain please?"

"When I was ten, I stole a model airplane kit from a local hobby store. My dad found it hidden in the garage and when he asked me about it I lied to cover up what I'd done. I was a Cub Scout at the time and when he confronted me with the evidence and his questions, I was in uniform ready to attend a Den meeting. He allowed me to go, but upon my return he told me to change my clothes and bring him my Cub Scout shirt. When I did we sat on the front steps to talk so mom, who was working in the kitchen, wouldn't hear. He took the shirt from me. 'You lied to me, son.' I admitted I had. Holding the shirt up to me he asked,

"What shape are these badges on your pocket—the wolf, the bear, and the lion?"

"They're, ah—diamond-shaped."

"That's how they are sewed on, but no matter which way you turn them they are square. Do you know what that means, son?"

"No sir."

"That means a Cub Scout is square, with everybody, his father, his mother, his family, his friends, his fellow man and most of all, God. You should live your life as if the Lord was standing at your elbow every hour of every day, watching."

"Yes sir—I see—I'm sorry sir." (He was taught to say 'sir' and 'ma'am' when speaking to his elders).

"What do you think we ought to do now?"

"I don't know."

"Well, son, you are going back to that store, tell the owner what you did, pay for it and apologize. That's why I had you change clothes, so you wouldn't disgrace the uniform of the Cub Scouts of America. You must never again do anything that will disgrace that or any uniform you may wear in the future. Do you understand?"

Bill stopped for moment and then to the listening officers he said, "I never forgot that because it was a serious offense, but to a ten year old that was real trouble. I don't think my mother ever found out about it. At least she said nothing and for that, too, I'm grateful to my dad."

Major Buck looked Bill in the eye and asked, "How do you think you will react under enemy fire?" Bill paused in thought.

"I can't really say sir. Until it happens, I must have faith that soldiers are trained to function under just that circumstance and believe that I'll be able to give a good account of myself."

Captain Greenbaum asked, "Did your dad give you any advice when you decided to join up.?"

"Yes sir, two things I recall. First, always carry a book to read while waiting in lines—he said I'd have a college education in no time. Second, and he used other language sir; 'don't let illegitimate opinions of others get you down.' He was referring to peers, seniors, subordinates, the enemy or anyone else who by word or deed tries to have a negative impact on me."

Captain Gallucci agreed that it was sometimes difficult to maintain a positive mental attitude, and then asked,

"Bill, if we could recommend that you be given a Captain's commission immediately, would you accept?"

"No sir, I—I couldn't. "

"Why not?"

"Because sir, I'm not qualified to be a Captain. I have neither the knowledge nor the experience. No sir, I'd have to earn that privilege."

Captain Greenbaum thought, "neither–nor; seems well educated." He opened a book, giving the impression he was looking at the answer to the next question. "What are the characteristics of a good leader?" Bill was not unnerved by this tactic, but simply answered as best he could, counting off on his fingers,

"Professional knowledge, endurance—both physical and mental, fairness, concern for the welfare of his men, courage, resourcefulness, trustworthiness, and, generally set a good example."

To this point, his manner, presence and sincerity had impressed the board, but they were experienced in these proceedings and always used the tactic of rapid fire questions, giving little time to respond, in an attempt to rattle the applicant. Bill remained calm but alert and handled the questions with short, complete answers. Afterward, Major Buck complimented Bill and explained,

"In the heat of battle, you will have to make critical decisions, keeping your head when others are confused and looking to you for answers. That barrage of questions and your cool responses gives this board confidence in your ability to do just that." Major Buck looked to his right at Captain Greenbaum and then to his left at Captain Gallucci; then, having received a nod from both, spoke directly to Bill,

"We generally dismiss the applicant at this point and discuss our findings among ourselves in closed session before making a written recommendation. But in your case Bill, as President of the Board I can tell you we are happy to add our positive endorsement to your OCS application." Bill's emotions were joy and relief, in equal parts.

"We extend to you our heartiest congratulations, but with a word of warning. The road ahead is tough, so tough that you will question your resolve more than once before finally winning your commission." Major Buck reached for his briefcase and pulled out some papers, continuing, "The next OCS class at Fort Riley, Kansas, doesn't start for another fifteen weeks. Your record shows you enlisted for airborne duty and that school starts in eight weeks. There is another requirement, however; officer candidates must complete a six-week leadership course prior to entry to OCS. The timing is perfect—you start Leadership School next week, go to Jump School at Fort Benning and then to OCS. Both these courses should help you prepare for OCS, since Jump School is fitness-oriented and we can all use leadership training. Again, congratulations and God speed you, Bill. Your orders will follow."

"Thank you, sir."

In Bill's mind, his future was assured. Yes, it will be tough, but this was his big chance and if thousands of men before him could do it, so could he. He's always known this was what he wanted to do—now was the time to do it. Besides, for a commission he would stand on his head for six months.

With basic training behind him and assurance of what was ahead, Bill was far from the callow uncertain youth of 14 weeks previous. He discovered, like many before him, that the army was a clean slate, a forgiver of past errors and every man was given the key to the door of opportunity, if he cared to use it.

CHAPTER 4

THE OPPORTUNITY

Leadership school caused Bill to regret his lack of effort in high school. His weaknesses, which he worked hard to remedy, were reading speed and mathematics, but his strengths were uncommon common sense and an outstanding geometric perception. He quickly mastered advanced map-reading and gained, without coaching, a clear understanding of trajectory and angles of fire. Nevertheless, he struggled with a lack of reading speed with comprehension, so he enrolled in an after-hours speed reading course, offered at the Post Education Center, and tripled his reading speed.

Leadership School separated Bill from much of the mediocrity of basic training. But as he developed, so did his new peers. No longer part of a pack of recruits, his abilities were less conspicuous and, as part of the elite, he was spurred from within to work harder. Leadership School was designed to develop Non Commissioned Officers (NCO) and to be a prep school for officer candidates; therefore, most of his fellow students would be returning to their units. The school was patterned after OCS, with formal classes, field exercises and opportunities to act as instructors without prior notice, on the spot, under close observation of the Tactical Officers and NCOs. This required the students to diligently prepare, the night before, to teach any class or a portion thereof on the next day's schedule. Each time a student was selected a detailed Observation Report (OR) of his performance became a part of his academic record. In addition, each student was rotated into leadership duties at various levels for a period of three days each and the usual ORs were completed. Students in these positions wore distinctive arm bands identifying the position and were watched by the cadre. One three-day tour of duty would often be documented by ten or twelve ORs, good or critical. The pressure was tremendous. One student was so intimidated by seeing cadre constantly bobbing their heads taking notes on his every move that he resigned. As it turned out not one OR was derogatory, but he had cracked and the natural selection process continued as he reported back to his unit. It would be a full year before this man would be allowed to reapply for Leadership School.

If you spent the evening at the movies or otherwise loafing around you were certain to be called upon the next day—it was spooky. We began to believe the entire post was an espionage network to catch lazy students from Leadership School. So a new institution was born—the latrine study hall—the only room where light was permitted after "lights out." Bill awoke one night to answer nature's call and couldn't find a seat unoccupied.

Bill's ability became recognized even in this group as he demonstrated that he could lead, give instruction clearly and effectively and command decisively. Groups under his leadership performed admirably regardless of the task set before them. During the final two weeks, the students were individually assigned temporary duty (TDY) to units conducting basic training. Here they were afforded the opportunity to perform outside the school atmosphere. ORs were completed here also and were used in determining final grade and standing in the class. Bill's temporary unit commander was so impressed he recommended Bill's immediate promotion. Upon graduation, the school commandant followed suit, and Bill was promoted to Private First Class.

PFC Bowman was now on his way to the Infantry School at Fort Benning, Georgia. He traveled coast to coast by Pullman. He found train travel a delight, enjoying the time to become acquainted with fellow passengers, the good food in the dining car, the luxury of the club car, and, contrary to expectations, he slept soundly—something he has always been able to do while traveling. However, all this was but a temporary diversion; his mind was on the future. The prospect of leaping out of an aircraft in flight intrigued him and he was excited as he anticipated his first jump.

In contrast to the cool, often foggy weather of the Monterey Bay, stepping out of the air-conditioned train in Georgia was like walking into a hot oven. It temporarily sapped Bill's strength and made the adjustment to the rigors of Jump School difficult. Making great demands on the body, the physical fitness program was extended to every minute of the day. The slightest lapse in discipline or hustle brought the too familiar bellow, "Drop down and give me twenty!" If you were alert and lucky, your push-ups were confined to physical training class, but few were so lucky. The class seldom moved at a walk; it was double time everywhere and from the sidelines the veteran troopers laughed and shouted, "So you want to be one!" This got old pretty fast so the stock answer became, "So how's it feel?"

Indoctrination consisted of a welcome to the Infantry Center by the Commandant, and a lot of action filled history, illustrated by WWII film footage of airborne operations in Europe and the Pacific. Each time a film was scheduled, it was said they were getting another shot of the "glory gun." It did build pride and esprit de corps because, in its glorious history, the airborne earned status as the elite of the army and the paratroopers were a proud bunch.

A popular story going around at the time (and still is) was about a trainee, prior to his first jump, being reassured by his Sergeant,

"What if my chute doesn't open, Sergeant?"

"Just pull the reserve chute ripcord, son."

"But, what if the reserve chute doesn't open, Sergeant?"

"Oh don't worry, there'll be an ambulance waiting to rush you off to the hospital."

Over the drop zone (DZ) the trainee stood in the door ready to jump, remembering what he had been told, when he got the command "Go!" He jumped and his main chute failed to open.

"Fool sergeant." He pulled his reserve chute ripcord and it failed to open.

"Fool sergeant." He looked down at the 1000-foot fall beneath him. "I bet that ambulance isn't there either."

For Bill, Jump School was fun, the most fun yet, and he enjoyed the physical challenge. During the week before "jump week" he and a buddy set a trainee record for packing a T-7 parachute, just 18 minutes. That was just the sort of thing Bill ate up. The big day started in the pre-dawn hours, with breakfast at 0400, after which Bill and his buddies boarded "deuce-and-a-half" trucks for the ride to the airfield, arriving before sunrise. In the hangar, the parachutes had been unloaded and lined up on the hangar floor as if in platoon formation, each tagged with a name. Bill had placed a red mark on his tag and there it was in the first row. Just then the Jumpmaster barked,

"OK, fall in on you chutes." When everyone had located their chute, the Jumpmaster commanded,

"Secure your chutes and stand at attention." Everyone picked up his chute and slung it over his right shoulder and the assumed the position of attention.

"Open Ranks, March!" The first rank stepped two paces forward, the second rank one pace, the third rank stood fast and the fourth rank one pace backward. This spread formation allowed room to don the chutes and to await the Jumpmaster's safety inspection.

"From right to left, Count off!" Each man shouted his number in succession.

"OK, you odd numbered men get into your harness with the help of the even numbered man. See that it is done right. Then reverse the procedure." There was much milling around and talking as the nervous men made ready. Finally,

"AT EASE" The Jumpmaster made his way down the ranks checking each rig with an expert's eye, making comments calculated to raise the spirits.

"Tighten that helmet strap soldier. We don't want to give someone on the ground a headache." And "That's way too much slack in that static line. How can you learn if you lose your head exiting the aircraft." And, "Let's insert that safety fork in place before you quick release yourself right out of your harness at 1200 feet. It's not the fall that kills—it's the sudden stop."

Shafts of sunlight now showed through the hangar doors. Dawn had broken on a fine day, widely scattered clouds and little wind; a perfect jumper's day. As we marched to the flight line, we saw our aircraft for the first time—a C-82 "Flying Boxcar." Like a bee, it didn't look like it could fly. These were high winged, twin-engine aircraft with twin tail booms high above the jump doors at the rear of a fuselage suspended between; ideal for jumping. Large clam shell doors formed the rear of the aircraft permitting vehicles to be driven on and off. Today, however, the cargo would be troops only. Jumpers looked forward to a one-way trip because to return meant a waste of time and fuel, not mention the psychological letdown of an aborted jump, due to high winds.

Jumpmasters saw to it that parachute harnesses were tight to the extreme to insure safety and comfort during decent, so when it came time to board the aircraft men in harness could only waddle like ducks. The four steps up a ladder were awkward to climb with 65 pounds of gear on the back. Once inside they were struck by the enormity of the cargo bay. Aft, near the large clam shell doors, now closed, were the two troop exit doors, one on each side, allowing two "sticks" of jumpers to exit the aircraft simultaneously. Beside each door were red and green signal lights operated by the pilot. There was no soundproofing in the cargo bay and the ribs and stringers of the fuselage construction formed a complicated backdrop to the scene. Two steel cables ran fore and aft about seven feet above the deck, one on each side of the plane, on which to hook the static line which enabled the chute to open automatically five seconds after jumping. Some of the men remained silent, considering their own thoughts, fears and anticipations while others tried to make conversation, but all were nervous. The turning over of the two powerful Pratt and Whitney engines put an abrupt end to all conversation. The noise and vibration only heightened everyone's natural fears.

What would it be like to jump off into nothingness? Bill thought of home and the many times he and his friends had put on a diving show for the paying patrons of the local swimming pool. It didn't pay anything, but it got them in free. They'd clown around on the one meter board, and the three meter board and climaxed the act with comedy routines from the 30-foot platform; all the time wearing colorful turn of the century bathing costumes. Recalling the act's finale he decided to himself, "Nothing to it."

The noise was deafening as the big plane began to move, and for those who had never experience flight it was gut wrenching, but to the rest flying was the least of their worries on this special day. As the plane reached the end of the runway and turned into the wind, the pilot revved the engines to a high RPM until the noise was almost unbearable; it felt as if the aircraft would disintegrate as it stood poised for flight. Then, the pilot released the brakes and the thrust from a standing start caused the troops to lean heavily toward the rear of the plane. They were off!

As the runway rushed by they bounced along for an eternity but still the big awkward C-82 was not airborne. Bill hoped the runway was long enough. Finally, as the big bird lifted off the pavement, Bill could see through a small round window its long legs being drawn up into the tail boom just behind the engine and the gear doors closing upon them like a pair of feathers. Once they reached altitude the noise level dropped perceptibly as the pilot throttled back to cruising speed for the short flight to the DZ.

This was to be an individual tap-out exercise meaning that as each man entered the doorway, the Jumpmaster would check quickly for the correct door position and stance and then slap you on the butt, shouting, "GO!" At that point you'd better be gone. They had heard of men freezing in the door, but that just couldn't happen, for the man's sake as well as the men behind him. If it appeared to the Jumpmaster that there was hesitation, the slap on the butt became a push. On the next jump the man was OK—usually.

Exiting the aircraft they counted aloud the five seconds and if the main chute failed, they activated the reserve chute with a pull of the rip cord. Main chute failures were extremely rare, even the T-7 which had a propensity for blowing panels owing to the violent opening shock. If your body wasn't in just the right position and attitude as you fell, you could be jerked around quite severely when your canopy "popped." Suddenly, Bill's thoughts were interrupted by the Jumpmaster's warning, "Ten minutes!" Everyone unbuckled their seatbelts. The Jumpmaster moved to a position in the center of the cargo bay where his commands could be heard by all. Then, over the drone of the engines came the sequence of commands, with appropriate hand signals, so familiar to paratroopers:

"STAND UP!" Everyone stood and turned facing the jump doors.

"HOOK UP!" Each man attached the snap fastener at the end of his static line to the cable overhead and inserted the safety pin.

"CHECK YOUR EQUIPMENT!" Each man inspected the chute pack and snap fastener of the man in front of him. Then the last man turned about to be inspected by the second to last man.

"SOUND OFF FOR EQUIPMENT CHECK!" From the last man to the man at the door, each called out his number in turn and slapped the butt of the man ahead— i.e. "12 OK!"

"STAND IN THE DOOR!" Whereupon the first man on each side took his position in the door with one foot ahead of the other ready to push up and out on command. The red warning light flashed on and the Jumpmaster told the first man to get ready. Looking down at his check points on the ground he could see the edge of the DZ pass below. He looked up for the green light. It flashed on and he commanded with a slap,

"GO!"

Bill was the third man in his stick, and he had shuffled closer to the door as each man exited the aircraft. His eyes met the eyes of the jumpmaster,

"STAND IN THE DOOR!" Bill assumed the position in the door.

"GO!" Bill felt the prop blast hit the side of his face and his clothing ripple as he push into the slip stream. Bringing his feet together and placing both hands on his reserve, he counted: one thousand, two thousand, three thousand—and falling—four thousand, five thou—his voice was stilled with a jerk as his main canopy opened. True to his training, he reached high on his risers and leaned back to check his canopy which had no blown panels and opened normally. He looked around to stay clear of the two he followed. Turning in his harness, he caught sight of the aircraft overhead releasing its human cargo one by one. Bill found himself thinking about what a great ride it was as the ground came closer. He assumed the proper landing attitude and fixed his eyes on the horizon, ready to execute his first real parachute landing fall (PLF) in any direction his oscillation took him. The ground was plowed soft to minimize injuries; he was surprised at the softness of the landing at a 16-feet-a-second decent. He sprang to his feet running down wind to collapse his chute, not difficult in a mild breeze, and feeling quite proud of himself, he asked a nearby ground instructor,

"How'd I do?" Expecting a lengthy and detailed critique, he got only a terse,

"You're walking away under your own power aren't you?"

Bill thought, "He's right. I guess that's what really counts. What a ride!"

There were no injuries, and there would be none. Each of the 152 men made all five qualifying jumps without so much as a sprained ankle, a tribute to thorough training and Corcoran jump boots.

With six months in the army and sporting the newly-won wings of a qualified paratrooper, Bill was ready for Officer Candidate School. But, he learned that the only constant in life was change, and OCS was not quite ready for him. The scheduled class was postponed for lack of applicants. While he waited, he was assigned to Company L, 325th Airborne Infantry Regiment of the 82nd Airborne Division, the famous "All American" Division. The "3-2-5," stationed at Fort Benning, was serving as school troops, providing troops for demonstrations and assistant instructors as needed. This afforded Bill a great opportunity to gain valuable experience observing the best instructors in the army at work and assisting them when called upon. Also, the classes taught would be part of the OCS curriculum. Bill looked upon this turn of events as a head start on OCS. Besides, the regiment was on jump status, and he could use the extra 50 bucks a month. All in all, that was a very happy circumstance.

Bill prided himself on his appearance; with spit shined boots, tailored uniform almost wrinkle free, he made a habit of winning the coveted position of Colonel's Orderly awarded by the Officer of the Day (OD) to the outstanding soldier at guard-mount; determined by a highly competitive inspection.

The uniform for Colonel's Orderly was Class A with pistol belt. As the appointed hour for Bill to report to the Regimental Commander neared, he found himself in the PX. If he was to report promptly he had little time to spare, but he was out of uniform—no pistol belt. Faced with a choice of being on time and out of uniform or returning to the barracks to secure the pistol belt and being late, he recalled an officer in basic saying, "It's better to be a half hour early than one minute late. Tardiness in the army can cost lives." Bill chose punctuality. Reporting to the Adjutant, he noticed a pistol belt hanging on a hook and asked to borrow it to report to the Colonel. The Regimental Commander was very impressed with Bill's military bearing and appearance, proper uniform and punctuality. He asked a question or two and told him to report for duty at 0730 the next day. Bill returned the belt to the Adjutant and departed, walking across the parade ground. The Colonel, looking out his window, observed Bill marching back to his barracks and noticed something was amiss. "Get that soldier back here!" he commanded. Bill hurried by the Adjutant's office, grabbed the pistol belt and reported to the Colonel as before. After another close inspection, the Colonel muttered a bit and dismissed him. Bill returned the belt to its hook and again headed across the parade ground. Standing at his window the Colonel summoned his Adjutant and asked, "Look at that soldier. Is he wearing a pistol belt?" Knowing the situation, the Adjutant replied. "No sir, he isn't." To this the Colonel observed, "The heck he isn't; you just can't see!"

In Leadership School and Jump School, Bill had seen quitters, men who gave up and returned to their units, fated to be lesser men than they could have been. Bill couldn't understand this at first, because "quit" just wasn't in him—his goals were always in sight. His credo seemed to be *It's always too soon to quit*. And, if he had anything to say about it, those around him wouldn't quit either. As he learned to understand men better, he began counseling those weaker men in his unit. Once, while on loan to a training company, he observed a young man having trouble with just about everything and recognized it as an attitude problem. While on the rifle range Bill realized the man would not qualify with his rifle unless there was a change. He questioned the trainee at length and found that his mother and father had been killed in an auto accident when he was seven and he was raised by an elderly aunt, a wealthy widow. She spoiled the boy and was too weak to challenge his unwise decisions. He developed bad habits, the worst of which was not finishing anything he started. He would not complete chores, he quit school and was either fired or quit several jobs. Now, following his pattern, he was ready to quit the army too. He finished by saying he just wanted out. Bill listened attentively to all this and then asked,

"What kind of man are you, average, above average, outstanding, below average or far below average? Where would you put yourself on a scale like that?" In barely audible tones the young man answered,

"Average, I guess."

"What?"

"I said average." Bill looked at him and said,

"Look at me!" The boy looked up, and in a soft voice Bill said,

"Do you have any idea how many millions of men in the history of our country have completed basic training?"

"No."

"Neither do I, but I've an idea that if you quit now that would put you far below average on our scale, if not the very bottom. You see, you've got a bad habit here. You don't seem to be able to finish anything you start. Now if you keep that up, life will be a dead end for you; you'll be a loser from now on. But, I don't blame you, because you were an under-privileged kid."

"Huh?'

"I'd be willing to bet that if your parents were alive today we wouldn't be having this conversation. Your attitude would be completely different because of strong parental guidance as you grew up. So what can we do about it?

"What?" the young man asked a bit suspiciously.

"When you graduate from basic training, for the first time in your life you'll have finished something important and it will be a great personal victory you'll never forget. You'll have reversed this pattern of failure, set a precedent, and you can always say, whatever the task before you, 'I finished basic training—I can surely get through this." Well, the young man went on to a fine army career and when they met again, years later, he told Bill that their little talk on the firing range that day was the turning point in his life.

Bill received several written commendations from both officer and NCO instructors for his conscientious effort as an assistant instructor, which culminated with his promotion to Corporal. Since the accepted picture of a Corporal was a bandy rooster who liked to flaunt his new-found authority, Bill's ability was recognized in an off-handed way by his Platoon Sergeant in a comment to the C.O., something to the effect that PFC Bowman would make a great Platoon Sergeant or even an officer, but he just wasn't Corporal material. But to nobody's surprise, Corporal was just another rung on the ladder upward.

Then came that fateful day, 25 June 1950, when without warning or provocation, the communist North Korean Army crossed over the 38th Parallel with 10 divisions and invaded the Republic of South Korea. The Korean War, characterized as a police action by President Harry S. Truman, was the first test of U.N. resolve to enforce its charter. Absent from the proceedings, having walked out of the Security Council in protest over another matter, the USSR was not able to cast its veto. It was a noble episode after which, in its efforts to keep world peace, the UN became ineffective. With the superpower's veto, a fatal flaw, came impotence. To accomplish its goals of world peace and security, America would be forced to resort to other means—means which would be highly secret and provide an important role for Hunter William Bowman in future years.

Unprepared for war, the U.S. response to North Korea's aggression was two understrength and poorly equipped divisions, already on the ground, the 7th and the 24th, eventually joined by the 1st Cavalry, 2nd, 3rd, 25th and 40th Divisions, brought to strength by the draft and taking troops from units in the states including the 82nd Airborne Division. In Bill's company several NCO position vacancies were created as a result. Experienced NCOs were transferred to units in or on their way to Korea. Bill was considered a logical replacement for one of these vacancies and was promoted to Sergeant ahead of his contemporaries.

With the growth of the active army under combat conditions, there was a critical need for Platoon Leaders, Second Lieutenants. Therefore, OCS for Infantry opened at Fort Benning, and Bill submitted his application, which was accepted in time to enter Officer Candidate Company Number 4. As an officer candidate, Bill was now scheduled for subjects he had been teaching only weeks before. His grades in these classes were perfect, giving him extra time to devote to his weak areas, thus converting them to strong subjects. This fortunate opportunity gave Bill one of the highest grade averages in the school.

Tactical Officers were always at hand to critique, find fault and otherwise keep the pressure on the candidates. Here, the need for numbers of new Lieutenants was subordinated to the requirement for quality officers. To help keep up the pressure and to maintain high standards of housekeeping, personal appearance and conduct, there was established a demerit system, a gig list if you will. Gigs were classified according to their seriousness:

- Class III   Minor infractions   1-5 demerits
- Class II   Serious infractions   6-24 demerits
- Class I   Cause for dismissal   25 required demerits

In the early weeks of the six-month course, candidates were restricted to the post, so there was little to do but study and avail themselves of the on-post recreational facilities. One candidate was designated by daily roster to be Barracks Orderly. It was his job to clean up and keep in order areas of the barracks outside the personal areas of each candidate. One Saturday night, the candidates in Bill's platoon left the barracks hastily to attend the only showing of a much anticipated film, leaving the place in a shambles. The Barracks Orderly on duty that day was pondering the futility of it all when he heard the Candidate Charge of Quarters (CQ) in the next building sound off with the command, "Attention!" He looked out the window to see the Officer of the Day (OD) striding briskly toward the First Platoon barracks with the CQ, clipboard in hand, hurrying to keep up. The Barracks orderly panicked and hid himself in a wall locker. During the subsequent inspection, the OD opened only one wall locker. Monday morning a rather lengthy gig list was posted on the platoon bulletin board. Contrary to popular belief, officers, even Tactical Officers, are not without a sense of humor as indicated by the manner in which the demerits were posted.

CANDIDATE DELIQUENCY REPORT
FIRST PLATOON

NAME	OFFENSE	CLASS & NUMBER
Jones, R.B.	1. Barracks Orderly failed to report.	III-2
	2. Barracks Orderly failed to keep barracks orderly.	III-5
	3. Barracks Orderly Panicked	II-8
	4. Barracks Orderly in locker	III-4

Bill's area looked good by comparison, but he didn't escape the OD's penetrating eye for detail. Bill had left a dime on his footlocker.

NAME	OFFENSE	CLASS & NUMBER
Bowman, H.W.	54. Dime on footlocker.	III-1
	55. Dust on dime.	III-1
	56. Head of former Commander-In-Chief turned downward.	III-1

Twenty-five demerits in one month were cause for dismissal. Bill was never over 12, but Candidate Jones picked up 19 in one embarrassing and humiliating night. Fortunately for him, with two days left in the month he had accumulated only 23. Virtually no one escaped the "Saturday night massacre" without a demerit.

Aside from physical fitness and academics, leadership was a separate area of emphasis and grading. It was quite possible and not at all uncommon for a candidate to rank in the top 20 percent of his class academically and fail to graduate because of leadership shortcomings. For example: there was the "do-as-I-say-and-not-as-do" type who failed to set a good example. And there was the candidate whose offense in that climate and in close living quarters was intolerable—he disliked bathing. Close observation of his platoon could tell you which way the wind was blowing. Some suffered from stage fright when required to step forward and instruct the group, and did a pathetic impression of a comic TV character of that era, Don Knotts, trembling from head to toe.

Time after time the company would return to the barracks at day's end to find an empty space where once had been a bed, wall locker and footlocker. The candidate had been dismissed and reassigned to troops without so much as a "so long, fellas." These disappearances had a strong psychological effect on the remaining candidates, especially those who had held the missing man in high esteem. The feeling that anyone-could-be-next added to the pressure.

The pressure had its effect on Bill, whose feeling of insecurity persisted despite his nearly uninterrupted string of positive accomplishments. He felt as if he was on the knife edge from where he could step into glowing triumph or slip into the abyss of abject failure. He saw no middle ground; therefore, it was difficult for him to relax. A very alert Tactical Officer recognized this flaw in Bill's make up having experienced it himself, and took Bill aside one day and counseled that if he didn't find a way to relax he could snap from the tension. He demonstrated an effective technique, learned in the Far East, which Bill would use the rest of his life. Twice a day for a period of 15 to 20 minutes each, sit or lie down, clear the mind of everything but one meaningless item, maybe the number one or a contrived word having no meaning to stimulate the mind. Then gaze at a fixed point and breathe deeply, inhaling for about two seconds and exhaling slowly, about five or six seconds. Repeating this begins the relaxation process. Turning the palms up, symbolically releasing your grip on the world, concentrate on the extremities, the toes and fingers; picture them relaxed. Soon your eyes, fixed on a stationary point, will want to close as the eyelids grow heavy. Allow them to close. In this state of ease, keep the mind at peace, whatever images that brings—a sunny meadow, sand and sea—anything to keep the mind relaxed for 15 to 20 minutes. Soon your metabolic rate slows, the heart beat and breathing drops to a relaxed pace. Bill's image of peace was the face of Jesus, so he combined this newly-learned technique with his spiritual meditation. This resulted in a relaxation response done twice a day and worked so well that tension simply could not build within him as a destructive force, no matter how hard he worked.

As this ritual took its disciplined course, the quality of everything Bill did improved and slowly the knife edge disappeared and he found himself standing on a broader avenue of life, able to distinguish clearly between the important and the trivial. He became more affable, gregarious and good-natured. More of his acquaintances began to add affection to their respect for Bill Bowman.

To the mental strain of OCS was added the physical exertion in the stifling summer heat and humidity of Georgia from May through October. The morning runs to Victory Lake and back before breakfast while it was still cool (78 degrees), some four miles round trip, took such a toll on the heavier men that they couldn't eat. I don't recommend this as a diet. When they weren't running to, from and between classes, the candidates marched at a fast pace, an impressive 140 steps per minute instead of the usual military cadence of 120.

During the last four weeks, the candidates traded their everyday olive drab helmet liners for liners of infantry blue which designated them as Senior Candidates. Along with this status came certain privileges, such as weekends in town or with families and salutes from junior candidates. Seniors were also permitted to conduct Saturday morning inspections of junior companies, a duty some disliked because it meant handing out demerits which, in their eyes, was harassing junior candidates. Seniors hesitant to serve in this capacity failed to appreciate two things: first, their attitudes cost them leadership points, and, second, it was necessary for their own development and that of the junior candidates.

Cooperate and graduate was the slogan among the candidates. Peer pressure to play the game was intense. No one purposely made another look bad; if one did present a negative impression, it was usually his own doing. Periodically, candidates were required to rate their peers in numerical order with comments to justify their rankings: these written ratings were called "buddy reports." Candidates were not permitted to discuss or compare ratings with others, so there was no collusion to "stick it to someone." A unanimous or near-unanimous bottom rating could be reason for closer scrutiny by Tactical Officers and possibly eventual dismissal. The mavericks, social outcasts and sometimes the brilliant were spotlighted in a negative manner by the "buddy reports." Although a poor report served to focus attention on certain candidates, it was never the sole reason for dismissal. A poor report had to be substantiated by below-standard ORs and performance. While most "buddy reports" were accurate, some candidates were absolved by closer evaluation; usually, a word to the wise was sufficient and an otherwise outstanding candidate's career was saved from the effects of petty jealousy, envy or the personal inability to picture the subject as a commissioned officer where the very attributes objected to would actually serve him well. Judging from the "buddy reports," his fellow candidates had no trouble visualizing Bill with gold bars on his shoulders.

Bill observed that some of the older men had seen lengthy service and viewed the war as an opportunity for advancement, but allowed pride to defeat them. They just could not, or *would not*, adjust to the constant harassment and pressure, preferring the comfort of the positions they had already attained. Some might do well as officers in another, perhaps non-combat, branch, but Infantry OCS was training Rifle Platoon Leaders, a position of acute stress and the one officer position with the highest casualty rate. It would not be fair to be easy on them. Yes, OCS was no country club; it was 24 weeks of nerve-wracking, stimulating, muscle straining, bone crushing work, and its graduates were specialists who had become Second Lieutenants preferred over ROTC and even West Point officers by some field commanders in Korea because they were ready to do the job in combat without missing a step, and they weren't looking past the job to future promotion.

Bill wondered if individual class standing had any correlation to mortality in combat. He was to discover that with few exceptions where fate intervened, the harder-working, better-trained would survive the carnage of combat. Most of the men in his class had no prior service. With nothing to compare, they worked hard and maintained a positive mental attitude (PMA).

One evening, Bill and some friends worked on a grounds-beautification project until after dark. His Tactical Officer decided to see what Bill was made of and made a note to call on him to give instruction the next day. Would Bill study the next day's subjects or let it slide because he'd worked so late? Tired, Bill gambled and did not study. When called upon to instruct the group in the manual of arms, he could have gotten by, faked it, but with characteristic honesty, he replied to the calling of his name, "I'm not prepared, sir." Bill felt humiliated and angry with himself. This was the first and only time he was caught unprepared. He couldn't forget the incident, and his future efforts, six opportunities in all, were outstanding and overcame that one unsatisfactory grade.

A few days later, Candidate Bowman was called upon to instruct his platoon in the use of the bayonet. He knew his subject, and his ability to teach it had even the most clumsy performing well before the hour was up. Bill's performance was observed by Lieutenant Arthur Kincaid, a veteran of the early fighting in Korea. His OR read as follows:

"Candidate Bowman demonstrated aggressiveness, a thorough knowledge of his subject and a superior ability to impart that knowledge to his men. In the time allowed, he demonstrated and conducted practical exercises in the short thrust-and-parry, long thrust-and-parry, vertical butt stroke, horizontal butt stroke, smash and slash so effectively that each man mastered the techniques. Bowman was quick to spot individual problems and correct them in a manner easily understood. His men responded enthusiastically to his instruction,"

At the bottom of the report an overall rating was circled and initialed: "SUPERIOR. AK."

Observation Reports weighed heavily in compiling the overall leadership grade for the course. However, candidates were never informed of the results; they knew only that they were observed and, in their own minds, had done well or poorly. This area of the unknown was calculated pressure. The outcome of any written exam was published in a day or two, so academically each candidate knew where he stood, but there was no hint of a leadership grade until the individual's standing was quietly announced by means of a figure penciled at the corner on the reverse side of the diploma. Class standing was not emphasized; only the outstanding candidate was announced publicly at the ceremony.

Fifteen months after the commencement of hostilities in Korea, OC#4 graduated 126 of its original 184 candidates. Bill's mother and father were on hand to do the honors—pinning on the gold bars of a Second Lieutenant. The ceremony, held at the main post theater in the presence of family and friends, was opened by a military band, followed by the invocation by the Post Chaplain and remarks by the Commanded General of the vast complex that was Fort Benning, who stressed the responsibilities of rank while wishing them well in their future careers. Then he said,

"At this time it gives me great pleasure indeed to announce the name of the Outstanding Candidate of OC#4..." with a flair for the dramatic, he paused for a deep breath and announced the name. "...Candidate Charles R. Elliot." Cheers and applause exploded from the assembled candidates and their families. Some who were near reached over and patted Bill on the shoulder sympathetically. Candidate Elliot rose and stepped smartly towards the stairs on the right of the stage; he was followed by the remainder of the class assembled alphabetically. Approaching the General, Bill snapped to attention, saluted, shook hands and accepted his hard-earned diploma.

"Very well done Lieutenant Bowman. Congratulations and good luck."

"Thank you, sir." *Lieutenant Bowman,* Bill hadn't expected that; it sounded good. The diplomas were rolled and tied with a ribbon of infantry blue. Bill would not look at the penciled number until he returned to his seat. The General's "Very well done." was inspired by the number he had seen on Bill's diploma: 8. Bill was happy. *Lieutenant* Bowman, a dream that persistence and hard work had made a reality in only three years in the army. At 21, he had matured beyond his years, thanks to a positive mental attitude, an unexpected opportunity and hard work.

After the ceremony Bill was approached by his Tactical Officer, Lt. Kincaid, who congratulated him and told him that a vote had been taken among the Tactical Officers and NCOs to select the Outstanding Candidate from the top ten in the class. The vote having gone to Elliot, the remaining nine remained deadlocked so their names were to be drawn from a hat. Lt. Kincaid told Bill that with a little luck he might have been number two. But Bill's incredible luck would come later and mean more.

After congratulating many of his friends, Bill spied his parents standing a little apart quietly observing the celebration. He broke away and walked toward them, smiling. His mother ran to him and embraced him with tears in her eyes, "We're *so* proud of you, dear." It was at this point that his father finally appreciated his son's unacknowledged latent ability.

"Son, when you decide to do something, you don't stand in your own way, do you? You know…to tell the truth, I was afraid you'd wash out." He had overheard Lt. Kincaid's comments and asked, "Where did they rank you in your class?"

"Eighth." His dad's eyes misted and, reaching out and hugging his son, he said, "Eighth, out of 126... how wrong can your ole man be?" Never before had his dad hugged him. It was a very special moment for Bill.

"Well dad, these other guys didn't have the advantage I had—your training."

CHAPTER 5

THE MAN

Owing to excessively high casualties among Second Lieutenants in Korea, the army adopted a policy requiring assignment of new officers to troop units in the states for at least six months prior to ordering them into combat. This provided an opportunity to adjust to their new status and to command troops without the added pressure of combat. During this period, Lt. Bowman learned to delegate tasks, call on veteran's experience in his decision making and to supervise without harassment. He was well aware that a commander is ultimately responsible for all his unit does or fails to do. Confident assignment of tasks required him to know his subordinates well, their strengths and weaknesses and the degree to which each could be autonomous. Bill's unit was receptive to his common sense approach, worked well with it, which enabled him to devote more time to the important tasks of leadership. He had seen the undesirable results of micromanagement.

Upon assignment, again to Fort Ord, he was given additional duty as Company Mess Officer. He really knew nothing about mess operation, but there was to be a school for mess officers at post headquarters to round out his education. Bill harkened back to the notion he had held before entering the army: if they wanted you to do something, they'd first train you to do it. So, for the next two weeks, it was back to the books.

Completing the course and, anxious to begin supervision, he inspected the mess and found it a very competent operation. The Mess Sergeant was a pro, and Bill was hard-pressed to find fault, so when he opened the big five-door refrigerator and saw a stainless steel pitcher two-thirds full of milk, he jumped at the chance to call this deficiency to the attention of the Sergeant,

"Sergeant, don't you know regulations call for milk to be stored in its original container?" Taking off his hat and scratching his head, the Sergeant looked at Bill and inquired,

"Aw sir, where will we keep a cow around here? Bill smiled and, realizing this was not OCS, said,

"You know what I mean Sergeant—good job."

Yes sir. Thank you, sir."

Bill grew to appreciate the sometimes irreverent humor of the NCOs. A trainee, dressed as an officer, had been picked up by Military Police in Monterey. Later, an officer's call was in progress in the CO's office with three Second Lieutenants, including Bill in attendance, when an MP investigator entered the Orderly Room. Addressing First Sergeant Dixon, he said,

"I understand you have a man impersonating a Second Lieutenant?" Without hesitation, Dixon pointed his thumb over his shoulder in the direction of the CO's office and replied,

'Yeah, I got three of 'um. Which one do you want?"

Bill was loyal to his subordinates and they responded with pride in themselves, high spirits and hard work. One soldier, who did well on a highly competitive physical fitness test, but not as well as he thought he should have, demonstrated his loyalty to the platoon by coming to Bill and apologized for letting down the platoon. Speaking of loyalty, Bill's definition came from a statement he read and memorized as a boy, by General H.H. "Hap" Arnold, Commanding the Army Air Corps and the man credited with putting America's aircraft industry on a war footing in WWII. Bill reached into his memory to lift the soldier's spirits:

"When you work for someone, for heaven's sake, work for him, speak well of him and stand by the institution he represents. If you must complain, leave and complain to your heart's content. But while you are a part of an organization do not condemn it. If you do, the first high wind that comes along will blow you away; and probably, you'll never know why."

In this connection, Bill told his NCOs not to blame him for any order, but to issue an order as if it was one of their own. There was none of this, "Well, the Lieutenant said we have to do this or that"—orders were issued straight from the shoulder, to be carried out vigorously. If one of his NCOs needed correction, he was careful to do it privately, but when he praised, it was done so all could hear. The respect and affection in which his men held him would best be illustrated by an incident which took place at the end of a basic training cycle. At the last formation, Bill had given the men a little pep talk and wished them well in their new assignments. Turning the formation over to his Platoon Sergeant, with an exchange of salutes, he turned and walked toward the Orderly Room, hoping his farewell remarks had been appropriate, when an acting Squad Leader led a spontaneous and rousing "Three cheers for Lieutenant Bowman." Looking back, he waved acknowledgement, visually moved by the gesture.

So far Bill had been required to perform duties for which he had been trained, and his resulting confidence was apparent in the outcome. In assigning tasks to subordinates, he kept this lesson in mind and was careful to take into account their strengths and weaknesses, thus insuring a good result while simultaneously challenging them. So it was that a key to Bill's success was to know his men and knowing how to get the most out of them. The other side of the coin was high morale and respect from seniors and subordinates alike. But the real test of his ability was imminent, in life-and-death combat situations which can only be simulated in training.

Bill would pass his 22 birthday while under fire in Korea and also vote in his first presidential election by absentee ballot—voting age being 21 at the time. But first, his orders directed him to report to Camp Stoneman, California, for overseas processing. During his brief stay, a letter caught up with him, for inclusion in his 201 file, signed by his former Regimental Commander: it stated that Bill's performance of duty placed him in the upper five percent of his contemporaries and recommended his immediate promotion to First Lieutenant. However, since he was in transit status, no action could be taken; it would be up to his new commander to evaluate the performance of the young "hot shot." Therefore, Second Lieutenant Bowman departed Travis Air Force Base aboard a Boeing C-97, the military version of the Stratocruiser (first cousin of the B-29 Superfortress) for the long flight to Japan, via Hickham AFB, Hawaii, and Wake Island in mid-Pacific.

Wake Island was more than a refueling stopover in Bill's mind—it was a battlefield. As a boy of 11, he had followed reports of the Marine's heroic defense of the tiny atoll during the dark days following Pearl Harbor when the unprepared U.S. suffered a succession of defeats at the hands of the Japanese in the Pacific. Marine Major Devereaux's stout defense surprised the Japanese with its ferocity and repulsed their first attempt to take the island. They retired from the scene only to return with a stronger force with far superior air cover and eventually occupied Wake.

After touchdown on the island, Bill decided to make the most of the little time he had and asked the base commander for the loan of a jeep to visit key points of the battle. As he surveyed the island with no elevation higher than 21 feet, he asked himself what he would have done in Devereaux's place with his resources. Then he determined in his mind what would be needed in men and resources if he were asked to defend the island today. He remembered this exercise to gain the most from a study of military history.

After takeoff, while on the next leg of his journey to Japan, Bill talked at length about the battle for Wake with officers seated with him. Soon he had a rapt audience of five or six, all amazed that he had accumulated so much knowledge in that short two-hour fuel stop. Most had never heard of the triangular strip of coral and sand. Bill explained that while defeat was inevitable, the island had surrendered while it still had means to resist; only destroyed communication lines kept Major Devereaux from knowing the true situation, therefore, he assumed the worst and surrendered. After the first Japanese assault the second Japanese force unknown to itself was in a race with a U.S. navy relief force heading for Wake, however when the U.S. force paused to refuel at sea, the Japanese arrived first and the U.S. force was recalled rather than risk a small but vital carrier task force; thus sealing the fate of the heroic Marine Detachment.

Setting the scene in the chronology of the Korean War prior to Bill's arrival, the South Korean Capitol city of Seoul had fallen in the initial onslaught and the North Korean People's Army had pushed back the ill-equipped South Korean Constabulary and under strength American units. American help arrived piecemeal and could only trade space for time. Fighting from successive delaying positions, our forces eventually were ordered to a final stand along a 140 mile perimeter around Pusan, the port in southeast Korea, so vital to the build-up necessary to resume the offensive. General MacArthur's brilliant and gambling end-run landing at Inchon, near Seoul and the 38th parallel enveloped the North Koreans, trapping their fighting units between two forces facilitating the breakout of the Pusan perimeter. From there the

US mounted an offensive to the Manchurian border and the Yalu River. Here, the Chinese hoards, using human wave tactics, intervened at a time when our troops were expected to be home by Christmas. Pushing the US back again, Seoul fell a second time and the United Nations forces withdrew to a line 35 miles south of the capitol where we were to begin an advance on January 25th, 1951, which would develop into OPERATION KILLER and liberate Seoul once and for all. Eventually we established a static defense line about the same distance north of the city. It was here that a demarcation line was agreed upon through negotiations at Panmunjom.

In a message to the troops, it was specified that the cease fire agreement was good for 30 days, after which, if there was no cessation of hostilities, units could expect "adjustments" to the line. There would be more than a year and a half of violent adjustments in that line before the protracted negotiations would bring about an armistice. It was during these battles of the outposts that Bill Bowman found his life in frequent jeopardy.

This was, in many ways, a more difficult time for a leader in a combat zone because now men were being asked to fight and die while "peace talks" were in progress without a cease fire. Although all deaths were tragic, it seemed a greater tragedy to be killed in action during the days or weeks before the armistice. Even so it became clear that the enemy, by using their fabled oriental patience, protracted negotiations to accomplish that which was unattainable by force of arms. It remained a test of wills to the very last moments until armistice. The Chinese Communist Force (CCF) leaders showed their lack of respect for human life by sacrificing many thousands of men in a vain effort to improve the strength of their position at the bargaining table, agreeing only to that which was to their advantage—the only reason a communist will agree to anything. *Compromise* is not in their manifesto. The US fear of a third world war and our resulting attempts to confine allied operations to an enclosed geographical area, no matter how artificial and strategically infeasible, only encouraged Soviet adventurism elsewhere in later years.

Lieutenant Bowman had been assigned to the famous 3rd Infantry Division, "Rock of the Marne," which won its nickname from action at the Marne River in WWI. The regiment he was to serve would be one of the nation's oldest, the 7th Infantry, "Cotton Balers." This nickname surfaced at the Battle of New Orleans during the War of 1812, when under the command of General, and later to be President, Andrew Jackson, the 7th, using cotton bales for cover, repelled the British. Its motto, "Volens et Potens" (Will and Power) was most appropriate for the test of wills yet to come. Over the years, the 7th had distinguished itself in many battles, some 54 battle streamers flying from its colors. So heavy were the Regimental Colors that only a very strong man was selected to carry them in President Eisenhower's inaugural parade. Bill was impressed with the proud heritage of the 7th Infantry and vowed only to contribute to its honor, or at least not to tarnish it.

During the long and tedious rail trip from Pusan, delayed by torrential rain and washed out rail beds, Bill had time to reflect as he watched this strange landscape of the heartland of Korea pass by. Aboard the train, there were a few officers and NCOs returning to duty from R&R and hospitals in Japan and, by this time of the war, there were those returning for a second tour. Bill listened to their war stories with a grain of salt. The most outlandish tales came from those who never saw action and manufactured war stories out of sheer boredom. For every front line soldier, there were ten in support rolls who had never fire a shot. Still, Bill listened with interest to a veteran Infantry Captain offering advice to young shave tails, "If in doubt, seek advice from the experienced, then make your decision. Your men will be looking for strength in you. A platoon reflects the personality of its leader. I have seen the same 40 men transformed from a confused rabble into a fighting machine with only a change in leadership.

If you are smart and have a choice, ask for the worst platoon in the company. It's not only an opportunity to show everyone the greatest amount of progress and establish your good reputation early, but you will be instrumental in saving lives by turning the platoon into an efficient team, thereby assuring its survival in combat and the accomplishment of our mission in Korea."

Bill knew a Rifle Platoon Leader's chances of returning home in one piece were slim indeed, and this would be the ultimate test of his young life. He knew his best chance for survival was to throw himself into his work wholeheartedly and apply all he had learned since entering the service. He felt the army had the most effective curriculum of any institution, a course of study aimed ultimately at only two objectives: mission accomplishment and survival. He made up his mind to work as if his death in Korea was a certainty. It would he unhealthy, indeed, to allow himself the luxury of looking past Korea, past the job at hand. His worst fear was an ignominious death with a whimper. If he was to give up his life, it would be in a good fight. He did not call that fatalism; on the contrary, he knew that attitude was his best chance at survival.

The other passengers were a fair representation of the United Nations; there were Australians, Brits, Canadians, Irishmen and Africans of the Commonwealth Division, Greeks, Turks, Belgians, and of course, the largest contingent, the Americans, all united in a common cause. No one asked why they were in Korea; naked aggression was self-evident. Bill looked at the crowded rail car and tried to imagine the same car a year hence and how many of seats now occupied by these men would be empty owing to casualties.

Colonel Fleming paused in his story and asked,

"Would you care for another cup of coffee, Scoop?" I accepted and he continued his narrative,

"Finally arriving at Division Headquarters, Bill and his fellow arrivals were fed and briefed on the big picture and the division's part in it. At the briefing Bill and three others assigned to the 7th were greeted by the Regimental S-1 and taken north for more briefings at the Regimental Command Post (CP). It was here that Bill and I got together again."

"How'd you get separated in the first place?"

"I had been called home on emergency leave after basic training and then entered Leadership school, the class behind Bill's. Upon graduation from OCS I was sent directly to Korea just before the inception of the six months in the states policy. I had almost completed my tour in Korea and was Executive Officer of Company K when Bill arrived. We were reunited by a collision as Bill was leaving an operations briefing.

"Bill...'ol buddy! What in the world are you doing here?"

"Hello, Matt. Boy, it's good to see a familiar face. I'm a replacement. What are you doing here?"

"What luck! You're coming to KILLER KING if I have anything to say about it. I'm the XO. Wait here, I'll talk to the S-1."

It took some fast talking because we were not yet scheduled for another officer, even though we had a vacancy. Coming back to Bill, I recall saying something like, "Watch out, you're mine now!" The 1st Platoon has been without a Platoon Leader for nearly a month now, and you're it, ole buddy! Will Sergeant Caruth be glad to see you! He's been carrying the load alone—a good man. You couldn't have come at a better time to get your feet wet."

"Yeah, doesn't it ever stop raining? It's been a downpour since we left Pusan."

"A couple more days of it are in the forecast, but what I meant was we're in battalion reserve now so you'll have some time to get to know your men before we go back on the line."

"That's a break."

"Bill, it's nearly 1200, so let's have chow and talk. By the time we're finished, your orders will be ready and you can ride back with me in the jeep. We'll check in at the Battalion CP and move on to the company."

The officers mess tent was erected on a wooden floor and tent frame and was very attractive inside with a string of lights and Korean waiters. I noticed Bill looking around.

"Enjoy it while you can, my friend; where we're going, it'll be C-rations or worse, but you won't starve. As exec I'll see to that."

"Tell me about the company, Matt."

"Well, we have a veteran CO, Captain Kennedy, a retread from WWII who knows his business, He just got back from *R&R* in Japan. He was on your train; you might have seen him. His driver met him at the rail head so he's back at the company now. KILLER KING is the best outfit in this war. I guess you know by now our regiment is code named KILLER. Added to KING Company, it has a fighting ring to it, wouldn't you say? Your Platoon Sergeant is from Beaumont, Texas, Master, has three years of service, twen..."

"Whoa..." Bill interrupted, "...Master Sergeant in three years? How'd that happen. Matt?"

"Bill, this kid is something; he's twenty-two and out-soldiers any NCO in the unit. He came to Korea 13 months ago as a PFC and worked his way up under the accelerated promotion system in combat. He refused a battlefield commission offered after he won the Distinguished Service Cross (DFC). He also has a Silver Star to his credit. I can best describe him as an Audie Murphy type—Murphy too was a Texas boy, you know. Anyway, he came to us as an enthusiastic kid and developed rapidly into a responsible NONCOM. He's well liked, humble and unassuming, but, when there's a job to be done, he's a fireball and always seems to have an alternate plan in a crisis—*just in case*. He sets a good example for the platoon. You'd do well to listen to him and seek his advice as long as you have him."

'What do you mean, as long as I *have* him?"

"As a condition of his last promotion, he agreed to extend his tour of duty in the combat zone for six months. In five months, he'll rotate home."

"Oh, so in the next five months I'll have to learn all I can from Caruth *and* find a replacement."

"He can't be replaced, but I wish you well."

"What do you mean?"

"Your predecessor, Lt Burke, who incidentally caught a .50 caliber in the leg and sent home, told me that Caruth is so good that all the Squad Leaders feel inadequate and are afraid to take the job. He said Caruth did most of their thinking for them. There's another problem: of your four Squad Leaders, two are also short timers. SFC Burba leaves in two months and SSgt Brown in three. Yep, this is not a very efficient way to fight a war, the point system. It goes like this: you get four points a month while on the front line, three points in support areas subject to enemy artillery fire, and two points a month in the rest of Korea. When you accumulate thirty-six points you rotate home and take your combat experience with you. Replacements are green kids who take up to two months, if they survive, to be battle-wise. When the end of their tour is in sight, they acquire the "short-timer's" syndrome, regarding themselves as people with a special kind of hide to be saved and begin slacking off. It can be a problem. All this info may be useful to you, but the best advice I can give you is this: you were trained to be a Platoon Leader—remember your training and be one."

"Thanks Matt."

"Hey, no charge, ole buddy."

As we walked toward the S-1 tent, we encountered the Regimental Sergeant Major who snapped a salute. I introduced the two and the SMAJ asked, "Welcome aboard sir. Ah, how tall would the Lieutenant be, sir?" directing his question to Bill in the third person as was the custom among the old timers.

"I'm six-four, Sergeant Major."

"The average life expectancy of a Rifle Platoon Leader in combat is six weeks, sir. The Lieutenant is a big target—keep the head down, sir."

"Thank you, Sergeant Major. I'll try to remember that."

The road was muddy and rife with potholes created by torrents of rain and heavy truck traffic. The jeep had no top and the windshield was down as required in the combat zone. We stopped at battalion long enough to meet Lieutenant Colonel Butler, the CO, and phone ahead to the company. Approaching the company bivouac at dusk, we had to ford a rain swollen stream to reach the CP. In the dim light, Bill saw steep hills and narrow valleys stripped of trees, either destroyed by artillery fire or cut for firewood, with deep water filled shell craters all around. This ground had witnessed a desperate battle; he wondered how long ago. He could see, nestled on a bulldozed notch in the hillside, three large squad tents and a smaller five-man tent. Stepping out of the jeep in front of the first large tent, I cracked,

"This is it, no reservations required, but I did call ahead. Ah, here comes the bellboy" Approaching the jeep was a Korean in uniform, a KATUSA (Korean Augmentation to the US Army). He reported smartly and announced that he was Kim Yong Cho, a soldier in Bill's platoon. I told him to put Bill's stuff in the officer's tent and dismissed him.

"Yes sir" addressing Bill he said with a smile "Welcome sir."

"Thank you Kim. I'll see you later."

We ducked into the company headquarters tent where there was something of a reception awaiting us. The interior was brightly lit with three Coleman lanterns making that familiar rushing noise which could be heard over the beating downpour.

"Captain Kennedy, this is our new 1st Platoon Leader, Hunter William Bowman, but he goes by Bill. Bill reported to his new commander with a snappy salute. The Captain looked at Bill, trying to place his face, "Don't I know you from somewhere?"

"We met on the train, but not formally. I'll try to follow your advice, sir." The Captain took Bill's hand in both of his and, with a firm handshake, said,

"I sure am glad to know you, Bill." Turning to me he asked,

"How'd you manage this, Matt? I thought we weren't due for a replacement for another two weeks or so."

"I had a little talk with the S-1 after I bumped into Bill at regiment. We took basic training together. Bill, let me introduce you to your colleagues, Lt Freeman, 2nd Platoon; Lt Gordon, 3rd Platoon; Lt Wosniak, Weapons Platoon; and someone who is really clad to see you, MSGT Caruth, your Platoon Sergeant. Bill was struck immediately by the effect combat had on the 22-year-old soldier—*old* being the operative word here. Aged beyond his years, he had lost his youth, but gain maturity due to the war. Bill extended his hand and, placing his free hand on Caruth's shoulder, he said,

"I've heard only good thing about you, Sergeant; I'll need your help." Caruth was pleased with Bill's request and replied,

"Thank you, sir. I'll do my best."

"From what I've heard, your best will be more than enough." Then, looking up at Bill, the 5' 10" Caruth added,

"Speaking for the platoon sir, we'd all appreciate it if you'd keep your head down so you don't give away our position."

"You're the second NCO to tell me that. I think I get the hint." Captain Kennedy interrupted,

"This is the first time in nine months that we've had a full complement of officers. This calls for a celebration. I'd like to keep it that way for a while. This guy pushing a beer in your face is our top soldier, First Sergeant Robert Fields."

"Glad to know you, Top."

"Sir it's my pleasure."

We all grabbed a beer and a toast was offered by Lt Freeman, most appropriate to the occasion, and one which would be repeated each time we were able to get together and relax.

"May the next man we lose have 36 points and return home safely."

"Hear, hear."

When the hour grew late and it was time to sack out, we had stepped into the rain to move across to the officer's tent when Bill observed,

"Here it is, the dead of night, in a downpour, and I can see just fine. What's the deal?"

"Artificial moonlight." I answered. "Look behind you and up." Bill turned and saw two anti-aircraft searchlights at the top of a distant hill directing their beams against the low hanging clouds in the direction of the front lines.

"The reflected light creates a moonlit night, every night, rain or no rain and permits easier maneuvering for night patrols forward of the main line of resistance (MLR). Also, it discourages large enemy troop movements. You treat the searchlights as artillery illumination and call for it as you would a fire mission. If it becomes a problem just tell them to douse the light."

Suddenly, there was the sound of distant artillery, a preparation on friendly positions about a mile to the north. It continued for about twenty minutes with the furious rattle of counterbattery fire passing overhead from positions nearby. Then silence, lasting some few seconds, then friendly artillery opened up with a vengeance, creating a racket which would not permit sleep without earplugs, which I readily inserted.

"The classic pattern; they hit us in preparation, they attack and we hit their attacking troops. Somebody's clobbering somebody up there." Even at that distance, at night, in spite of the rain, small arms fire could be heard chattering away. The firefight lasted until after midnight, and then in a few seconds, thanks to those earplugs, sleep finally arrived.

Bill awoke before dawn and, except for a few clanking noises nearby, it was quiet; the rain had stopped. He was comfortable in his sleeping bag and just lay there in the dark listening to the activity outside, concluding that the field kitchen was nearby. He looked at his luminous dial watch, 0505. In the quiet of predawn, noises were clear, easily penetrating the tent's thin canvas walls. Just outside the tent, he heard the muffled explosion of someone igniting an immersion heater for hot water. He thought he smelled a faint aroma. Yes, coffee! That did it, there'd be no more snoozing; time to roll out and face the new day. He got up, stood at a roughly-crafted stand built for shaving from one's steel helmet, dressed and walked toward the smell of food. He was joined by Lt. Wosniak, who explained,

"Bill, you and I can have a cup of coffee anytime, but in this unit officers eat only after the last man has passed through the chow line. So let's have that cup while we wait...oh, here comes the ole man." Captain Kennedy approached the two and smiled,

"Good morning, gentlemen. Sure glad the rain stopped. We might have been stranded on this hill by the rising creek."

In spite of the early morning activity, dawn broke in eerie silence and the countryside seemed to stand still in time as Bill spoke,

"Quiet, isn't it?"

"Welcome to the *Land of the Morning Calm*." Captain Kennedy replied. Lt Wosniak added,

"Your first day here and you're witnessing a perfect example of why they call it that."

Just then the First Sergeant approached quickly, and addressed the CO, "There's a company commander's meeting at battalion at 0900, sir—just got the call."

"Something to do with that commotion at the front last night," the CO speculated with characteristic understatement.

The line of men moved slowly in the chow line. Trays were used in rear areas and the men appreciated that, but no dining hall here. Most men filled their trays, looked for a level spot on the ground and sat on their helmets while they ate. Sergeant

Caruth arrived with the 1st Platoon, scheduled to eat last that day, and approached his new Platoon Leader,

"Good morning, Sir."

"Good morning, Sergeant Caruth. While I've got you here, let's have the platoon assembled at 0830. I want to meet them."

"Very well, sir," said Caruth pointing, "our platoon area is over there. See you at 0830, sir."

Breakfast was well prepared and tasted good to an appetite whetted by the fresh outdoors. The menu was C-rations of course and served in bulk, consisting of canned orange or tomato juice, powdered eggs, corned beef hash, sausage patties and recombined milk. We didn't know at the time that it was to be our last hot breakfast for some time to come. Bill and his men would not sleep again for thirty-six hours. As they ate, Lt Gordon, 3rd Platoon, edged closed to Bill and, in low tones, told Bill he wished he could command the 1st Platoon. Bill asked why.

"Your platoon was the last to see action. They were on a night combat patrol and had temporarily occupied an abandoned outpost to regroup before moving on. It so happened that *Joe*, a slang we use for the enemy, intended to capture the hill that night. Just as the patrol left the hill to continue its mission, it came under heavy artillery fire in preparation for the attack on what the Chinese Communist Force (CCF) considered a permanently occupied hill. Caught in the open with the only cover being the shallow trenches of the hill, the platoon raced back and took what meager cover the old run down position provided, and there sweated out a fifteen minute enemy artillery and mortar barrage which, miraculously, barely scratched them. The platoon was then attacked by two companies, a force six times their number, rushing the hill with bugles blaring. Some Chinese penetrated their position but were killed in close hand-to-hand fighting. The enemy fell back to regroup and attacked again only to be repulsed again. With each new assault, Sergeant Wilson, your machine gunner, was the first to take the enemy under fire and Corporal

Rathbone, with his automatic rifle, kept the trenches clear of enemy infiltrators in the rear of the tight perimeter. Both men were recommended for Silver Stars. Wilson kept moving his gun between assaults so Joe couldn't get a fix on his position until it was too late.

"Ole *just in case* Caruth did a superb job commanding, assuring that the platoon's fire power was used to its maximum effectiveness. He called for artillery early and, quite by mistake, the mission was fired with white phosphorus (WP) and overshot the enemy troops catching Joe standing silhouetted against the white smoke like targets in a shooting gallery and were promptly cut down in great numbers, making it a reasonably fair fight. During a grenade duel, a concussion grenade, which is like a tin can filled with black powder, landed between Caruth's legs, exploded and threw him backwards against the trench wall unconscious. Slowly regaining his faculties, he saw his trousers had been blown away to mid-thigh, his boot laces were shreds, and he suffered second degree burns on his legs, but, except for a terrible ache in his groin, he was otherwise unhurt and continued to direct fire until the enemy finally broke off the attack.

At first light, seventy-one enemy bodies were counted, all of which were too close to our guys to be recovered by the Chinese, who make a habit of removing their dead before withdrawing. And here's the amazing thing: every member of the platoon walked off the hill under his own power and returned to our lines. Only six required treatment at the battalion aid station. Sergeant Caruth's DSC is pending. So you see Bill, you've got a pretty confident group there. There's no enemy boogie man for them. Sure, they were lucky, real lucky, but they did the job."

"When did this action take place?" Bill asked.

"About three weeks ago. Oh, they're all still here."

"Thanks Gordon, that's useful information, I really appreciate it."

Later, Bill walked to the platoon area, arriving precisely at 0830 to find his men in formation at attention. Sergeant Caruth reported, saluting sharply,

"Sir, the platoon is all present or accounted for."

"Thank you, Sergeant. At ease, men. Break ranks, gather around and sit down." He paused to let them get settled and have a good look at him—then he smiled.

"Good morning, men."

"Good morning, sir." They replied loudly, in unison.

"That's the spirit. My name is Bowman, your new Platoon Leader. The last rank I held was Sergeant, E-5. I was a Squad Leader in the 82nd Airborne Division before applying for OCS. All my training, from basic to Leadership School, to Jump School to OCS has prepared me for just one job—Platoon Leader. However, I like you, have arrived in Korea missing one important thing—combat experience. There is where I'll need your help. I'm very impressed with your combat record, especially that most recent fracas—that was nothing short of miraculous. So you have no doubt where I stand, you should know my priorities: the mission is number one, and number two is returning each and every one of you safely home to your loved ones. Realistically, I know number two will take a miracle. There is no question in my mind about whether we will accomplish our mission here, but that won't be without casualties; it is my conviction that training and functioning as a team, as a platoon should, saves lives. You all have had a vivid illustration of that recently. No man could have walked off the hill without having done his part. Combat offers the best training there is. The little things that can mean the difference between life and death are the things I need time to learn. I don't want to send any of you into certain death situations because of my inexperience and I don't want to become another platoon leader casualty statistic either. So if you see me doing something dumb, please don't stand on ceremony—let me know. There may not be time to be polite about it. I'll understand and take it as counsel. In return I hope to prove that you are better off *with* me than without me. That's about all I have to say to you as a group..." Bill paused for a moment..."except this: I'd like to give you a motto that fits this platoon in every way; Semper Primus—always first. Sergeant Caruth."

"Yes sir. Attention!"

"Dismiss the platoon, but have the squad leaders stand by. Then join me over here, please."

One by one, Bill interviewed his NCOs, each for no less than fifteen minutes with Bill asking the questions and listening closely and carefully to the answers he got. The senior NCO in terms of age and length of service was Sergeant First Class Burba, from Columbia, South Carolina, who was due to go home soon. At 31, he had twelve years' service and was a veteran, surviving landings at Anzio and Omaha Beach. He had been a Squad Leader for nine months and had been a SFC for almost two years in an era of accelerated promotions. This puzzled Bill, so he asked Burba point blank, and was told,

"That's easy sir. I don't hold nothin' agin' Sergeant Caruth. He's a born leader, sir, and when he was a Squad Leader he done a better job than me. When the Captain asked me 'bout takin' over the p'toon, I told him flat out, Caruth was his man. We had no Lieutenant then, and to tell the truth, sir, I figgered I'd have a bettah chance comin' thu' this here war with Caruth in charge. Besides, I figgered he'd get a battlefield commission and I might git promoted anyway. Any other way jest wouldna' be best for me or the p'toon, sir." Bill had long since learned the army was full of smart men who, for one reason or another, lacked a formal education, and that actions spoke volumes in evaluating men.

Bill asked Caruth why he had refused a battlefield commission. He explained his feelings this way,

"I was proud and flattered, sir; but army policy requires transfer to a new unit, where you haven't been 'buddy-buddy' with the men—a fresh start. That's probably a good idea, but I have a lot to learn to be an officer. Besides, I didn't want to leave these guys. I guess I have as much confidence in them as they have in me. I think we're a good team, sir. I've heard of battlefield commissions going to a new unit and getting killed before they had time to know their men. I felt I'd make it home if I stayed on the team, *just in case* what I heard was true."

Aside from Caruth and Burba, each NCO had been promoted only once since arriving in Korea, and they were competent Squad Leaders. They were SFC Holmes, 1st Squad; Staff Sergeant (SSGT) Aldridge, 2nd Squad; (SFC Burba had the 3rd Squad) and SSGT Browne, Weapons Squad. Bill had just begun to get an idea from Caruth about areas of training which needed emphasis during the next days when the conversation was interrupted by a runner from company who announced an officer's call, immediately.

CHAPTER 6

THE LEADER

Captain Kennedy stood in front of a battle map posted with the current situation, a half chewed cigar jutting from the corner of his mouth—I never saw him smoke one. He believed that the more his people knew about the situation, the smarter and better motivated they'd be in a fight.

"OK, listen up! That action we heard last night was serious; so serious it has put an end to our rest period." Pointing to the map, he continued, "The fight took place on Hill 250, designated OUTPOST QUEEN. Our guys were a company from the Belgium Battalion, attached to our division, and they took a terrific pounding last night fighting off an attack of battalion strength. So, they're coming off the hill tonight. We are to affect a relief no later than midnight." Using his pointer, Captain Kennedy continued, "QUEEN is one of a line of seven outposts approximately seven hundred yards forward of our Main Line of Resistance (MLR) stretching from the Imjin River, on the west, to a point here, about three miles to the east. The brass hats consider three of these terrain features critical enough to be occupied 24 hours a day—QUEEN is one of the three. The other four are occupied by patrols only at night; whether these are friend or enemy depends on who gets there first. The other night, a patrol from G Company had just reached the summit of Hill 195 when it spotted a CCF patrol coming up the forward slope. Our patrol won the day, or rather the night, taking only three hand grenades to decide the issue. OUTPOST QUEEN, however requires a full company for 30 days at a stretch, and *we* are it. KING on QUEEN. That sounds like a normal, healthy situation to me. Knowing the S-2 as I do, he'll wait nine months and put us on OUTPOST PRINCE." In a situation like this, any attempt at humor, no matter how feeble, was welcome and the men chuckled as the Captain continued,

"The Belgiques will leave on position whatever ammo is remaining from last night's firefight, but that won't be much, so each man will carry a double basic load and one day's C-rations. We'll be resupplied tomorrow after dark by KSC. These are Korean Service Corps, men and boys unfit for military service by reason of age or physical or mental deficiencies not affecting their ability to act as bearers. They will bring food, water and ammo. Trucks will be here at dusk to transport us to a point as far forward as possible without being seen by enemy observers; we'll assemble behind the MLR in G Company's sector. Just after dark, they will guide us through their defensive barrier of barbed wire and mines. Then we'll move to a point 300 yards behind QUEEN and wait. If Joe wants to hit them again tonight, they should attack about an hour after dark, and we'll be in a position to launch a counterattack, if needed. If Joe had enough last night, and S-2 thinks they'll stay home licking their wounds, we'll begin scaling 250 at 2100 hours. If all goes as expected, the surviving Belgiques will be heading back to our lines by midnight. Are there any questions?" The Captain looked at Bill who was shaking his head no.

"Sorry Bill. I had hoped to give you more time with your troops."

"Can't be helped, sir. I'll just have to learn quicker."

"That's the spirit. OK, we leave the camp just as we found it; the Belgiques will be sleeping here tomorrow night. The password sequence for tonight is: sign, PLYMOUTH; countersign JALOPY." Bill was struck by the difficulty the Chinese would have with that one even if they knew it.

By 1830 it was dark enough to begin the slow trek through G Company's defenses. Careful to follow in the tracks of their guide, KILLER KING slowly negotiated the narrow serpentine safe-lane between the barbed-wire entanglements, mines and booby traps. Artificial moonlight was providing the light of a half moon—just about right. They could see their way, but it was too dark for enemy observation, except at close range. They were a little early arriving at point "wait," 300 yards behind QUEEN.

By now Bill was used to the smell of Korea, but here and now was the smell of death at the bottom of this narrow valley. He felt it was close by. He didn't want to, but looking about he saw it; a Belgian soldier, spread on his back, missing the left leg at the hip, his lifeless eyes seemingly staring at Bill. Stepping out of the dead man's gaze Bill found his rifle and bayonet, plunged it into the ground marking the remains so the Belgians could carry it back on their return trip.

All was quiet except for distant small-arms fire to the east like a clash of patrols because of the distinctive "burp" sound of CCF submachine guns. Eventually, Bill would learn to recognize the distinctive sounds of various weapons being fired, even at some distance away, a "little thing" which would help when required to make quick decisions in combat.

The company began moving the final 300 yards to the base of Hill 250. Bill looked up and gasped, "It's straight up!" At precisely 2100, Company K began the precipitous climb. After climbing the steep slope for 10 to 12 minutes, it became even steeper. By cutting into the side of the hill, crude steps had been fashioned using wooden ammo boxes filled with earth and held in place by steel barbed wire pickets. It wasn't long before Bill's leg muscles were burning under the weight of his equipment load. Each step became agony, and he could only take three steps at a time before resting momentarily. He looked down at Sergeant Caruth following behind him and said breathlessly,

"I can't believe I'm so out of shape." Caruth, not letting on that he too was hurting, and grateful for the slow pace, replied,

"Don't worry, sir, you'll get used to it. In Korea everything is either up or down. Without all that weight, you'd scramble up this hill like a goat."

Finally, the agonizing climb was over and Bill was greeted at the top by a Belgian Lieutenant, who whispered in good English, colored by a heavy accent,

"1st Platoon?"

"Yes." Bill replied in a low voice.

"When all your men are up, stay in line and follow me." They entered the trench, defining the circumference of the entire hilltop, at the reverse slope and moved to the left for about 25 yards, stopping at the entrance of a bunker covered with sandbags and earth.

"This is your CP. You can drop your pack here; we will continue to post your men." After a few feet he stopped again.

"This is your first position." The Lieutenant pulled his own man and Bill replaced him with one of his own. This procedure continued, position after position, until all the 1st Platoon was in place. Then, the officer turn to Bill and said,

"During last night's attack, most of the enemy came from your left front, up that draw, so I recommend that you move your machine gun over there. We started a covered bunker. You can finish it tomorrow."

"Thank you. By the way, at the bottom of the hill, about 300 yards back I found one of your dead. I marked the body so you can find him."

"Merci. Bon chance—good luck."

In a few minutes the Americans were alone on the hill. Bill thought that had the enemy been only 50 yards away they would have been unaware of the change in units on the hill during the night. It was a text-book relief. He thought also that if Company K were pushed off the hill, taking it back would be costly; he'd hate to make that climb again under fire. He vowed then and there to organize the strongest defense possible, but not in the dark. He'd just have to trust until morning that the Belgians had done a good job.

At first light, he and Caruth took stock of the situation as they made their way from position to position. Naturally, in war, there is the belief that devastation, skillfully inflicted, will eventually bring an end to fighting; hence, after expending a terrific amount of professional skill and energy in the preparation of fortifications which seem impregnable, the soldier is apt to look upon his handiwork with confidence and finds himself almost wishing the enemy *would* attack—the expected victory being the pay-off for his exhaustive effort. This attitude lingers only until he finds himself in the thick of an all-out assault. But, if the enemy's battlefield intelligence is good, such well-prepared fortifications are avoided and the point of attack shifted to softer sectors of the line. Appreciating this, the battle-wise infantryman needed little prodding to dig in. Bill made certain that each man placed firing stakes in front of his position, marking the left and right limits of his sector of fire, and that range cards were prepared for automatic weapons, which made for effective and accurate fire at night. When he was finished with the last man's position, his platoon had a solid front with interlocking fields of fire and was tied into the platoon on the right. His left flank curled around to a nearly-sheer drop-off at the rear of his position. Two men stationed at the top of the steep climb would be sufficient protection there.

The forward slope was gentler and covered with barbed wire entanglements. On the left flank, at the middle of the curl, was a mound about 50 feet out which offered good cover for an approaching enemy; Bill would have it manned as a listening post each night. Daylight brought an unexpected discovery; during the past three or four months, units on the hill disposed of their C-ration cans by throwing them out in front of their position or over the side of the steep rear precipice, as if aboard ship. Although Hill 250 had become a tremendous trash heap, fortunately, it had at the same time, provided early warning of an enemy advance; the empty cans making stealth impossible; attested to by the nightly sound of rats rummaging around feasting on the leftovers. One way the CCF would learn a new unit had occupied the hill was the occasional firefight against rats by nervous gunners inexperienced with the position. But, on the whole, fire discipline was maintained by KILLER KING.

Bill was uneasy and looked forward to the night's resupply; he'd feel better with more machine gun ammo and grenades. At about 1500, the password was passed to Bill who made a mental note to circulate it to his troops before dark. Bill prided himself on his memory and often used word association as a memory device. A couple of hours later he passed the word to his NCOs and then began his nightly ritual of checking individuals to assure himself all had it. Most of the Korean War was fought with equipment, vehicles and ammunition which had been stockpiled on Pacific island bases for the invasion of the Japanese home islands. Just after dark, Bill was in his bunker enjoying a hot can of spaghetti and meat sauce, vintage 1943, when his field phone rang. It was Captain Kennedy's voice issuing a terse, "Report to my bunker immediately!" Bill wasted no time getting there. Captain Kennedy looked up from his map and asked in a stern tone,

"Lieutenant Bowman, what is the password for tonight?"

"ICY PEAK, sir." Bill responded without hesitation.

"Lieutenant, you'd better get the *correct* password to your people before someone gets shot." Puzzled and alarmed, Bill asked,

"What is the correct password, sir?"

"You were close, but no cigar. The correct password is..." One could see Kennedy was enjoying this, "...FROSTY SUMMIT!" Now get outta here." Bill would never again delay dissemination of the password.

As he and Sergeant Caruth moved to correct the situation, they passed around the "curl" when Bill thought he heard the wind pick up. Instantly, two hands between his shoulder blades sent him sprawling face down in the trench as five tremendous explosions straddled the trench shattering the quiet night air, narrowly missing them.

"Did you hear anything just before I pushed you, sir?"

"Yes, now that you mention it, I heard a rush of wind."

"That was five mortar rounds falling on us. It's a good thing it was quiet. You can hear incoming artillery easily, but mortars are sneaky, harder to hear in day light, and in the noise of battle, you can't hear them at all. I pushed you *just in case* you didn't know what you were hearing."

"Thanks for the lesson and the push, Sergeant."

"Oh, that's OK, sir. I kinda enjoyed it. I'll always remember the time I decked an officer and got away with it."

"Thanks anyway." Bill had learned something that night which would save his life long after Caruth had returned stateside.

At night it was fifty percent alert. Bill and Caruth alternated shifts; dusk to midnight and midnight to dawn. Kim Yong Cho always had coffee and hot chocolate waiting at the midnight changeover. Bill had a taste for chocolate and Kim's was the best he ever drank. Kim's secret belonged in the G.I.'s handbook of combat cuisine, if there was such a publication. He collected the unwanted soluble milk packets from other men and mixed them with C-ration cocoa—just like home. The routine was coffee when getting up and cocoa when going to sleep. In battle, Bill discovered Kim made himself responsible to protect Bill's back. While Americans come and go, this was Kim's country; for him there was no escaping the ravages of war, even for a short time, so he was allowed to act as orderly for the platoon headquarters in the field, a role in which he delighted; but Bill would discover Kim was more than worth his weight in a fight.

It was the tenth night on OUTPOST QUEEN when a whistle was heard on the sound-powered phone connecting the CP with the Listening Post (LP) to the front, about 40 yards out. Bill grabbed the phone, "CP."

"Sir, we got somethin' goin' on out here…" Bill recognized the nearly whispering voice of SSGT Aldridge, "…cuz we can hear troops to our front and left, but we cain't see nothin'."

"Are you certain?"

"Yes sir, this is a large force, by the sound of it."

"OK, you've done your job, now come on back—fast!"

Bill called Captain Kennedy, who had just received a report from the 3rd Platoon on the extreme right and was calling for Illumination over that position. The company's provisions for detection and early warning had picked up the scent. Suddenly, the entire hill came under intense enemy artillery and mortar fire. Bill joined his men just as Aldridge and his two men arrived back safely. Friendly artillery placed the star shells accurately and turned the scene into near daylight exposing CCF in great numbers. Bill estimated a battalion, about six or seven hundred troops following close behind their own artillery barrage. Bill's baptism of fire had begun, and he tingled with fear and excitement as his adrenalin surged.

Overhead, a C-47 from an Air Force unit called "The Fireflies" dropped flares lasting much longer than star shells. With no fewer than five in the air at all times, the battlefield would not grow dark during the fight. Prearranged artillery support was called for and adjusted by the Forward Observer (FO) on the spot. The noise of artillery from both sides at once was deafening, and all heads were down except those in covered automatic weapons positions. Bill had joined his machine gun crew in their new bunker so he could observe the front from under cover. His first indication that CCF was close was a grenade bouncing off the chicken wire apron over the bunker's firing aperture.

"They're coming at us inside their own artillery barrage..." Reaching over and touching Sergeant Wilson's shoulder he commanded, "...COMMENCE FIRING!"

The machine gun bursts alerted the platoon and heads began to come up to observe and take under fire the enemy, now attempting to break through the barbed wire barricades. In seconds the full and awesome firepower of Company K was added to the booby traps and anti-personnel mines exploding at the feet of the attackers. It was a devastating display and one which would have stopped most any enemy a good distance off, but the human wave tactics of the CCF left the issue in doubt for most of the battle. Before the night was over Bill realized that the CCF meant to take all of the outpost line, of which Hill 250 was a key, probably in preparation for a general attack on the MLR. As far as the eye could see to the left and right, the outpost line was illuminated.

Enemy bodies began piling up on the barricades, cutting off fields of fire, allowing third-and-fourth-wave attackers to close in greater numbers, having sustained only artillery casualties. As the CCF scrambled over the bodies of their dead and wounded which now were holding down the wire, they came at Bill's men not only in larger numbers, but from very short range. While moving up and down the line commanding his men to fix bayonets, Bill bumped into his platoon medic,

"What's the casualty situation, doc?"

"Two wounded, but fighting—we haven't lost anyone yet, sir."

"Thank God."

"Amen, sir."

The main battle developed by degrees into Bill's personal battle and he and the enemy were face to face. He had already shot several, without hesitation; his mind had dehumanized them—they became demons bent on killing him and he reacted with a soldier's instinct to protect himself and his men. There was no time for "buck fever" nor thoughts about taking human life; hesitation would probably get him killed. He had heard that on the battlefield there are only the quick and the dead.

While moving to his left near the "curl," he suspected something—it was just too quiet on the left flank. Taking Kim, with a dozen grenades between them, they dashed out to the mound which had been a close-in LP, and jumped into the two-man foxhole. His gut feeling proved accurate. He observed approximately 200 of the enemy forming below him in position to menace his flank. They had not attacked from this direction before, so the barricade was free of bodies which revealed a clear field of fire. Most of his men were staving off the frontal assault, some in hand-to-hand combat. If the enemy was permitted to reach the mound, their flanking fire would devastate his platoon and probably mean the loss of the hill. He turned to Kim and told him to leave his grenades, tell Caruth to get some mortar fire on the enemy and bring help. Just as Kim sprinted away, the enemy launched their assault toward Bill. Setting his M-2 Carbine on single shot, he began picking off enemy—one falling with each shot. Noticing two separate groups bunching up, he took advantage of the thirty degree slope increasing the hand grenade range, and began throwing with deadly accuracy. Many had come within 20 yards of his position and a few began to scramble up the mound toward him. To prevent his own grenades from being thrown back at him, Bill allowed two or three seconds to burn off the four second fuse before rolling it down the mound. CCF grenades were crude, and often unreliable, especially the powder train fuse in the wooden handle which when it became wet dampen the powder turning the grenade into a dud. One such dud landed at Bill's feet, unnoticed; another came flying at him end-over-end, which he fielded like a first-baseman. He hurled it back, killing two of the enemy. Continuing to fire his carbine with telling effect until his ammunition depleted, Bill used all his remaining grenades. Exhausted, with the enemy still coming, he called upon his last resort; a personal .45 automatic pistol he had purchased before leaving the states. The .45 had enough hitting force to knock a running man backwards. Bill proved that fact to himself, six times at close range.

SFC Burba arrived with help just in time to see Bill, using his bayonet as a dagger, stab to death the last enemy soldier. The threat to the flank had been reduced single-handedly by Bill Bowman in less than eight minutes of furious effort. Although his actions were ferocious in appearance, his quiet courage, born of confidence in himself and his weapons, enabled him to act with precision; coupled with his extraordinary skill at arms, his efficiency was machine-like. The enemy's only chance of survival was to destroy the machine, which they very nearly succeeded in doing. Looking Bill over, Burba pointed out matter-of-factly,

"Sir, y'er hit—y'er bleedin'...MEDIC!"

"Where?"

"There." Bill had sustained a flesh wound on his upper arm just below the shoulder and his sleeve was saturated with blood, dripping from the elbow. But that wasn't all, as Burba observed while tying a compress bandage in place.

"We'd be carryin' ya off'n the hill if it warn't fer yer flack jacket—look here." Bill had been hit four times during the fight; beside his shoulder, one bullet and two jagged pieces of shrapnel were dug out of his armored vest, any one of which, had it penetrated, could have been fatal. At this realization, Bill broke into a cold sweat, paling a bit,

"Thank you, Lord. I nearly didn't make it to six weeks." Burba looked around, and then, holding up his hand, he said,

Don't move, sir; I'll jest git rid o' this dud grenade fer ya." Tossing it down the hill he said it all:

"Don't ya think that's cuttin' it kinda fine, sir; runnin' outta ammo an' enemy at the same time? Y'all must have a friend upstairs, sir."

There were 56 enemy dead inside 30 yards of Bill's position. Because his act of heroism was so extraordinary as to set him apart from his comrades, Bill was awarded the Distinguished Service Cross.

Sporadic fighting continued for another hour, but the enemy plainly had no stomach for further bloodshed this night and withdrew around 0200, after a six-and-a-half-hour struggle; the battlefield went dark as the Fireflies turned for home. Soon the Chinese, groping in the darkness, removed their dead so we'd not know the full extent of their defeat. But we *did* know. An occasional star shell lit the area briefly, but the Chinese didn't bother to take cover while they continued to cart off their dead and wounded. They seemed to know there was no further danger from us, or didn't care if there was. Nonetheless, KILLER KING kept a watchful eye on them, carefully counting the bodies through binoculars when there was light.

At first light, it was clear they had done a good job, leaving only the close-in bodies for us to bury. They had tried to capture a well-defended, company-sized outpost using two battalions—a six-to-one advantage, but we had the advantage of defensible terrain and a highly trained Company K. A prisoner revealed that they thought they were attacking the Belgians again. The company suffered fifteen percent casualties, 29 men, but only two were killed, by artillery. The 1st Platoon had six wounded, including Bill; four were evacuated, but returned to duty in four to ten days. Bill's luck was there in spades, when he really needed it, and he felt touched by the hand of providence.

Their remaining days and nights on OUTPOST QUEEN were uneventful, with only small reconnaissance patrols at night, held to a couple of hundred yards ahead of the position. When their 30 days on Hill 250 expired they were relieved by Company B and returned to the MLR where they improved the main defense positions and patrolled at night.

The 7th Regiment next saw action in the area of the infamous "Iron Triangle" formed by Chorwon and Kumhwa in the south and Pyongyang in the north. They spent most of the winter on White Horse Mountain, scene of heavy fighting a month earlier by the 9th Republic Of Korea Division (9th ROK) which the U.S. 3rd Division relieved after the battle. Henceforth the 9th was called the White Horse Division.

It was on Whitehorse that Bill was summoned to the company CP once again. Inside, there appeared to be an officers call, with the First Sergeant present. The Captain was uncharacteristically tough on Bill, accusing him of being 10 minutes late and keeping everyone waiting. Bill didn't understand; he'd only just received the message and came instantly. Captain Kennedy voiced his irritation,

"There're only three things I hate..." he bellowed, "...warm beer, wet toilet paper, and Second Lieutenants!" The snickering could be heard all around, so the jig was up and Kennedy lowered his voice and said,

"I guess there's only one way to remedy that...so if First Lieutenant Bill Bowman will step forward we'll bleach his bars to silver. This is long overdue, Bill, congratulations."

It was the spring of 1953, and peace talks were stalled with no hint of a cease-fire. There would be one last desperate and convulsive effort by the CCF before the armistice, and First Lieutenant Hunter William Bowman would be caught in the thick of it.

At best the MLR was a bulwark of defense which the CCF attempted to pound into impotency at selected locations. In all-out war, fixed fortifications are considered "monuments to the stupidity of man" by offensive-minded strategists; but this was a political war in which the fighting and dying participants were hamstrung by policies having nothing to do with sound military strategy. Paraphrasing Winston Churchill, it set a precedent which in another day and time would embalm principle.

The regiment now occupied positions near Kumhwa, with the 1st and 2nd Battalions on line and the 3rd once again in reserve. Our front line was on a low, boomerang shaped hill mass (Hill 256) with its two ends swept back, southward. Just to the northeast, towering over the BOOMERANG was the key terrain feature which anchored the "iron triangle," a mountain 1062 meters high from which the enemy had a commanding view of the entire region. The 3rd Battalion was kept busy rehearsing counterattack plans which prepared them for just about any enemy move.

The call came at 0245 hours, 15 June, two days before Bill's scheduled rotation home:

"*Execute Counterattack Plan NEW YORK. You will cross the initial point (IP) at 0600 and be in the attack position no later than 0630.*"

It came as no surprise, since a battle had been raging in the 2nd Battalion's sector for two days, spilling over the division's right flank into the 9th ROK's sector. At night, the main supply route was heavy with traffic carrying vital munitions under blackout conditions to forward supply points to sustain the battle. Companies F and G had been badly mauled taking the brunt of the assault. The situation had become so desperate that G Company's CO called for friendly artillery fire on his own position. This last resort measure consisted of warning your own troops to stay under cover and calling for timed fire over your position; the air bursts rained down shrapnel on the exposed enemy. There is always some trepidation because inevitably, there are friendly casualties among the few who, in the confusion of battle, don't get the warning.

It was during this fire mission that all communication was lost with F and G Companies, leaving the fate of about 500 yards of the battle line in doubt and the regiment's position vulnerable to breakthrough, if the enemy were prepared to follow up their success. But, at this point, the real situation on the BOOMERANG was unknown, and delay could mean disaster, so Counterattack Plan NEW YORK was implemented to restore that portion of the MLR.

The plan had been rehearsed by key people and the terrain was familiar and the objective clear. Even the weather cooperated. A smoke barrage, just prior to jump off, covered the advance of the 3rd Battalion up the cratered hillside from enemy observation from Hill 1062. As Bill and his men broke out of the smoke, they could see enemy milling about trying to organize a hasty defense against the expected counterattack. The 3rd Battalion, advancing with K and L companies abreast, was not detected until it was halfway to the crest, but then came under intense artillery, mortar and small arms fire from the entrenched enemy. Under this withering fire, the Americans hit the dirt, taking what cover the quaking ground could offer. The battle of OUTPOST QUEEN paled before the BOOMERANG's inferno.

"What happened next, Scoop, is best described in this citation..." said Colonel Fleming, "...but before you read it, let me explain that the Medal of Honor is awarded, in the name of Congress to persons who, while in the service, shall have distinguished themselves by gallantry and intrepidity at risk of life above and beyond the call of duty in action involving conflict with the enemy. Here's Bill's citation; you can read it yourself." I reached for my glasses, took the citation from Colonel Fleming and began to read aloud.

First Lieutenant Hunter William Bowman, 02028652, Company K, 7th Infantry Regiment, 3rd Infantry Division, distinguished himself by conspicuous gallantry and intrepidity above and beyond the call of duty in action against the enemy *near Kumwha, South Korea, on 15 June 1953. When his platoon was pinned down by intense fire, he completely exposed himself to move among and encourage his men to continue the advance against an enemy force which had become entrenched on Hill 256. Inspired by his courageous leadership, the platoon resumed the advance, but was again pinned down when an enemy machine gun opened fire, wounding six of his men. Lieutenant Bowman immediately charged the hostile emplacement alone, engaged the crew in hand-to-hand combat, and killed all three. Continuing on toward the objective, his platoon suddenly received intense automatic-weapons fire from a well concealed hostile position on its right flank. Again leading his men in a daring bayonet charge against this position, firing his carbine and throwing grenades, Lieutenant Bowman personally destroyed four of the enemy before he was struck himself by submachine gun fire. Completely disregarding his wound, he continued to lead his men to the objective and worked to consolidate their position before he would accept medical aid. The extraordinary heroism and outstanding leadership of Lieutenant Bowman reflect great credit upon himself and are in keeping with the highest traditions of the military service. Lieutenant Bowman entered the service from California.*

I could feel the hair stand up on the back of my neck as I said, "Incredible, utterly incredible."

"There are a couple of footnotes to his story in Korea. Again, his new model flack jacket had stopped two submachine gun bullets at the chest and stomach, but a third caught him in the left hip, spinning him to the ground. Kim Yong Cho, following close behind, killed the enemy soldier who had shot his Lieutenant, preventing Bill from being finished off as he lay on the ground. Ignoring his wound, Bill got up and continued on. Reaching the positions on the MLR, it was not difficult to piece together what had happened. The CCF had overrun F and G Companies by sheer weight of numbers in furious hand-to-hand fighting, in and out of the trenches. A few or our troops had been caught by our own artillery fire, but many more Chinese were slaughtered by the air bursts. Bill began placing his men in position and, in doing so, found several men of G Company still fighting from inside weapons bunkers, unaware their position had been overrun. Outside, killed by airbursts, were several CCF soldiers with grenades and satchel charges which could have finished off the survivors.

Then, CCF artillery and mortars resumed the fierce barrage in preparation for yet another assault. It became impossible to hear and, to finish placing his men, Bill was forced to dash across open ground where there was no trench or cover. Still bleeding, he signaled his men to follow when suddenly, a very strange thing happened. The din of battle was abruptly silenced for about ten seconds—just long enough. He dove to the ground yelling, "Hit the dirt!" Three 120mm mortar rounds struck, detonating within killing range. Two of his men were hit but Bill, hugging the ground, escaped further injury. He struggled to his feet, nearly passing out from loss of blood. Just as suddenly, the battle resumed and continued for several hours.

The Chinese chose the point of attack carefully, where they had the advantage of terrain and numbers. Yet the stout defense by F and G Companies forced early commitment of enemy reserves so, once a hole in the line was opened, there was no significant enemy force immediately available to penetrate and pursue. This gave us precious time. The point of attack of Bill's platoon and his heroic action proved the key to foiling the enemy's hasty defense.

In a classic example of contingency planning, the 3rd Battalion had regained control of the BOOMERANG. What was left of Company F walked off the hill—the XO, who replaced the badly wounded CO, and 18 men of its original 165 three days earlier. The CO and 26 men survived from Company G. The CCF had squandered 12 regiments trying to strengthen their negotiating position, some 18,000 Chinese recklessly spent before the guns of the determined soldiers of the 7th Infantry Regiment.

Unsuccessful here, the CCF shifted its effort eastward to the sector of the Capitol ROK Division and, in heavy fighting, was allowed to penetrate to a killing ground where they were destroyed by waiting UN forces. Their forces significantly weakened, it was to the communists' advantage to sign the armistice, ending the three-year-old conflict.

Bill's wound was treated at the battalion aid station. The bullet had penetrated the skin at his left hip, causing a long shallow wound which exited his left buttocks cleanly. Bill once again sought solitude and thanked God for stopping the battle long enough for him to hear the incoming mortars which spared his life and the lives of his men. Miraculously, Bill lost several wounded, but not a single 1st Platoon soldier was killed in battle while Bill was in command; this, and Bill's example, convinced the platoon that surely a higher authority had been watching over them.

"Later, word came that Bill had won the Medal of Honor, to be presented personally by the President at a White House ceremony. Bill was surprised because he wasn't told he had even been recommended. This announcement caught the attention of a young STARS & STRIPES reporter named Charlie Hall, based in Korea, who discovered Bill had already won the DSC and two Purple Hearts. During his interview, he asked how Bill could be so brave. Bill's unabashed reply was this; here's a clipping of the article. Read the underlined part aloud, please."

When I arrived in Korea I considered myself already dead, and, if it was God's will, I vowed to go out of this life as a soldier should; fighting the good fight. I simply believed the words of Jesus in Luke 9:24 which say, "For whoever desires to save his life will lose it, but whoever loses his life for my sake will save it."

His perilous passage through the incredible snares and pitfalls of the ultimate danger, emerging unharmed and victorious, was a clear message that his destiny lay ahead. He was convinced he had been saved for some more important work yet to come.

After the Korean War, like so many fighting men who stayed in the service, Bill lost himself in the comparatively mundane duties of the peacetime soldier, serving in the 11th Airborne Division at Fort Campbell, Kentucky, where he continued his college education in the evenings. A GED test started him at a two-year college equivalency. Through the study of mobile warfare in books by several military leaders: the German General Hans Guderian, General George S. Patton, General Omar Bradley and Brigadier Desmond Young, Bill developed a keen interest in armored warfare and tactics, which happened to coincide with a shortage of Captains in Armor Branch at the time. Responding to a Department of the Army circular calling for volunteers, Captain Bowman seized the opportunity (and so did I) to broaden his experience and attended the Armored Officer Advance Course at the Armor Center at Fort Knox, Kentucky, where we met again. Thereafter, he was assigned to the 2nd Armored Division (Hell on Wheels) Fort Hood, Texas, as a Company Commander. There he served with distinction for three years. Soon after, I lost track of Bill. Trying to find him, all I was able to learn was that he was on some kind of detached service with the State Department inspecting the Military Assistance Program around the world."

From what I knew so far, that assignment must have been a cover, but complying with my instructions from General Betancourt, I said nothing. So came to an end my very vivid and informative interview with Bill's good friend, Colonel Matt Fleming. My pursuit of the remarkable career of Bill Bowman would take me back to General Betancourt. His knowledge of the special operations which were to occupy Bill for the next few years should be fascinating and, I hoped not anticlimactic.

CHAPTER 7

THE RECRUITMENT

Moving now to highly classified information, I returned to General Betancourt to pick up the story. The army's chief historian ushered me into his private office. Locking the door to the outer office, Court asked me to follow him as we made our way into the secure conference room. I was heartened to see that, apparently, it was show time because the room was set up for a presentation. Just over the far end of the table on the ceiling was a battery of spot lights to illuminate maps and charts on a small speaker's platform. The General activated an electronic field, thereby shielding our conversation from eavesdroppers. Once seated at the conference table, he pressed a button on a computer-like console which opened the curtains and exposing a large rear projection screen. Pushing another button, he projected a notice in giant red letters:

**This material is classified
TOP SECRET**

Leaving it on as if to burn the message into my brain, he continued,

"I need not remind you of your sworn oath to the President, but MOPS could be placed in moth balls with the election of any future president and then you might be free to write your *now it can be told* book. But for the present, MOPS is strong and healthy. They say that in Washington the word 'covert' is a contradiction, because no secret can exist in this town. What you will learn today will refute that view. Shortly after I joined MOPS, the President spoke to us. I can still recall most vividly his saying,

'Freedom is paid for on the installment plan. Do you know what happens when you miss a payment?' He asked rhetorically. 'You must pay a big payment to catch up. In the past we have been forced to make some pretty hefty payments, like the Second World War and Korea, which were penalties for unpreparedness and failure to act. If we decide not to make the big payments, our freedom will be repossessed. Wendell Phillips said in 1852 that eternal vigilance is the price of liberty. We certainly must be vigilant enough to see when a payment is due. As President, it is my job to see to it the payments are made on time so that they remain within our budget and keep the peace.'

"Scoop, you are about to learn of a highly effective method we use to keep the collection agency from our door." He reached forward and pressed another button, and this time a briefing title flashed on the screen.

TOP SECRET

MILITARY OPERATIVES TO PREVENT SUBVERSION

(MOPS)

"The first thing you should know is that, in addition to my duties as Chief Historian, I am the Army Facilitator for MOPS, code name MULEY. Wearing that hat, I take my orders directly from the Chairman of the Joint Chiefs of Staff, code name CLIMBER, through the MOPS Chief of Staff, code name WIZARD. The Navy and Air Force also have facilitators and these are covert positions in addition to their normal duties. If the MOPS brain trust needs people and/or material from the Army, my job is to procure it for them through key army people. These, though ignorant of MOPS know I have the clout and the backing of the Chief of Staff and the Secretary of the Army, who, although they don't know why, do know that I am occasionally on temporary duty to the Chairman of the Joint Chiefs of Staff. I alert certain key people by beginning all my messages with: THIS IS A K-2 PRIORITY; K-2 being the exclusive MOPS priority and supersedes all others. It is then authenticated by computer without 'permitting the tabby to escape the sack,' and gets MOPS anything the army can provide.

Our recruiting effort, though not on a grand scale, nonetheless is thorough and meticulous. We make extensive background checks before we recruit our operatives. We look for someone with clear motivation. We do not want someone running away from something—an escapist trying to get out of a jam. We look for a particular kind of courage which can support a person through an ordeal in obscurity. An operative needs that cool, determined, lonely kind of courage, being a cross between an assassin and a saboteur, a diplomat and a soldier, a spy and a commando.

I recruited Captain Bowman personally from the 2nd Armored Division. Wearing my historian's cap, I visited Fort Hood ostensibly to observe the new M-60 tank on maneuvers, while in reality my only purpose was to buttonhole Bowman. I knew him only by his exemplary military record in war and peace, which showed him to be an intelligent man of action, a quick thinker on his feet and just the sort we'd need in a tight situation. He was also a bachelor.

Yes, he was qualified, but I felt Bill was happy with his career, and having accepted a regular army commission along with his CMH, he had set definite career goals. He had just been placed on the promotion list to Major and, at the current rate he expected it to come through in three or four months. The change of branch to Armor was a wise move because the branch was watching his career development carefully and had projected the best assignments in the coming years to enhance his qualifications. With all this going for him, I doubted he'd want to rock the boat. I felt the only chance was to appeal to his keen sense of service and patriotism by convincing him that his individual contribution to the security of our country, and therefore the world, would be magnified many times by joining us. I stressed the job's importance by explaining that his immediate superiors would be at the highest level. To my great surprise, knowing no more about his new job than that, he agreed by quoting Thomas Jefferson, 'Resistance to tyrants is obedience to God,' which, whether he knew it or not, cut to the heart of the matter. Also, the expectation that his most important work was still to come, as part of his manifest destiny, no doubt influenced his decision to join MOPS. It was as if he had foreknown my coming and let me speak only long enough for him to be certain it was I for whom he was waiting.

We were pleased to hear that Bill wanted no part of fame, riches and power—that trio of seducers which alienate the affections of men for truth, beauty and goodness. He did know that hereafter, from a career management view, his work would be both independent and anonymous, and for all intents and purposes, his record as an army officer would no longer reflect his true activities, but include false assignments and dummy efficiency reports so as not to draw attention to him. Future promotion boards would be fed fictitious records calculated to insure promotion along normal guide lines.

To get him started in our line of work, I arranged for him to attend the Army Special Warfare School at Fort Bragg, North Carolina, which, although overt, was the closest thing the army had for teaching the skills required for the job. Later, we could fill in the gaps which called for specialized education. As a Green Beret, he acquired expertise in the martial arts, communications, code training, guerilla warfare, handling all manner of specialized demolitions on land and beneath the sea, scuba diving, mountaineering, the rudiments of covert operations and establishing intelligence networks. Bill was a Master Parachutist with considerable experience in night airdrops, vital to future operations. By this time, Bill was a half-step slower than the Lieutenant in Korea, but more experienced, with mature judgment. Paradoxically, his future performance would be spectacular, if less conspicuous.

I interviewed Bill at length to learn more about what made him tick as a man, the inner Bill. On the one hand, he said this,

"We have been accused of looking for simplistic answers to the complex problems in the world today. However, I have discovered that living a good life is simple; so simple that many let their intellect stand in the way of their faith. They keep asking questions, the answers to which they need not know. God gave us the rule book—we need only to follow it.' Hearing this, I made note to myself that these were not the words of a fighter. I admired his faith, but wondered how this could be the same man who had won the CMH. Then he exposed the flip side of the coin as he continued,

'In the wilderness alone with Satan, Jesus commanded with supreme authority, "Get thee hence, Satan!" As mortals, *we* cannot command evil to disappear. Evil must be fought at every turn to keep it from insinuating itself into our lives. We cannot accomplish this by being idle. On the contrary, idleness invites evil to take power over us. We fight evil by doing good works at every opportunity.' The opportunity I was presenting him seemed to be in harmony with his beliefs. It was fundamental to his strong sense of patriotism, his purpose for being and his unshakable faith. He would blush to hear me say this, but he was a modern crusader for a righteous cause. For that reason, MOPS appealed to him: he could devote the remainder of his active service to combating Satan with every chance of winning. When you think of it, that was a powerful motivation to a man like Bill; one that would serve him well in his opposition to a demon who was Satan's first apostle.

Bill also felt strongly that a soldier's ambition should be limited to the ranks of the military. Historically, he knew that all the heroes who had been called upon by their countrymen to serve in the highest office in the land shared the belief that civilian control of the armed forces is absolutely essential in a free society; men like George Washington, Andrew Jackson, Zachary Taylor, Ulysses S, Grant, Theodore Roosevelt and Dwight Eisenhower. Bill felt that political objectives should not be allowed to conflict with sound military and strategic considerations, at least until victory is a certainty.

I think I discovered the key to Bill's positive mental attitude when he told me that whereas some men are better equipped physically, mentally and emotionally to handle adversity, he did not believe there were great men, only great challenges which face ordinary men. When they are successful, the greatness of the challenge is attributed to them. While a humble point of view, which I found refreshing, Bill had a confident 'can do' attitude toward his new and challenging job."

General Betancourt flashed onto the screen an organizational chart and the MOPS mission statement.

TOP SECRET

THE MOPS MISSION: At the discretion and direction of the President of the United States, conduct covert anti-terrorist and anti-subversion operations in support of U.S. foreign policy worldwide. Such missions will be accomplished in a manner as to hold secret the existence of MOPS from the enemy and friendly governments alike.

<u>**PRESIDENT**</u>
<u>**CHRM, JCS**</u>
<u>**MOPS C/S**</u>
<u>**TASK TEAM COMMANDER**</u>

Four teams to be tailored to the mission in terms of expertise, number of personnel and equipment required.

TOP SECRET

The code names of key people, not including K-2 contacts.

The President	EVEREST	(EV)
Chairman of the JCS	CLIMBER	(CR)
MOPS Chief of Staff	WIZARD	(WD)
Army Facilitator	MULEY	(ML)
Navy Facilitator	SWAB	(SB)
Air Force Facilitator	TALON	(TN)
CIA Rep	BLANKET	(BK)
FBI Rep	GANGSTER	(GR)
Task Team Commander	BUCKAROO	(BK)
Task Team Commander	SIDEKICK	(SK)
Task Team Commander	VICEROY	(VY)
Task Team Commander	WILLIAM TELL	(WT)
MOPS Base	MAGNOLIA	(MA)

TOP SECRET

"Now you can see why the Secretary of the Army and the Army Chief of Staff know nothing of this organization. They are conspicuous by their absence. Notice that the Chairman of the Senate Armed Services Committee is not considered an insider and is only told what he needs to know. Also the Secretaries of Defense and State are out of the picture. The chain of command is quite clear, beginning with the President, to the Chairman of the Joint Chiefs of Staff, to the MOPS Chief of Staff, to the Task Teams. The MOPS Chief of Staff, WIZARD, coordinates the activities of the Army, Navy, Air Force, State Department, CIA and FBI representatives, one per service, who have no idea of the character of the operations they are supporting; only that K-2 is the highest priority. So it boils down to the fact that operationally MOPS consists of only seven people plus highly trained men to make up the task teams—no empire building here—the larger the organization the weaker the security.

WIZARD, the MOPS Chief of Staff, was what they allude to in the navy as a mustang; a man who worked his way up through the enlisted and officer ranks to Vice Admiral. Respected by all for his effort, but especially for his kinship to enlisted personnel; his men knew he'd "paid his dues" and so they'd follow him anywhere. His broad experience, serving on and commanding ships of the line, in naval aviation and as military attache in embassies in Europe and Asia uniquely qualified him for the job. Socially, he was equally at home on the bridge or in the forecastle; his language refined or salty, appropriate to the moment. He and Bill, WILLIAM TELL (WT) as I must now call him, were kindred spirits, having begun as enlisted men, but he was careful not to show favoritism toward anyone. He was highly sensitive to the needs and abilities of his four Task Team Commanders and made every attempt to equalize their prowess so that commander availability would never be a problem.

MAGNOLIA is the MOPS base quarters, our safe house, and is located on a military reservation near the capitol. It consists of two large warehouses, the interiors of which were remodeled with office spaces, living quarters, kitchen, recreational facilities, and an indoor small arms range. The building is air conditioned and completely sound proof and without windows or doors except for a covered truck loading dock. Entry is gained through what looks like a water pump station in thick woods some 120 yards away, then through a concrete tunnel to a point beneath MAGNOLIA where an elevator brings you up to the office area. The two buildings are connected by an enclosed passage wide enough for a forklift to operate. The buildings are surrounded by a double-chain-link and barbed-wire fence equipped with state-of-the-art electronic intrusion detection and surveillance devices.

MAGNOLIA boasts a worldwide communications center, a conference room with the latest in visual aids, gymnasium and weight room, two bowling lanes and handball courts. Necessary to the mission is a political science library that would be the envy of any university. Service facilitators, when operating under the K-2 priority, do not work at MAGNOLIA; they only respond to render assistance as required and then return to their normal duties. Between missions the Task Teams maintain a staggered training schedule of two weeks on and two weeks off, keeping WIZARD informed of their location. Because missions are at the personal direction of EVEREST, they can be several weeks absent, so two of the four teams are normally kept on training status to stay sharp, each regarding the other as the enemy. This role-playing can become very realistic, depending on the imagination of team members and how far they wish to carry realism in training; there are no holds barred, short of causing casualties.

WILLAM TELL found the "chess game," as he called it, with the more experienced TTCs, stimulating and honed his skills at covert operations to a fine edge. But, still it wasn't the real thing, and he was becoming impatient for the excitement of action, so he asked WIZARD to declare his team operational. WIZARD, on the other hand, was about to do so, based on his own evaluation of the team's proficiency and reports from the other TTCs, but since the request came from WT, he asked for justification. Expecting a long explanation he instead got just four words, equally emphasized and distinctly spoken,

"Because we are ready."

"I came to that conclusion three days ago, but needed reports from the other TTCs. The last reached my desk this morning. You *are* operational, effective immediately."

"Thank you, sir. I'll alert my people."

Although WILLIAM TELL's team had trained together, in a sense they became operational as individuals from this point because the organization of each task team was tailored to the mission; one might require three men, another ten. One mission might emphasize demolition, another might require a blend of individual skills. Being operational meant his team was next up; two teams were on missions, real or drill, and one was on leave.

Elsewhere, sinister plans were on a collision course with WILLIAM TELL. The Cubans were crucial to Soviet Plans for the subversion of South America, one nation at a time, targeting the two most prestigious countries; reasoning that, without their protection and stabilizing influence, the remainder of the continent would fall like so many dominoes. But first, it would be necessary to obtain a foothold on the continent, quietly, so as not to arouse the world, the United States in particular. The U.S., the sleeping giant who has shown no signs of invoking the Monroe Doctrine against western hemisphere countries with internal revolutions, even if thought to be foreign-inspired.

I told you this was a story of two men. Enter now the evil one. The Cuban's Soviet adviser was non-other than Satan's first apostle, Vassily Karenski, an experienced and sadistic KGB agent who had been largely responsible for subverting middle European countries following World War II. He had been assigned to the highly sensitive western hemisphere because he was a patient but ruthless man capable of all sorts of outrageous attacks on the established social order and skilled at political assassination, often handling such assignments personally. He found a ghoulish excitement in killing and intellectual stimulation in devising methods which would leave him above suspicion and free to kill again. Karenski had become known to the secret services of the western community of nations by a universal code name, but little else was known of him. No one, as yet, could positively identify him. Later, when detailed facts about him came to light, we marveled at how accurately his assigned code name described him. This deadly snake who killed without warning was code named KRAIT—the deadliest of vipers.

The Soviet's master plan for the subversion and subjugation of South America targeted first the tiny democracy of Tierra Blanca for a coup d'etat. Possession of Tierra Blanca would facilitate the eventual conquest of the continent in years to come. It had been KRAIT's task to train Cuban insurgents for the job as a front for the Soviets. Events were proceeding inexorably toward a blind confrontation between KRAIT and MOPS in the person of WILLIAM TELL.

The MOPS TTCs were encouraged to keep tabs on likely candidates for recruitment to replace losses, by mishap or retirement. WILLIAM TELL was reading over service records of some of the best with whom he'd served. During his next time off, he would talk to them one by one. The other members, called by their code numbers, were around the complex using its various facilities when they were interrupted by an announcement on the intercom summoning the team to the conference room.

Upon arrival, it was instantly apparent that this was a mission briefing because both CLIMBER and WIZARD were in the room. CLIMBER move quickly to the platform over which was emblazoned the creed, borrowed from the commandoes of WWII, that the men of MOPS lived by: **PLAN CAREFULLY, EXECUTE**

BOLDY, RETIRE SWIFTLY. He took up position in front of a large map and, with a sense of urgency, began to speak,

"You've probably wondered why we have recently directed your studies to South America. Reading the papers and the increasing volume of intelligence summaries on that area, it's not hard to see that things are heating up there; Tierra Blanca in particular. This little country is the key target in the Cuban-backed insurgency effort to get a foothold in South America that can be used as a staging area for the eventual subversion and take-over of the entire continent. Historically, this tiny republic, with its splendid natural harbor, here in the bay of Salinas at the capitol, Buena Vista, has never required nor maintained a standing army, but has a militia with a small cadre of U.S. trained officers and pilots. It has never been threatened by her neighbors because they too have an abundance of the same natural resources and take their Christian faith seriously.

"Cuba saw easy pickings here and began a campaign to discredit the democratic government. Of course this is a classic ploy and not difficult to accomplish in a free and open society where the press can be counted upon to sensationalize and provide a free voice to a tiny but vocal minority, whatever their politics. Over the last two years the seeds of discontent have been sown with the help of a handful of vocal native turncoats trained in Cuba. Last night what looks like a successful coup took place. Under normal circumstances, that would be that—chalk up another one for the bad guys. But, we now have the leadership, the will, the ability and the means to turn this situation around so quickly, that when the dust settles, the coup will be regarded by the world as a mere incident successfully defeated by an alert government in power. A coup isn't a coup unless power can be consolidated and relations established with Cuba and the Soviet Union. We do not intend that either will take place.

"Fortunately, EVEREST has received a written request for assistance from President Armendarez. Our latest information indicates the government can regain control of Buena Vista by concentrating all their residual loyal forces. But they can be forced out again by reinforcements from the Cuban-controlled garrisons outside the city from four separate camps: here on the south coast, on the south plain, in the northern mountains and near the central area. Our contingency plans for this area call for insertion of troops within 24 hours of an alert, so the speed required does not concern us. We can deploy airborne troops in assault aircraft to neutralize these garrisons and their rough airstrips to prevent movement to reinforce Buena Vista, giving President Armendarez time to reestablish his government in power. We anticipate U.S. troops would be in-country no longer the three days, during which time we would turn over the captured rebel leaders to the government, at the end of which time, we will depart as quickly as we came in.

"What we cannot permit to happen, however, is for U.S. forces to get bogged down in a lengthy fight which would give Cubans time to mount an anti-American propaganda campaign in the U.N. and provide fuel for agitating anti-war activists in our own country. What is needed here is quick surgery, precise and effective, so the patient can be back on his feet and functioning in the shortest period of time. Therefore, it is mandatory to confirm that we have accurate, up-to-the-minute intelligence and assurance that everything is in place to guarantee success. So here is what EVEREST has directed MOPS to do:

1. Insert, covertly, a pre-strike reconnaissance team to verify and update current intelligence and contact resistance leaders;
2. Assess the ability and resolve of the Armendarez government to do its part;
3. Establish a mutually-determined D-day and H-hour;
4. Exit the country, undetected, prior to H-hour.

"In deference to WILLIAM TELL, our TTC, this mission is herewith designated OPERATION ARROW. Reference part 2 of our mission; this is a Tierra Blanca show at Buena Vista. No U.S. forces will show themselves anywhere near the place, and if we all do our jobs, neither will reinforcements which can hinder them. The MOPS team is given a 48-hour maximum in country, after which you will transmit by radio one of three code words:

- "WINDOW" is to be followed by the number of hours to H-hour. Example: WINDOW-41 means success and H-hour is mutually agreed upon to be 41 hours after this transmission.
- "SHUTTER" means you need twelve more hours to accomplish your mission, and can be sent only once.
- "CURTAIN" means abort mission; there is serious doubt that the mission can be accomplished within guidelines.

"I don't have to tell you this operation puts a tremendous burden of responsibility on MOPS. The whole show depends on the good judgment of our TTC, WILLIAM TELL, in whom EVEREST has place special trust and confidence."

CLIMBER yielded the platform to WIZARD. "For the next hour we'll bring you up to date on the latest information we have including high altitude reconnaissance photos and messages from in country which you must verify on the ground as soon as possible after landing. Our embassy cannot be of much help. The staff is under surveillance and is not permitted to leave the city. The MOPS team of nine men will infiltrate by night parachute drop, here;" with the pointer he indicated a centrally-located drop zone, and continued…"where you will meet your contact and four other guides." Once again he adjusted the position of his pointer… "the alternate DZ is here. Your contact on the ground will be a friend of our military attache and an English speaking citizen of

Tierra Blanca, Antonia Lopez; she knows the country and has arranged transport for you. Here is a recent photo of her." She was strikingly attractive and this evoked an enthusiastic response from the team, but WIZARD forged ahead. "Your recognition code is, DO YOU LIKE TO FLY? To which her reply must be, ONLY SINGLE ENGINE AND ONLY ON SATURDAYS.

"From the DZ you will split up in twos and obtain your confirmation of the following:

1. Intelligence indicates the four garrisons consist of 300 men each with ten Cubans leading. Are these figures accurate to within 20 percent?
2. Are troop dispositions, as we know them, accurate? Note any troop movements.
3. Are all four airstrips operational and free of obstacles?
4. Is President Armendarez ready to act decisively at H-hour and organized to do so.

If the answers to these questions are 'yes' send your success code, WINDOW, and make your way to the coast, here, where two inflatable rafts are hidden. You will rendezvous at sea in the manner we developed during your last training exercise.

"Let me emphasize that time is critical, but don't rush; sloppy work can't be tolerated. Be in and out in less than 48 hours. Don't even think about sleep until you are out safely. You will all wear casual clothing, just like that worn by natives, but you will carry concealed hand guns. Your radio transmitter is the AC/DC Paraset Mark-9 with telegraph key. Your message should reach me, but as a backup, SWAB has arranged for the navy to monitor your frequency and relay the message. Your twin engine aircraft will have commercial markings, courtesy BLANKET, and you'll refuel at Guantanamo Bay Naval Station, Cuba; again arranged by SWAB—a little irony there. Your plane's flight plan calls for Rio, and it will proceed there after your slight detour. Be at planeside in two hours—takeoff 30 minutes later. You are as prepared as we can make you and the opportunity has presented itself, so do it!" WIZARD didn't believe in luck.

At the airfield, the Task Team was dismayed at the sight of their transportation. It was a Curtiss C-46, and antique, a relic from the past first used in WWII flying the 'hump' over the Himalayas to help supply China. But on second thought, it was perfect for the mission because these old planes were still rather commonplace in South America having been made available at disposal prices after the war. Frequently seen flying at low altitudes, they would not be regarded with suspicion, even by trained observers. Further, the team's parachutes were free-fall models which would mean less time in the air, so the possibility of being observed was quite remote. They breathed a collective sigh of relief when the old plane's engines cranked over and the sound told them the engines were new. Not only new, but of recent design for more power and speed, and the fuel tanks had been enlarged for longer range. This old bird was a regular hot rod.

Meantime, in Havana, KRAIT beat his fist on the desk of Ramon Salazar, the Cuban Deputy Foreign Minister, in charge of the Tierra Blanca coup attempt.

"You must get moving to consolidate your power in the country. You are too slow in following up your advantage. You must not lose momentum."

"Set your mind at rest, comrade..." Salazar assured him,"...we are in total control in Tierra Blanca. You taught us well. We did not expect it to be so easy. Our timetable must be moved ahead but there is no urgency, Senor. We haven't enough air transport to do the job and the ships take time to load. Relax, the coup is over; Tierra Blanca is ours. In a few days we will land the troops and material to control the populace during the consolidation phase." An aide to Salazar standing by added,

"Comrade, there has been nothing in the foreign press about the coup; we have won. It is over."

"Nothing is over!" KRAIT warned, "The ships should have been loaded well in advance, have sailed and been ready to dock as soon as the country was seized. You must depart today or risk everything." Salazar paused in thought and then acquiesced,

"Very well, we have two ships two-thirds loaded, but not scheduled to depart until the day after tomorrow. I will order them to sail tonight with what they have."

KRAIT backed away from the desk and summoned up his very limited Spanish, "Buena." Admonishing himself for failing to check the obvious, he secretly yearned for the day when he could end this charade; the world would be under Soviet control and he would no longer have to cajole these Latin idiots to achieve his ends. Doubting the Cubans, he pinned his hopes on SWALLOW, his deep undercover agent in Tierra Blanca, to assure success. He could not afford failure, even if the Cubans were blamed. He gloated for a moment on how he had won so many victories at so little cost to mother Russia. Nothing in this world could stop him because no one was organized to do so. The great United States, so invincible in conventional warfare, still had not devised an effective defense against him.

The high-tech engines of the old C-46 droned sweetly and there was plenty of time to sleep, the last they'd get until the mission was accomplished. Nearing the end of the flight, the pilot called WILLIAM TELL forward and reviewed the prearranged signal to identify the DZ: five lights, shielded from ground observation, in the form of a "T." However, if they saw four lights in the shape of a square they must proceed to the alternate DZ. Looking around the crew compartment, WT was impressed by the advanced electronic equipment on board which contrasted with the rest of the aged aircraft. The plan was to fly south hugging the coast, using radar which was projecting a high resolution image of the coastline. The navigator had plotted a right turn due west when they reached a certain sleeping fishing village, then a straight line to the DZ, some 40 miles inland. Then, if necessary, a 20 degree left turn to the west-southwest another 8 miles to the alternate DZ. The navigator turned to WT and speaking loudly to be heard over the drone of the engines,

"Fifteen minutes to the DZ. Get your people ready!"

Returning to the passenger cabin, he could see that most of his team was awake and he shouted, "Fifteen minutes, get ready. He turned off the cabin lights and switched on the red night vision lights so eyes could adjust during the next few minutes. Another advantage of the C-46 was that it had doors on both sides which meant the team could jump five out one door and four out the other, holding a tighter pattern in the air and simplifying assembling once on the ground. WT checked his map and weapon, attaching a silencer, and stood up to initiate his sequence of commands.

"STAND UP!"
"CHECK YOUR EQUIPMENT!"
SOUND OFF FOR EQUIPMENT CHECK!"

Five OK! Four OK! Three OK! Two OK! One OK, shouted the two sticks in sequence. The red warning light flashed on.

"STAND IN THE DOOR!" WT waited, poised in the door watching for the green light, feeling uneasy about how long it was taking. Suddenly, the plane banked slightly to the left. Knowing something was wrong, WT looked toward the cockpit to see the navigator running toward him,

"No signal lights on the ground. We're going to the alternate—be ready." WILLIAM TELL warned his team to be alert for trouble on the ground.

In three minutes, the green light flashed on and in five seconds the nine men had exited the aircraft into the blackness. After a delayed count, each parachute opened, suspending the men in the air for only 15 seconds before landing: a great performance! The team quickly regrouped, buried their chutes and entrenching tool and moved off the DZ to the southwest corner of the field edged by a low rock wall. A woman appeared. Pistol drawn, WT challenged,

"DO YOU LIKE TO FLY?" In clear English came the reply, "ONLY TWIN ENGINES AND ONLY ON SUNDAYS." Without a word, WILLIAM TELL shot her dead with a single pull of the trigger. He produced the identification picture from his pocket to verify to the team what he already knew; there was no resemblance to the woman who was to be their contact. He looked around to assure that no one was close enough to have heard the muffled shot and, huddled with his men, explaining his estimate of the situation.

"Here's how I see it. Somehow our contact, under duress, gave this woman false information. She was probably instructed to lead us into a trap, either ambush or capture. Our contact gave her the location of the alternate DZ, knowing we would be alerted to danger by the lack of lights at the primary. If we stand any chance at all of contacting the Armendarez people, we must move out now and backtrack to the primary DZ. Now, let's get this body underground before her confederates come looking for her."

With only the light of the stars and some sky glow from the distant city to the southwest, the team covered the 8 miles cross-country in three and a half hours, arriving at the primary at 0430, just before dawn. Shortly thereafter, the team saw a shadowy form approaching, moving unsteadily, and falling headlong at the feet of a team member. WILLIAM TELL ran over to discover a woman, badly beaten about the head and bleeding from the mouth. He challenged,

"DO YOU LIKE TO FLY?" She replied haltingly,
"ONLY SINGLE ENGINE, AND ONLY ON SATURDAYS." He looked concerned for her, so she said, smiling, I'm OK, don't worry about me. I just escaped an hour ago from my home where they were holding me, a woman and two men. They knew I

was a friend of the Military Attache and came to my house last night before I was to join you here." A team member, agent 18, who was a qualified paramedic, examined her injuries as she continued, "They seemed to know *something* but wouldn't say what. Maybe they just expected trouble and thought I knew something. Anyway, they beat me and I didn't know what else to do, so I gave them the location of the alternate drop zone and the wrong password. The woman who met you intended to lead whoever she met back to my house. I think they were trying to be heroes and didn't notify anyone. After she left, one of the men ordered the other to stand guard outside the entrance and then forced me into another room, tried to rape me and, in the struggle, I killed him with a pair of scissors. Then I went to the front door and screamed. As the other man came through the door I struck him on the head with a heavy candlestick holder. I contacted my men, so they should be here before daylight. Did I do the right thing?" Looking at 18, she said, "Thanks."

"I don't see how it could have worked out any better. Don't worry about it. We're here and there's work to be done. Are you OK now?"

"Yes, I'm fine, just tired from running. Now that I've caught my breath, I'm OK."

"How did you dispose of the bodies? I don't want to alert anyone."

"That's been taken care of; they won't be found." As she spoke four police cars arrived and stopped near them. Seeing the startled look on the team's faces, she hastened to explain,

"These are your guides. The Assistant Chief of Police is loyal to the president and so are these officers. They can take you anywhere in the country without suspicion, but you must ride in back, like prisoners."

Two to a car, each team pair was given instructions to rendezvous at a point five miles inland from where were hidden their rubber rafts. Just as quickly as they arrived, the cars scattered, leaving Miss Lopez and WT to seek out and talk to the president.

"Please, we must hurry. My car is hidden down the road. The president is expecting us. He is in hiding at Rancho Tierra del Sol, in the hills."

As the sun began to rise, they got under way and Miss Lopez continued her explanation,

"My country is small, roughly 250 miles north and south and 150 miles across from the coastline inland to the border. We are now in the hilly north, good cattle country. The southern plains are ideal for sugar cane, bananas and pineapple. Our people consider themselves residents of paradise. The Cubans came to cause trouble because, in their twisted view of the world, they saw us as weak and vulnerable. But a free people can be strong when they need to be. Without a strong armed force, the president wisely prepared the country to fight an insurgency, and you represent the timely help we need from friends we can trust."

WILLIAM TELL wondered about his stunning companion. He was curious, but since he could not answer questions in return he thought it best not to be inquisitive—stick to business. Yet, she was beautiful; an actress perhaps, her classic features only partially diminished by her bruises. From her apparel, he concluded she had dressed for her mission, strictly business. She spoke with no accent and in American idiom, so he assumed she had been American-educated. She was indeed class, a woman of education and a devout Christian, judging from the beautiful crucifix around her lovely neck. For a woman her voice was low but still very feminine. It had a soothing quality; it was a voice with which one could not grow weary. He was struck by the perfect match, voice and features. She must be well aware of her attractiveness, he thought, but she appeared not to be affected by it. She was down to earth, with a job to do, and there'd be no nonsense about it. She wore no make-up except lip rouge sparingly applied. He noticed the graceful natural arch of her dark eyebrows, needing no enhancement, her high forehead providing the canvas which showed them off to perfection. Her dark eyes were not only beautiful, but expressive, and her long eyelashes proclaimed them most proudly, female. Never had his powers of observation been so pleasantly treated. Being a bachelor, and considering her figure, he found it difficult to stifle the temptation to mentally undress her. Still that wasn't his style.

She, in their very brief acquaintance, was impressed by his professionalism, his reaction to how she had handled a difficult situation, in particular. He seemed a gentleman, and obviously dedicated to his work. She would have to be content with her sketchy appraisal of this man with no name based only on observation of his mannerisms and speech because he wasn't trying to turn this into a social call. If he wished to remain silent, she'd respect that. Engrossed in her appraisal of him, she caught herself suddenly and thought to herself, "One thing at a time; mission first. But, gee, he's a hunk."

They were now on a gravel road, and off in the distance they could see a complex of adobe buildings which comprised the ranch headquarters, but at a junction in the road they turned away, prompting WT to ask,

"Isn't that the ranch?"

"Yes, but it is not safe there. The president is at a section foreman's home closer to the border. We'll be there in a few minutes."

As they drew closer to their destination, WT began to look for likely security outpost locations and, finding some occupied, he knew they'd been seen and were expected. He approved of the site for a resistance headquarters; close to a friendly border, it could be evacuated quickly, the terrain lent itself to defense by relatively few troops, and the only vehicular approach was under observation for a great distance. Yes, the selection of this site was no accident. Then they caught sight of the house, a modest stucco hacienda in a pastoral setting with a barn and a corral.

There was nothing out of place or suspicious about the scene. As they stopped, a middle-aged man stepped off the porch to greet them. Miss Lopez spoke in Spanish, and turning to WILLIAM TELL said,

"He doesn't speak English; we are to follow him on foot."

They walked around a hillock, losing sight of the hacienda, and into a grove of tall eucalyptus trees sheltering an out-building at the base of a sharply rising hillside. Once inside, he discovered the building concealed the entrance to a natural cavern, which they entered. They were immediately met by a militiaman, whereupon the first man returned to the hacienda. The tunnel was well-lighted and eventually led into a huge room carved by nature, with a ceiling over 30 feet high and about the size of a basketball court, with room to spare. It was alive with activity having been set up as a secret emergency operation center years before. There were wooden stairs to a cleft-like opening some 12 feet up the rocky wall leading to another, smaller room and overlooking the activity. As they ascended the stairs, a figure suddenly appeared at the top, looking down and smiling,

"Welcome to my country, senor. You are late."

"Thank you Mr. President, but there was an incident that delayed us. Miss Lopez's calculated risk counting on our alertness kept us out of serious trouble. She is to be commended." Antonia mused, "He didn't have to say that. What a wonderful guy." The president looked at her,

"Antonia, what happened to you?"

"I'm alright, sir. Please excuse me a few minutes, I need to freshen up a bit."

Looking at WILLIAM TELL, the president said,

"Come…come into my humble hideaway and be comfortable." Turning to an aide he said, "Bring coffee and some sandwiches" Then to WT, "Senor, you can eat while I explain our plan. We have no time to waste; I am prepared now to reestablish our government in Buena Vista, which you can see is still in operation, but each day we delay makes it more difficult. I must move within 48 hours to take advantage of the Cuban's cocky attitude. Once we knew the Cubans were active in our country, we purposely led them to believe we were a sleepy banana republic without the ability to resist. In this way we drew the enemy into the open and marked them for elimination—assassination, if you will. That is how we fight without an army. Every Cuban operative and turncoat has now shown his true colors. No trials are necessary because this is war. We are merely fighting it in our own way—to win. Our counterinsurgency plan calls for the elimination of the following people:

1. The three Cubans and one traitor at the TV and radio station.
2. The four Cubans and two traitors at the newspaper.
3. The Chief of Police and 10 Cubans at the Metropolitan Police Headquarters.
4. The 16 Cubans at the presidential palace.

We have led them all into believing our people will bend to the prevailing wind which now blows from Cuba.

We are counting on U.S. Forces to neutralize the garrisons outside the city. In time we might be able to do that too, but we have no time. If we are to be successful, we must strike now before the Cubans can consolidate their power. Most of my people will be concentrated to regain control of Buena Vista International Airport, the only paved runways in the country, and the Capitol Garrison, and are ready to turn on the Cubans when given the word. By concentrating my whole effort at Buena Vista, I regain the means to show my countrymen and the world we are still in control. In fact, it might work without your help, but I believe in insurance and, this way, we can capture and eliminate many Cubans schooled in insurgency, once and for all. Secondly, your president wants to demonstrate to other western hemisphere countries America's willingness to help those who can help themselves. The signal that will put our plan into motion is my prerecorded message to be broadcast from a secret transmitter inside the city. My key people are monitoring that frequency; their first move will be to recapture the radio-TV station from within and repeat the message to all the country. Now, do you have any questions?"

"Yes sir. There is a lot to be done here and, if it were done piecemeal, your chances for success are substantially reduced because, once alerted, the Cubans could foil your attempt. What is a realistic timetable for you to accomplish your end of the plan?"

"One hour."

"Mr. President, I mean a realistic timetable for you to regain control?"

"Without interference from outside the city: one hour. You see, every Cuban and turncoat has a shadow; a man who can pinpoint the location of each man or woman to be eliminated, and he is backed up by two or three others who will perform the actual assassination. No one will escape. When this specially-trained Cuban cadre is eliminated they cannot be replaced for some time, to try again here or elsewhere. Our success here will strike fear into the hearts of those who would play this game again, not to mention raising the morale and patriotism of my countrymen. Believe me, our hearts and souls are in this. Have no doubt about that."

"Very well sir, the rest of my team will be at the rendezvous point no later than 14 hours from now. I must have their reports before I can act, and the military task force needs 16 hour notice prior to H-hour. So that means the nearest time that can be set for H-hour is 30 hours from now."

"Buena, better than I had hoped. Let it be 30 hours from now."

"It is 0910 hours. H-hour will be 1510 hours tomorrow."

"Excellent, we will be ready. Ah, Antonia, you look yourself again." During the briefing Miss Lopez had her injuries attended to and put on a new face; even with a swollen eye, she was a lovely woman.

With the usual amenities, WILLIAM TELL and his charming guide departed for the rendezvous to await the return of the team. As they drove, the country seemed oblivious to the coup, and phase two, the ruthless consolidation of power, had not yet begun and would not if the Armendarez plan succeeded. As he thought, WT quickly and confidently struck *if* and substituted *when*. He attributed the ease with which he was able to move unmolested to the timing of the U.S. In a few days, this would have become a police state and very difficult conditions for resistance groups.

The first to report in at the rendezvous were agents 21 and 42, who were assigned to the north garrison, close by. Agent 21 rendered his report,

"Of the estimated three hundred men at north garrison, about twenty-five deserted into the hills when the Cubans arrived. There are eleven Cubans and the camp's second-in-command is a turncoat. The CO is being held under lock and key. The senior officer is a Lieutenant who is prepared to lead a handful of men against the Cubans. The airstrip can accommodate C-130s. In fact, they have prepared it for the arrival of re-enforcements, due in three days." At this point 42 added,

"There's only one road, and it ends at the camp. Block that road and they're boxed in. They have a conglomeration of nineteen trucks, of which four are light vehicles, a couple of Jeeps; they could effectively block the airstrip, but the Cubans have confiscated the distributer rotors until re-enforcements arrive. They have no armored cars or tanks and no weapons larger than .30caliber. The Lieutenant will be happy to organize a firing squad, but he and his troops expect more Cubans later in the week as promised by the Cuban in charge."

"OK, so we've confirmed the intelligence at north garrison."

"Yes sir."

"If all goes as expected, we should be hearing next from central garrison." At 1430 they did, and at 1845, 27 and 33 rendered their reports, followed by 18 and 40 at 1915 hours on coastal garrison. All airstrips were operational and troop strengths were within parameters. At 2010, the success message was sent in the clear,

"WINDOW19". The message was acknowledged and authenticated: "WINDOW19—ROGER, OUT."

The machinery was in motion. Next, having accomplished their mission, the team would immediately exit the country undetected. Antonia knew the road to the coast, and they were well within their operational timeframe. Finding their prepositioned rafts under some hay in a barn near the shore, they had only to inflate them and paddle out to sea for the rendezvous.

It was here that WT got a farewell he would never forget. Antonia came to him slipping both hands behind his neck, gently drew him close and kissed him long and passionately, and then breathed on his lips,

"When you come to my country again, I can be reached through your embassy." Then she pressed against his body and kissed him again, parting. WILLIAM TELL's head was swimming and his knees were shaky; when he regained his composure she was gone, into the night.

There was hardly a stir on the water's surface and WILLIAM TELL gave credit to the planners; they knew the hydrography of this part of the coastline. A cloudless night and a quarter moon setting, the team split up into the two rafts and began to paddle their way out to sea. The continental shelf ended abruptly about three quarters of a mile out and paddling became more difficult as they stroked through the choppy surface. Certain they were well out in deep water, they linked the two rafts together by the bow with a 60 foot line and began paddling away from each other until the line was stretched taut. Gently paddling to keep the line extended, with each raft showing a dim red light, they waited for fifteen minutes or so. Then they saw something in the water coming toward them from the direction of the coast. Like the head of some fabled sea serpent, it moved silently between the rafts intersecting the line between. The rafts began to swing back in an arch toward each other and picked up speed as they swung in behind the periscope. Dragged further out to sea, they soon slowed to a stop and the team maneuvered back to the intercept position, whereupon the submarine surfaced to a point where her deck was still awash by a foot or so. Then the team paddled their rafts to a position directly over the submerged deck, jamming their paddles into the deck grooves to maintain their position while the submarine continued to surface. Once high and dry, they deflated the rafts and stowed them in the sea locker of the conning tower and went below for a hot meal and some welcome sleep. They had accomplished their mission in 30 hours with no casualties. Correction: unknown to all, including himself, WILLIAM TELL had been pierced through the heart by an arrow from Cupid's bow.

Now the operation was in the hands of President Armendarez and the U.S. forces assisting him. Precisely at 1510 hours, airborne assault troops in C-130s unloaded along with command vehicles, and the aircraft were away. An aircraft carrier nearby flew air cover, just for practice; they weren't really needed. The tremendous show of force intimidated the Cubans, who scarcely fired a shot, and the four garrisons were returned to the control of the militia. Cubans and turncoats, with the Americans looking on, were summarily executed as a message not to try again. The next day at 0500 hours, the American Embassy radioed a success message, and the C-130s returned at 0900 to load up and were away by 0930. Just an overnight stay for the troops, a clean mission for MOPS, but a brilliant success in foreign policy which occurred so quickly it rated little space in the press and hardly a mention on TV. As a stern warning to stay out of the western hemisphere, the cost was negligible; no more than a training exercise. It was one of the cheapest victories in the cold war; which left KRAIT and the Cubans asking what happened.

In the aftermath, several Cuban ships already at sea bound for Tierra Blanca were intercepted by the navy blockade and turned back. Hereafter, the Cubans would focus on Central America, but without success."

My head was buzzing with questions, so I asked them.

"First, couldn't this job be handled by the CIA?"

"Our adversaries would expect that, and be looking for it, but also EVEREST felt it unwise to ask the CIA to verify its own work, particularly since he had the means to, in a very short time, not only verify, but update to the hour their information. The CIA had done its work well—intelligence was accurate."

"I see, but wasn't this a rather simple mission for MOPS?"

"That's just the point; timely action does make things easier and less costly all around. But even if the mission had not gone as planned, the team was capable of handling itself in a more fluid situation, or if there had been some resistance. Suppose the Cubans had been stronger, with a firmer grip on the country? Any number of things could have happened. I can't elaborate, but the team was ready for any eventuality. Also WIZARD was watching, as WILLIAM TELL's first mission, it was ideally suited to him, a test of sorts. Aside from that it became a personal milestone, although he was not immediately aware of it. Also, although they never met, he would one day confront his Soviet adversary in a way no one could foresee.

KRAIT, for the moment however, was left to ponder his misfortune.

CHAPTER 8

THE TEST

With the best sort of final examination behind him WILLIAM TELL fell to the bottom of the mission roster. He had been debriefed and full reports of the mission became history, buried history, but on the record nonetheless. Consequently, he had free time, at least two weeks. How would he use it? For two or three days he'd do some research in the MAGNOLIA library, a chore he'd put off long enough, and then he'd look up an old friend, a man he had not seen in years.

WILLIAM TELL relaxed in the library one afternoon. Wearing a stereo headset, he listening to the Saint-Saens Symphony #3 in C minor, Opus 78, oblivious to the world, his eyes closed, lost in the melodic strains of the kind of music he loved, the more dynamic of the classics, he felt a breeze on his face. Opening his eyes, he looked up to see 21 fanning his face with an official looking envelope. Lip reading produced "For You." He took the envelope with a nod, without removing the headset, and read the return address: Department of the Army, Office of the Adjutant

General. He shook the contents to one end and tore open the other, extracting the letter:

> *Dear Major Bowman,*
> *Reference your request to locate First Sergeant Billy R. Caruth..."* his eyes scanned the lines to... *"Company L, 12th Infantry Regiment, 4th Infantry Division, Fort Lewis, Washington"*

It was, momentarily, a sunny day as Major Bowman piloted the military Lear jet west over the smoky pulp mills of Tacoma and the Puget Sound looking toward the Olympic Mountains, snow-capped and crisp against the early morning sky. Banking to his left 180 degrees to an easterly course into the rising sun across the dark blue sound, he marveled at the breathtaking Cascade range and its most prominent feature, majestic Mount Rainier rising over fourteen thousand feet above the thick carpet of fir trees. He lowered the flaps and gear as he approached Fort Lewis and Gray Army Airfield. "This is some country," he sighed, giving inadequate words to his impression. Cleared to land, he was thinking that with all those trees, the air must be pure oxygen and looked forward to his first breath of it. At the direction of the ground guide he taxied to a stop near the hanger closest to Base Operations, shut down and opened the door. Stepping out, he drew a deep breath and gasped, "Wow, its cold for July." Then he recalled the words of Mark Twain: "The mildest winter I ever spent was a summer on Puget Sound." He knew now what that meant. The official temperature was 55 degrees. It had been 92 in the nation capitol the day before.

Looking around, he saw an old friend walking toward him. With a snappy salute he greeted,

"Good morning, Major Bowman. Welcome to God's country."

"Well, it's too cold to be the devil's country. How in the world are you, Sergeant Caruth?"

"Frankly Sir, I'm bored stiff."

"I gathered that from our phone conversation. Are you doing anything about it.?"

"I've a couple of irons in the fire, *just in case,* but I thought I'd hear you out first."

"Where can we talk and not be overheard?"

"There's an empty office in Base Ops, right over here. I got to tell you Sir, your phone call really piqued my curiosity."

"I'll start with some questions. You haven't gotten yourself married in the past few days have you?"

"No sir." Caruth replied smiling.

"Do you have special lady friend?"

'No sir, none willing to put up with me." They entered the empty office and closed the door as Bill continue,

"How would you feel about disappearing from view for a while—like until retirement?"

"That sounds downright clandestine, sir."

"More than you can possibly imagine. I'm in a completely different business now. I perform missions for people at the highest level of the service, in secret." Sergeant Caruth let out a low whistle and asked,

"But why do you think I'd be a good fit sir?"

"A look at your service record only confirms what I already know; you're as trustworthy and dedicated as ever—a consummate professional. You think quickly under pressure and you've always been officer material. Now hear me on this; if you want to join me, I'll be happy to take you as you are, but would you accept a commission? I can arrange it."

"Not yet, sir. I'd be more comfortable in a new job just as I am. Could I have a rain check on that?"

"Certainly, you just say the word when you're ready to be a Captain."

"Captain? What happened to Second and First Lieutenant?"

"This is a high powered outfit—no time for shave tails. We have Captains and above and senior NCOs."

"Still, I'll wait 'til my feet are on the ground, but you're making it sound very attractive."

"Does that mean you're ready to join me? Your value to the service will be greatly multiplied?"

"Before I commit myself sir, I have a couple of questions."

"Go!"

"Is there any special training I'll need?"

"Yes, six weeks at the Special Warfare School and specialized training with us until you can be declared operational. Altogether, 14 weeks of intensive training, then special studies for each mission, if there is time."

"I see. Do you guys appreciate the need for R&R from that pressure cooker of yours?"

"Indeed we do, and you'll like the schedule. It's better than the rest of the army, but it's all to insure that you are sharp physically and mentally for your next mission." Pausing a moment, Caruth looked at Bowman,

"I trust you sir. If you think I'm right for the job—OK." Reaching into his briefcase, Bill came out with a fist full of papers.

"Here are your orders. You report to Fort Bragg in two weeks. Incidentally, upon completion of your training there, I'll see to it your promotion to Sergeant Major is automatic."

"Pretty sure of me, weren't you sir?"

"No, but years ago you taught me to be ready...*just in case*. I saw the kind of opportunity I was looking for in the job and it's everything I'd hoped it would be."

"Can't you tell me more about the job?"

"Not here and not now, but I'll personally brief you after you win your Green Beret. By the way, why did you go to Jump School after Korea?"

"Oh...I had a pretty good Platoon Leader in Korea who was a jumper; besides you know how it was after Korea, I was looking for excitement."

"Still looking?"

"Yes sir!"

"You found it, my friend."

Major Bowman boarded his refueled plane for the return flight and turned to wave goodbye to his old comrade in arms who was standing at attention saluting. He returned the salute and closed the door as rain began to fall once more in the great northwest.

In contrast, it was a warm, clear summer day in the nation capitol, a day when you're glad to be alive, a day to spend in the park with your family, a day to get out and relax, a day to go to the ballpark and cheer for the Senators. This was not a day to be spent in the oval office with the immense burden of responsibility heavy on one's shoulders. Nevertheless a tiring President serious and worried but attentive, listened closely to the advice of his closest confidants concerning the weighty matter of yet another crisis in the middle east.

The USSR was probing for a soft spot again. The troubled area this time was around a point where the borders of three countries came together. Russia to the north, bordered both Sahbidad on the southwest and Tibistan on the southeast. This oil rich area had long been a powder keg with a short fuse owing to an ancient blood feud between two nomadic Bedouin tribes, traditionally observing no national boundaries. The tribes, the Shiminites and the Zirkas, are legendary for their fierceness in battle and hot tempers, more likely to indulge in inquiries after the bloodshed. The Soviets intended using this feud to their advantage, hoping to foment trouble and provoke open warfare between the tribes to create a situation which would give the impression to the world at large of open aggression against them, providing an excuse to occupy and seize the oil fields and the much coveted Indian Ocean port in Tibistan.

KRAIT, now superintendent of the KGB Academy as a result of a power struggle within the organization during which he narrowly averted banishment to Siberia, reported to his superiors that conditions would be right momentarily to invade Tibistan on the pretext of armed provocation. Based on his report, a timetable for occupation troops to cross the border was established, to be implemented the moment the world press announced open hostilities between the Shiminites and the Zirkas, which KRAIT promised was imminent.

American interests in the Middle East were assuredly in jeopardy, and reports from the CIA painted an alarming picture of possible Soviet intentions in the area. Only a month before, in a peace initiative, the President invited the Foreign Ministers of Sahbidad and Tibistan for a relaxing week at Camp David, where discussions revealed that the Shiminite and the Zirka tribesmen were certainly a large part of each country's population, but by no means a majority and there was no boundary dispute between the two countries. The problem centered on controlling the two fiercely-independent tribes each of which, in the eyes of the world, was identified with its country so closely that an action by either tribe would be construed to be an action of their nation. The Soviets understood this situation well and planted secret agents, selected for their cruel and sadistic natures, to stir up unrest by the commission of particularly heinous atrocities and leaving behind false evidence implicating the other tribe. KRAIT, the instigator, specialized in just this kind of operation. Under his direction, they had been successful, and individual family vendettas had been savage, brutal and bloody. It would take full mobilization and open warfare between entire tribes to provide the Soviets with the pretext they needed, and the violence was indeed escalating. Counteraction was required, and quickly.

It was agreed between the President and the Foreign Ministers that, because the tribes distrusted their governments, help was needed to keep the situation from exploding into open conflict, and, if the President of the United States could guarantee such help would be covert and show no signs of foreign intervention, they would thankfully accept it.

Later, as he sat in the Cabinet Room, listening to the various comments, opinions and warnings from counsels of both the positive and the edge of despair, the president became certain of the action called for. Most of the eleven officials present had no knowledge of MOPS. Giving the impression of doodling as he listened, all could see the president draw a circle with an X inside. To those in the know, it was the signal to return to the President in an hour's time. He thanked them all for their input and bid them good-day. Outside, the group was besieged by the White House press corps, and the morning papers and the 6 o'clock news roundly criticized the president for his lack of decision and weakness on the issue of peace in the Middle East.

An hour later, the president looked up from his desk in the Oval Office at the three men standing before him, rose to his feet and walked to a group of chairs at the opposite end of the room.

"Sit down, gentlemen. Thank you for your promptness. I didn't want the others to speculate as to the nature of our response to this Middle East situation. Had I asked you to stay in front of the others, they might have speculated to the press. No offense, Senator, but this is an election year and politicians tend to grab air time when they can get it."

"Understood Mr. President; no offense taken."

"The Secretary of State and I have discussed the subject at length and agree. As I see it, in order to defuse this situation quickly, we must do four things immediately: 1. Teach the Soviets a lesson, cheaply and quietly; 2. Eliminate their covert team at the scene, making it look like an accident; 3. Discourage them from future tampering by effective action now; 4. Show our allies we are willing to support our friends anywhere in the world, even to the Soviet's doorstep. Gentlemen, I'm handing this one to a special warfare unit. I am confident they can do the job quickly and quietly. Their success rate has been phenomenal indeed, and I'm sure you will agree that this should be our first response and, if they succeed, it will be the only move required in this situation.

Gentlemen, let me emphasize secrecy. Are there any questions or suggestions?" He paused for an answer and got none. "Very well then Admiral, if you will stay a minute or two…" Looking at the other two, "…thank you, gentlemen." When the door closed behind them, the President turned to the Admiral and asked, OK CLIMBER, who's up?"

"WILLIAM TELL; Mr. President. You'll recall the Tierra Blanca mission, OPERATION ARROW: he was our TTC there."

"Oh yes, splendid job. He sounds like just the man, but under our policy it doesn't make much difference, does it? The next man up is the next to bat. No pinch-hitters in this game. When can you get underway?"

"Not by coincidence, his team has been on a program of middle east studies, so no more than a few days. We have trained them for this type of scenario, Mr. President. You can be confident of a good result."

"I would guard against overconfidence, CLIMBER, but that sounds encouraging. The necessary clearances have already been obtained from the host governments. Your people will enter the countries as geologists, under a government contract to survey for new oil deposits. They'll need a crash course in geology before they leave. I'll loan you an expert from the Department of Interior. He's an old wildcatter and a PhD in rock hunting. Here's a list of books and equipment they should carry with them."

"That's helpful, sir. I'll set up the class away from MAGNOLIA, at the Education Center at Fort Eustice, Virginia; home of the Army Engineers. That shouldn't look like anything out of the ordinary. I'll get our people busy rounding up the items on the list, but the stuff should be used and dog-eared if it is to lend authenticity to our group. I'm sorry sir, I don't mean to burden you with the details—just thinking out loud. WIZARD and I will work out the particulars. Is there anything else I should know, Sir?"

"Only this, CLIMBER; impress upon your people that this is a hazardous mission and represents a dangerous situation for compromising MOPS. That must not happen under any circumstance, even if it means death. Arrange a fallback story of gun running, but only use it under torture or real threat. I'll leave to you the details of making the gun-running story plausible, if and when it's checked out by the enemy. In that regard, if you need coordination with the government involved, let me know so we're all building from the same set of plans. That's it CLIMBER: good luck."

Later, at MAGNOLIA, the usual background briefing was given to the team by CLIMBER, and the proceedings were turned over to WIZARD, who began with the overall mission.

"Code named OPERATION ARROW II, your mission is to prevent warfare between the Shiminites, a Bedouin tribe mostly in Sahbidad, and the Zirkas, another tribe mostly in Tibistan, by exposing, discrediting and, if the opportunity presents itself, eliminating the communist thugs behind these provocations."

When WIZARD was serious and said something he wanted to stick, he expressed himself dramatically. He hadn't lost a team yet, although there had been casualties, and he didn't want to start with this one. He was more than ever concerned with the dangers involved with this mission because they would face not only the enemy, but also dangerous "friends" in the tribes until they were won over. So, he cautioned the team in stern language, to emphasize the hazard.

"You guys are going to step off that plane into deep trouble and you won't get out of it until you leave safely for home. So, remain alert and watch yourselves. This close to the Soviet border it's no trick at all to whisk you away to spend your retirement in Siberia. Your cover, the Great Eastern Petroleum Corporation, is in California; its chief operations officer works for the CIA and will back your cover with detailed employment files and job titles. Of course, you're on the company payroll, but don't expect a payday. This has been arranged by BLANKET. FOREIGNER has arranged for your authentic passports with false identities to correlate with your Great Eastern records. During the timeframe of your mission, those of you who are supposed to be married, including you, WILLIAM TELL will have "wives" in residence at the addresses shown in your company files. They will have your cover story, but will have no knowledge of your real mission. These women and children are professionals at this game and when you return they will disappear, never to be heard of again. Their names, also fictitious, will be provided to you. Phony birth certificates are also on file at the appropriate county and Social Security numbers have been assigned. You are, literally, the person on your passport, but evidence of that person will remain for 30 days after the mission ends, just in case they check later.

"Beginning immediately, you will address each other by your new names. I want you so accustomed to them you can be awakened from a sound sleep by being called by your assumed name. To further imbed this cover story and identities into your subconscious you will use the usual hypnotherapy techniques. A cassette tape has been prepare for each of you, which will be returned to me personally prior to your departure. Here are your names; your ten-man team will be split as follows."

TOP SECRET

Team A	Team B
Sahbidad	Tibistan
WT-Edward Miller	21-Charles Taft
34-Robert Bright	24-Guy Vosberg
42-David Randall	26-Patrick O'Malley
51-John Kellogg	44-Artis McGregor
57-Donald Johnson	45-Gerald Yukness

TOP SECRET

"Mr. Miller, you have been assigned to the Shiminite tribe because their Sharif, Eleazar Shillem, is an obstinate and fiery hothead with a hair trigger temper. He needs to be handled diplomatically, flattered, cajoled and otherwise bought under control. Once he closes his mind on a subject you'll need a claw hammer to pry it open again. Mr. Taft, your man, Sharif Ramah Ben-habib, is more reasonable, slow to anger, western educated, but a weak leader whose vacillation, fortunately, has delayed open warfare.

"Your transportation is courtesy of Great Eastern; a conspicuously-marked commercial version of the C-124 Globe Master, so you will carry your company vehicles, each loaded with all your equipment. Team A will land at Shadri, the Capitol of Sahbidad, and Team B will land at Llamahn, the Capitol of Tibistan. You are expected and will receive the red carpet treatment, the usual round of wining and dining before you are permitted to start "explorations." Here you must be especially on your guard. In this social setting you all will be questioned casually by everyone, but you'll have no way of knowing who is asking the questions the enemy wants answered. Watch the native booze; it can not only loosen your tongue but also your bowels and knock you on your ear. The minute you arrive in the country, you'll be under enemy scrutiny, so appear relaxed but be wary and observant. Identify for future reference, if you can, all those who appear a little too inquisitive. Once you are released from government protocol you're on your own. Remember, stick to your cover story and identities and you will be accepted by friend and foe alike as oil men. If it comes to life or death, your fallback is gun running. There are guns in crates, marked electronic equipment spare parts, to verify that story if needed and, while an embarrassment to the U.S., it would not be the disaster your discovery would be; so try to stay oil men. After a cram course in geology, oil exploration and refining you will be ready to depart, so study hard and talk oil amongst yourselves every chance you get.

"In both these countries oil was discovered and developed by a foreign power. When the political situation changed foreign control of the industry was released to the Arabs who inherited a functioning industry manned by their own people who were trained, only marginally, by advisors to perform those jobs necessary to operate facilities already in existence. They know little of theory or the techniques of oil exploration. I have high confidence of your success."

The enormous four engine plane with prominent blue and black markings of the Great Eastern Petroleum Corporation rolled to a stop on the concrete apron in front of the Shadri air terminal, where Sahbidad's Assistant Oil Minister and customs agents waited to board and inspect. As the last of its engines shut down, the group boarded. Customs inspectors began checking and the official introduced himself, "Mr. Miller?"

"Yes, I'm Miller." WT replied, stepping forward.

"Salaam, welcome to Sahbidad. On behalf of the Oil Minister of my country, Imnah Asani, it is a pleasure to greet you. My name is Shabi Asim, assistant to the Minister."

"I'm happy to meet you, sir."

"Your party is larger than expected, Mr. Miller."

"Oh, no, there are only five of us. The others will continue on as soon as we are unloaded. Allow me to introduce my crew, Mr. Bright, Mr. Randall, Mr. Kellogg and Mr. Johnson. The first two vehicles belong to us." Asim passed the information to the customs men, and they proceeded feverishly to complete their inspection, slapping a sticker on the windshield of each truck and stepping away toward the door.

"Very well, you may unload now." said Asim. Miller gave the signal to the aircraft crew chief and the gigantic clam shell doors in the nose began to open. Wheel ramps were lowered as Bright and Randall started the trucks, a pair of four-wheel drive off-roaders with hard tops, and drove them unto the concrete apron, whereupon the mammoth aircraft closed its big mouth restoring its shape for flight. The engines turned over, and it taxied for take off.

"Big plane." commented Asim.

"Yes, we call it 'the aluminum overcast.'" replied Miller. The prop wash felt good in the heat. Then, Asim said,

"You will follow me to the hotel. Please, Mr. Miller, will you ride with me?"

"Yes, thank you." Miller continued, "I'm surprised to see you in a business suit."

"Oh yes, during the business day, we find it very practical, but we wear traditional robes after work and to special ceremonies. Tonight, at your welcome party, I dare say your crew will be the only men in suits. In that regard, I will be around to collect you about 8: pm and we will go to the Foreign Minister's reception at his residence by limousine—room for all in that car."

"Do I detect a British accent?"

"Oh, I do hope so. Cambridge, Class of '53. I'm afraid my accent was dampened a bit at the Colorado School of Mines."

"It would appear you are eminently qualified for what you do."

"Thank you, Mr. Miller, but I'm afraid I have no head for figures, finished rather low in my class, you know. Sometimes I think my graduation was a courtesy, really."

"I like your honesty. I think we'll get along fine."

"Jolly good. Where is your home in the states, Mr. Miller?"

"Oh, please call me Ed—all my friends do. My home is in San Bernardino, California."

"The weather there is much like ours, I think. Are you a married man, Mr. Miller—ah, Ed?"

"Yes, with two boys, 7 and 10."

"I have three children, one son. How long have you worked for Great Eastern Petroleum?"

"About seven years. I can't help but be impressed with how new and clean your capitol looks." said Miller, changing the subject.

"It is a completely new city built in the last 20 years by oil money. There was nothing here before that. The old capitol was mostly crumbling ruins before the discovery of oil. We are very proud of Shadri, but we are already making plans to develop our country's other resources as a hedge against the day the oil is gone. Our strikes were not as rich as the other Persian Gulf countries; that's why you are here. I hope you are successful in finding more for us."

"We'll do our best, and I wish I could promise results, but oil is very elusive."

"Yes. I understand. Ah, here we are the Shadri Grand Hotel; our biggest and finest. You will be comfortable here. They have valet parking, scrupulously honest people and an underground garage—all that sort of thing. Your rooms are ready, I saw to it, and you needn't worry about someone pinching your belongings; in my country the penalty for stealing is amputation of the hand, you know." Assuring himself, the hotel staff had the new arrivals well in hand, Shabi Asim bid Miller goodbye with,

"I'll be back to collect you at 8 sharp."

The hotel was world class with slightly better service. In no time they were in their rooms, a three bedroom suite with a large sitting room and a luxurious bath for each bedroom. It was midday and the trip had been tiring so all relaxed, cleaned up, went down to exchange currency and have a bite of lunch, leaving Johnson behind to search the rooms for bugs and phone taps. If the room was to be searched, Miller wanted it done while they were at the reception, after they had systematically prepared the room to detect tampering.

Shortly before 8: pm, the five departed for the lobby. Shabi Asim had arrived and was waiting for them, resplendent in full Arab regalia. He wasn't recognized until he spoke,

"I say, here I am; you're right on the dot." Miller chuckled to himself at the Cambridge accent coming from under the robes, like a character out of a badly cast movie. They walked out into the night air to be greeted by a very long white Cadillac limousine. It was apparently a custom design, judging from its extreme length, unusual even for a limo. It seemed to fill the hotel's quite sizable driveway. Asim was right, there *was* room for the entire team and no one had to sit up front. No sooner had they moved away from the hotel and proffered a few compliments about the car, than they stopped in front of the Foreign Minister's residence. Kellogg observed that they could have walked the three blocks; to which Asim replied,

"Our Capitol is small, but we like to go first cabin."

The residence was a large white building of modern architecture, two tall stories with a colonnade all around supporting a tremendous flat roof overhang designed to prevent the hot sun's direct rays from penetrating inside except in the morning and the late afternoon near sunset. It was as practical as it was beautiful. The lavish manor had two main entrances, one on the west and the other on the east. These were actually the opposite ends of a great hallway designed to take advantage of the prevailing breeze. The entrance in use was chosen simply because it was the one in the shade. The second story was for family living with a private entrance on the north side of the structure. The great entry hall had three enormous crystal chandeliers. The floor was white Italian marble with streaks of aqua polished to a glass-like surface. First cabin, indeed. It seemed a Hollywood flight of fancy straight out of the Arabian Nights. The great hallway was flanked by a series of massive double doors twelve feet in height. Midway down the hall on the left, the door was open and, led by Asim, the awestruck crew entered.

The crew was greeted by a formal reception line at the entrance to what was an immense state dining room, devoid of women. Asim introduced each member of the crew, in turn, to the Foreign Minister, His Excellency Ismael Ben-hadad, whose greeting to Mr. Miller had a double meaning,

"My country deeply appreciates your service to us and we wish you God speed. Please join me later in my office across the great hall and we will talk."

"Thank you, Your Excellency, I'd be delighted." Next in line was the American Ambassador,

"It's a pleasure to meet you Mr. Miller. I've heard good things about your work. Congratulations on that new offshore strike of yours." Turning to the Foreign Minister, the Ambassador continued, "All the other so-called experts said there was no oil there, but Mr. Miller persisted and found a sizable strike."

"You are well informed, Excellency." Miller complemented.

"The President himself told me when I heard you were coming to Sahbidad. If there is anything I can do to assist, please don't hesitate."

"Thank you, sir." Next, the Oil Minister, Imnah Asani, greeted Miller.

"I have hopes for your success, Mr. Miller, but alas, our methods have produced no new oil."

"The recent acceleration of oil exploration in my country has led to the development of one or two new techniques which may prove useful here."

Content with working their established oil fields, the Sahbis continue to use 25-year old technology. Feeling inferior and a little intimidated by the speed of new developments, they didn't choose to disclose their ignorance by asking too many technical questions. This reticence turned out to be a break for our crew who, only on rare occasions, had to demonstrate their newly acquired knowledge of the oil business.

After a sumptuous meal, the entertainment began with no shortage of women here. At this point, the Foreign Minister excused himself and sent an aide back to invite Mr. Miller to join him in his office. Striding across the great hall, Miller was led through an anteroom to the inner office.

"Ah, Mr. Miller, do come in and sit down. Would you join me in a brandy and a cigar?"

"Thank you, Your Excellency, a brandy would be fine." The aide handed Miller the brandy and left the room.

"You may speak freely, Mr. Miller, no one can hear us in this office. Among the members of my government, only the King and I know of your true mission. As I explained to your president at Camp David, we suspect enemy spies are in high positions in our government. We are working diligently to identify them. No wonder my country has become a trouble spot, and I hope you are able to help single out those of my countrymen who might be aiding our enemies."

Miller replied, "Of course, and I'm sure some will turn up, but discovering who they are, the situation may dictate we use that knowledge against them to help us. But, before we leave, you will be provided with names. Is that agreeable?"

"Mr. Miller, suppose your team is lost…your knowledge goes with you. I must insist on prompt notification of any government official you determine to be an enemy agent. However, I will promise to take no action against them until you say so. Let me emphasize that my immediate concern is with government officials. I can wait for other names until you complete your mission. Is *that* agreeable?"

"Yes, Your Excellency, agreed."

"Good. Now about Sharif Eleazar Shillem; he is a firebrand. You must be careful he doesn't lose his temper with you. If he thought I sent you to help with these tribal disputes, you wouldn't stand a chance with your mission. He'd call it meddling. Therefore, he has been notified that a government oil crew will be working in his territory and that his cooperation will bring his tribe a share of the profits. Knowing him, he won't get too excited about that prospect until the oil is actually flowing, and he knows that can be years away. To be successful, you must undertake the difficult task of becoming his friend. It is customary to pay a courtesy call on the Sharif before you start work in his territory. If he should discover your presence in any other way your mission could be doomed. When you go to his camp, tell him you have done so out of courtesy, as if it is your own idea. Another thing, he has a passion for marksmanship; the only oil he knows anything about is gun oil. I presume you, too, know something of guns."

"Yes Excellency. Anticipating the need, I have brought with me the latest model Winchester rifle with a telescopic sight, which I will present to him as a gift when the time is right. We didn't know he was particularly fond of guns, but we thought any Bedouin chief would appreciate a fine rifle. Having the interest, he will especially appreciate this one."

"Very good, you may have already won a friend, but let me warn you. Don't give it to him straight away, or he'll look upon your motives with suspicion. Wait until you have established a rapport and then you may cement that relationship with the gift. Remember, here in the Middle East, bribery has been an art for centuries. We consider an honest man to be one who, once bought, stays bought. And finally, anything you can do to make him look good to his people will make you his friend, and friendship once given, cannot be taken away except by betrayal."

"You have been very helpful, Excellency."

"Let it not be said that we sent you on your mission without cooperation. Now, there is the matter of our future communication. Once you leave this office, you are on your own. You have my letter of authority, regarding this oil business..." Ben-hadad handed Miller a sealed envelope, "...but we shall not communicate by phone or radio until this matter is settled. However, I have instructed my staff to grant an immediate audience to any member of your crew who might have news for me, day or night. If needed, my messenger to you will have this business card with my personal seal on the reverse side, like this. The United States is a true friend; may Allah go with you."

'Thank you, sir."

"Let us now return to the festivities. There is a special dance of my country I wish you to see."

Upon their return to the hotel, the five were intent on whether their rooms and vehicles had been searched in their absence. Miller sent Randall and Bright to the parking garage to check the vehicles while he, Kellogg and Johnson inspected the rooms for telltale signs of intruders. In both locations, the tests were positive; somebody was checking on them. Tiny hairs at doors and drawers were broken and certain items were ever so slightly out of place, but nothing was missing. Finding listening devices concealed in their rooms and in the 4x4s, the five met in the hallway outside their room. So as to not arouse suspicion, it was agreed to leave all devices in place for the duration of the mission. This of course, meant from here on, while within earshot of the devices, there'd be only small talk, mostly conversation commensurate with their cover story. Then Randall volunteered,

"I'm not sure if it means anything, but I saw Asim in the lobby talking to a bellboy. Didn't think much of it at the time, being our host and all—figured he was just making sure we were taken care of. But thinking back on it, that was a pretty intense conversation, complete with gestures, but they were too far away to hear."

"Could be significant." commented Miller. "Don't forget, we have an unseen audience, and be careful what you say. Now, let's get some sleep."

The next morning Shabi Asim stood knocking at the door of the crew's suite with the bellboy at his side. Johnson opened the door,

Hello Asim you're on time as usual." The bellboy pushed the baggage cart into the room, bumping Asim aside. Asim stepped in, talking to him in an irritated manner, as Miller entered from his bedroom,

"What's the trouble, Asim?"

"Oh bother, it's nothing to concern yourself about..." Asim was looking angrily at the bellboy, "...it's this worthless cousin of mine, a family matter."

"I see you're in your travelling clothes, too."

"Yes, actually I'm instructed to escort you to the Shiminites and return here. It's a long journey, about a day and a half's drive, so I took the liberty of having the hotel prepare some food to take along."

"Well now, that's downright thoughtful of you, Asim."

"Nothing at all. Come, the lift is waiting."

When the vehicles were loaded, Asim announced he would lead the way in his Jeep and that the paved highway ended about halfway there, so traversing open country could be a "bit sticky" in the desert and to stay close behind him. He then told Miller that he seldom journeyed out of the city, but the driver was a Shiminite and knew the country well.

Soon the comfort of Shadri was behind them and out of sight. The crew was struck by the enormity of nature's desert desolation and its stark beauty. As the day wore on and the temperature climbed sharply, the shimmering heat rising from the desert floor obscured all but the closest landmarks, of which there were few and subtle, making navigation tricky for all but the desert-wise traveler. The highway was asphalt, while it lasted, bubbling with the heat and free of traffic; a highway to nowhere it seemed. Their air-conditioners appeared to have little effect; merely thinking seemed to break a sweat. One had only to roll down a window to realize just how much better off they were inside the trucks. The crew had seen desert like this only in the movies, and it was easy to see that without gasoline and water, they would perish quickly.

After nearly two hundred miles in open desert, they reached the low rolling foothills climbing to the plateau. The vegetation was sparse, poor grazing land mostly, with few sheltered draws, occasional dry stream beds and, in the distance, low mountains with some scattered scrub trees could be seen. This was inhospitable terrain but, knowing nothing better, the Bedouin found it to his liking. This was land which man and herds shared carefully and roamed by necessity because no one piece of it could sustain them for long. Tents were pitched, to be struck after only a few days, a necessary sort of land management.

At sundown, the party stopped at an oasis sheltered by precious few trees in clusters around it. Situated in a deep draw, one could see a dry creek bed on the high and low ends of the pond. Taking Bright aside and speaking in low tones, Miller said,

"These desert nights get very cold, later we'll have to build a fire, so have the fellows search the area for some fuel. Tonight, as a precaution, I want you to watch for a chance to search Asim's vehicle; I want to know if he's listening in on us."

When the opportunity came, it was easy. Both the larger 4x4s were parked between Asim's jeep, and the camp. Bright pretended to be searching for something in his own vehicle, next to Asim's. The rest of the group sat around the fire, talking. The next time Bright had a chance to talk to Miller alone, he reported,

"Asim's jeep is clean. If he's listening in on us, he has to be wired himself."

"No, I just saw him washing up. He's not wired."

"Well, somebody's listening to us."

"Or will be, perhaps, when we come within range of their monitors."

"Do you think Asim is OK?" asked Bright.

"I see no reason to doubt him. He's been a good host and a likable guy, but that's as far as it goes. The jury is still out."

"Right." The two men walked back to the water hole and Miller addressed the group,

"It's time we got some sleep fellas; we've a long day ahead of us. Since this is a known oasis, I think one man should be awake at all times. What do you think, Asim?"

"A wise precaution, indeed, Mr. Miller; I was just going to suggest that myself. There are bandits in these hills, desperate men cast out of their tribes. They would cut your throats as you slept, just to acquire your boots."

The night passed quietly and without incident. Before long, the small caravan was on its way again through the rolling rock-strewn hills. After a couple of hours, they had completed the climb to the plateau and began to see small, isolated family camps of the Shiminites. It was near one of these camps they saw vultures circling in the air. Asim's driver changed direction abruptly toward a column of rising smoke to investigate what had attracted the scavengers. Rolling over a slight crest, their eyes beheld a ghastly sight, turning their stomachs. The tents were still smoldering and the stripped bodies of two men, two women and seven children had been impaled on pikes stuck in the ground. The women had been mutilated, with numerous knife wounds over their bodies, inflicted in such a way as to bring a painful death slowly. The men and children all had their throats cut—the only mark on them. It was a savage atrocity, calculated to inflame the spirit of revenge already instilled in the Shiminites by previous outrages.

Asim's driver jumped from the vehicle and ran to the carnage. Certain they were all dead, he began looking at the ground for tracks, which he found and followed to the east for fifty yards or so, returning with a dagger which had been dropped, apparently by one of the assassins. Then he walked to one of the pikes and cut a length of rope which bound the hands of a child. Walking toward the vehicles he said something to Asim who interpreted,

"Zirkas! Sharif Shillem must hear of this."

"How do you know it was Zirkas? Miller asked. After a short discussion with the driver Asim replied,

"This is a Zirka dagger and this is a Zirka rope. Look, do you see the one black strand in the rope? The Shiminite rope has a red strand. For centuries, the ropes have been used to identify tribal property bound with it. There is never deviation from this custom."

Engrossed in conversation, no one noticed the twenty mounted riders slowly showing themselves in a line from behind a nearby crest to the east, until, "Oh-oh, we've got company." observed Randall.

Asim's driver turned and cried out, "Shillem!" as the riders broke into a gallop and reined up in front of the seven men. The driver dropped to his knees in front of the Sharif's horse and, with head bowed began to speak rapidly of what he had found. Two horsemen broke away from the group and moved to the bodies and returned to report to Shillem. The driver handed the Zirka dagger to Shillem, who examined it carefully before passing it among the others. He was astride a majestic black stallion with red tasseled bridle and saddle, a fitting mount for the imposing figure of a man arrayed in traditional Bedouin robes of a Sharif with shining black boots showing from beneath. He spoke with the booming voice of a basso from a tragic opera emanating from a mouth surrounded by a well-kept beard.

"Americans, you would be dead now, but for your company trucks. We have much trouble here; soon there be war I think." He then barked some orders and three rode away tracking to the east; five stayed with him and he turned to the Americans and commanded,

"Follow me. My camp is not far." Looking at Asim he ordered sharply, "You, go home." Showing due respect and obedience, Asim and his driver were gone in a flash and without a word.

Now it was one-on-one and Miller had not been formally introduced. Stepping forward to remedy the situation, all he got for his trouble was the dust of Shillem's departing horse. Quickly, the crew scrambled into their vehicles and gave chase, eating dust all the way. Fortunately for Miller and his friends, the way the Shillem's camp was suitable for vehicles and they were able to keep pace with the horses.

The Shiminite's camp was a small city of tents which at first sight gave the impression of some permanence, but in reality, the entire area could be given back to nature in thirty minutes without a soul, animal or tent to testify the camp had ever existed. Miller looked at the site through a soldier's practiced eyes. It would be hard to surprise the camp and it could be defended easily from an attack such as might be expected from another tribe, but a modern force would have no trouble overrunning the place. The herdsmen, old men, women and children, doubled as security outposts, sounding the alert by blowing their rams horns and flashing their heliographs from hilltop to hilltop with impressive speed. It would seem that a Bedouin chief would have to be a pretty fair general to protect his people.

As Shillem rode into camp, his magnificent stallion, sensing the opportunity, put on a splendid show with his ears up and tail held high as he pranced proudly among the shouting women who welcomed home their leader. Miller wondered, from the show of adoration, if they were all family or possibly wives. The great steed wheeled and paced over to Miller's Vehicle.

"M. Miller..." Shillem began, as he pointed to a large tent. "...you and your men will use that tent while you are in my camp. I beg you accept my humble hospitality. If you need anything, please let me know. And Mr. Miller, join me in my tent in one hour and we will talk." So, he not only knew the name but had correctly singled out Miller from the others.

Later, as Miller was led into Shillem's tent, he was impressed by the large and colorful carpet which spread from wall to wall. Ventilation panels were open in the ceiling and the incoming light was defused by a white liner creating a soft effect. The hanging partitions of colorful and intricate patterns divided the great tent into separate chambers. Miller recalled living in a tent or two in his career, but the Shiminites had taken tent living to its ultimate. Then again, he thought, they've had thousands of years to perfect the nomadic life. To one side of the main room there were nine chairs, one larger than the others, but all had stubby legs only two or three inches in height and were covered with throws. Around the remainder of the room were sitting cushions in many colors and patterns. But where was Shillem? The question was answered almost as it was asked when he entered clean and relaxed,

"Salaam, Mr. Miller. Let me apologize. I hope you can understand why I was so abrupt with you earlier; my men expect me to be a strong leader. For their benefit, I am a different person and, I am told, my acting role is also my reputation."

"Firebrand was the word used to describe you, sir." Shillem laughed robustly,

"Good, good, then my reputation is untarnished." Miller smiled, somewhat relieved at his joviality, and asked,

"Sir, how do I address the Sharif of the Shiminites?"

"You Americans seem comfortable with 'sir' and so are the British. That will be fine."

"Thank you, sir." Replied Miller who was still a bit uncomfortable trying to reconcile what he had been told of Shillem with the man who now stood before him. He felt as if he was being set up for something.

"I was told of your coming…" said Shillem, "…you have a letter from the government?"

"Yes sir." Miller handed him the letter from the Foreign Minister. Shillem reached for it while at the same time, he fumbled under his beard to reach a pair of spectacles and, looked every bit the ancient scholar as he read, frowning.

"I don't trust the government." Then he looked at Miller suspiciously and asked,

"What do you do beside look for oil?"

Shrugging his shoulders, Miller replied,

"Look for more oil."

"Many have looked but have not found. Why are you here, American?" Miller ignored the inference of an ulterior motive.

"In my country, once much richer in oil than now, we are busy with new explorations. The easy oil has been found and now, we must look harder and deeper and in more remote areas. In recent years, we have developed new ways to detect the presence of oil, and we think these techniques can be used here with success. We are attempting to locate possible reservoirs and make tests in the ground using new electronic instruments. These tests require the use of small amounts of explosives. You can warn your people in advance so they won't be alarmed."

"I will send with you a guide so you will not become lost in my territory. I owe the government that much."

"This afternoon you said there might be war. What is the trouble?" asked Miller in feigned ignorance.

"You saw the trouble, but do not concern yourself. Look for oil. I will protect you until you leave my lands."

"Our guide, Asim, said it was the Zirkas who killed that family."

"Yes, and that was only one of several attacks on my people. Years ago, the Zirkas and the Shiminites were blood enemies, but after so many years of fighting and hatred both sides grew weary and eventually the killing stopped. I cannot understand why it has started again. They are in Tibistan and we are in Sahbidad. I recognize their right to continue to use ancestral lands on both sides of the border, just as they let us. Until three months ago, we had not sought a fight. And then these cowardly acts…I cannot understand it, but I also cannot permit it to continue. My people expect me to protect them and keep them safe."

"Have you spoken with the Zirka leader?"

"Ramah Ben-habib? No, I will not talk to that pig who murders women and children. For every life, I will take five, ten, twenty—I must avenge my people!" Eleazar Shillem sat in silence for a moment following his outburst and then apologized,

"Forgive me. I should not burden you with my troubles." Still, Shillem appreciated the opportunity to vent his rage to somebody who would listen, and he found Miller to be a good listener. Miller advised,

"I have an oil crew operating in Tibistan also. We are scheduled to make radio contact every night at 8: pm, and when required, to coordinate our findings. I want you to know the purpose of these transmissions and to whom we will be talking. Also, one of my men, Mr. Johnson, is a qualified medic—doctor..." Miller hesitated to use the term, but paramedic was too complicated, "... and if you have anyone sick, he can treat them in return for your generous hospitality." Shillem smiled, seeing a chance to help his people, "I will bring the sick and lame to your tent tomorrow. Thank you."

"Mr. Kellogg is an explosive expert. If you would like one or two of your men to learn about explosives, he would be glad to teach them. You might find this knowledge useful in the future. As long as we are here, we'd like to help where we can."

"I would like to meet these men." Clapping his hands, he sent a servant for the rest of Miller's crew, as well as some of his own subordinates. "Do you ride, Mr. Miller?"

"Not often." Miller exaggerated.

"Tomorrow we ride together. I show you the land."

The men arrived and Miller introduced each one in turn. They were invited to be seated, each next to one of the subordinate tribal leaders, and they enjoyed a late afternoon and evening of food and entertainment. Randall, the crew communicator, excused himself temporarily to make his scheduled radio contact with Taft's crew. He sent his message in the clear, knowing his vehicle was still bugged. Returning to Shillem's tent, he found the party over and only Miller and Shillem still talking. He handed Taft's message to Miller.

> HELD UP BY RECEPTION. WILL ARRIVE ZIRKA CAMP TOMORROW A.M. ALL BITTEN BY INSECTS. WILL CALL ON ARRIVAL. TAFT.

From the message, it was apparent Taft's vehicles also had been bugged. Miller looked up from the message at Shillem,

"My other crew will be in the Zirka camp tomorrow morning to begin testing. I'll know more tomorrow." Miller knew he had planted an idea in Shillem's mind, but did not press it. Shillem, preoccupied in thought, bid him goodnight.

The next morning, the line of sick and lame was long and serpentine under a fly canopy to shade them from the sun. Johnson was administering everything from aspirin to antibiotics, treating all manner of ailments from skin diseases to dysentery. Shillem was impressed and grateful. According to the latest report from the World Health Organization, this area had a typhus problem, so Johnson had brought with him enough vaccine to inoculate the entire camp, including a somewhat reluctant Sharif who was called to demonstrate his courage before all.

Bright and Kellogg had departed camp with a couple of "explosives apprentices" to perform tests at designated locations. Shillem excused himself, saying he had to meet with his subordinates to plan reprisals against the Zirkas and walked away to join a group entering his tent. At this point, Randall handed Miller another message.

> ARRIVED ZIRKA CAMP 9:45 AM. OBSERVED RESULTS OF TWO SEPARATE MASSACRES COMING IN. ONE: FIVE ZIRKA CHILDREN FOUND HANDS TIED BEHIND AND THROATS CUT. TWO: A FAMILY OF SIX FOUND THE SAME WAY. EACH VICTIM'S HANDS TIED WITH SHIMINITE ROPE—RED STRAND. ADVISE. WILL BEGIN TESTING IMMEDIATELY. TAFT

Miller wrote out a reply concerning the Shiminite family atrocity, advising Taft to notify the Zirka Sharif, Ben-habib, and requesting they exchange information promptly of each new incident. Miller then begged an immediate audience with Shillem.

After some resistance, he was admitted to the tent, interrupting a council of war. Apologizing and taking Shillem aside, he explained the message and asked quickly,

"Did you know of these two incidents?"

"No, Mr. Miller, I did not order any such action." Shillem turned and questioned his subordinates. "They know nothing of any such incidents."

Miller whispered, "I thought not. Someone is trying to start a war."

"But who?" Shillem asked.

"Your friends the Afghans could tell you. Please, I have an idea. Give me a couple of days to compare notes with my crew in the Zirka camp and we will know more." Shillem, who had already understood the advantage of rapid communication with someone in the Zirka camp, as well as that Miller was trying to help, quickly agreed to delay action, and dismissed his lieutenants. Clapping his hands, he instructed a servant to bring the Black Pearl and Ruby and, turning to Miller, he announced,

"And now we will ride."

Followed at a respectful distance by three of his personal body guards, the two men rode away from camp to the base of a large butte, at least 150 feet high. Following it to its end, they doubled back on top and climbed to a point that overlooked the plain below. Dismounting, they sat on a boulder and talked for a while. Shillem pointed to a small bush on the ground below some distance away, and walking to the Black Pearl, he took a rifle from under his saddle blanket. He fired from the offhand position creating a puff of dust two feet in front of the bush. A second shot hit the base of the bush. He handed the rifle to Miller, who fired and missed the bush by seven or so feet to the right. Firing again he narrowly missed high. It was not yet the time to demonstrate his skill with firearms.

That evening an exchange of messages began building a picture, but still Miller was missing pieces. The next day he carried the Winchester with him on their daily ride. The new day found the two men riding side by side with the usual entourage trailing behind.

"Sir, have you considered the possibility that you have a spy in your camp?"

"Under the circumstances I have to think of all possibilities. But no, I have not." Shillem admitted.

"If someone is trying to stir up trouble by committing atrocities and placing the blame on the other side, they would need help from the inside, and that person or persons would know how to find the culprits. My information confirms that the Zirkas could not have killed that family three days ago. Also, two of Taft's men found an abandoned camp site, large enough for no more than five or six people. Appearances would lead us to believe they broke camp in a hurry, because in their haste they carelessly left behind a mixture of Shiminite and Zirka goods, including small lengths rope which they had been burning, scraps of blankets and clothing as well as three damaged daggers from both tribes."

"Who are you, Mr. Miller?"

"A friend."

Shillem believed Miller, "What do you suggest we do, Mr. Miller?"

"Wait, don't contact Sharif Ben-hadad; you must continue to appear hostile to him. He will be getting the same advice from my man. Be patient, your time will come." The two rode on until Miller pointed to another bush growing out of the face of an escarpment some 500 yards away and challenged,

"Let's see you hit that bush."

"Very long range, but I try." Shillem raised his rifle and firing from horseback, missed by three feet left and low. Miller produced the Winchester and place three shots in succession into the bush. Shillem's body guard, watching from a distance, rode forward out of curiosity about the weapon. Shillem couldn't believe his eyes and showed his astonishment. Miller waited until he closed his mouth and handed him the Winchester saying,

"Here, you try." Whereupon Shillem fired one shot and hit the bush. He turned back to Miller with disbelief and yearning in his eyes. Miller smiled, "Try again." The second was dead center in the bush.

"You are a fine marksman." Miller complimented.

"With such a rifle I cannot miss. I must have one."

"You have—look at the stock." Shillem looked at the plate on the stock and read the engraving done in Arabic script:

pRopeRty of shaRif eleazaR shillem

Miller thought he saw a glaze in Shillem's eyes when he realized it was a gift from his new friend. He quickly composed himself and showed unbridled joy by turning to his bodyguard and raising the rifle high over his head. Standing the Black Pearl on his hind legs and, giving out a hoop that echoed across the plain, he dashed off in the direction of the camp. Ruby was no match for the Pearl in a hurry.

The Red Army was poised for action, awaiting the word to go. KRAIT felt pressure from his superiors; what was taking so long getting this fraud started? Thousands of men and machines were ready to execute a carefully devised plan that would quickly steal the long coveted warm water port, but where was the provocation which would legitimize the theft? Something was wrong—again. KRAIT, controlling the plot from Moscow, decided to get closer to the action in order to keep the scheme on track. He flew to a base near Samarkand to take personal charge of the operation. He could not understand why his specially selected agents were having so much difficulty. The tempers of the tribes must be strained to the breaking point if the descriptions of the atrocities were accurate. Why aren't they at each other's throats?"

Upon his return to the camp, Miller noticed a helicopter had arrived and found a messenger from Foreign Minister Benhadad. Showing the card with the seal, he handed Miller a coded message. In a few minutes Miller had fully deciphered the message and read that enemy agents in the states had been busy authenticating the oil crews, and Miller's "wife" had been visited by an agent conducting a "public opinion survey." Afterward, the Great Eastern personnel files were checked, and a message was sent to Moscow declaring the crews legitimate. Miller burned the message on the spot and decided to send Bright to Shadri with a message to the Foreign Minister, but not in writing. He sat down with Bright and explained his suspicions.

"On the way from the airport to the hotel, Asim and I made small talk. He is the only man to whom I talked about my "family." If agents checked my family first and then the company files, Shabi Asim is a spy. Have that sequence of events confirmed to make sure. Now on your way and get back as soon as you can." Bright and the messenger left together in the government helicopter.

Miller began formulating a plan to trap the spy in camp and get information they needed to locate and eliminate the trouble makers from north of the border. After the evening meal, Miller took Shillem aside far enough so no one could hear their discussion. He explained his plan to nab the spy: Shillem would call a council of war to plan a reprisal raid and put the word out to his men. Then using his most trusted men they would picket the camp in order to catch the spy when he left to notify his superiors. Shillem volunteered that he could probably narrow the odds of catching the spy by concentrating on the two most likely routes of escape. Then he selected and stationed his men at key points and called the conference to outline the plan for a raid on Zirka peripheral camps to take place the following night. Miller did not attend; after all, why should an oil man be in on a war council? Miller was on the radio to Taft talking business as usual during their scheduled 8: pm contact.

The next morning, it was feared the spy had slipped through the net because no one was caught leaving the camp and all Shillem's key people were accounted for. Shillem and Miller assessed the situation on their morning ride, an exercise Miller had begun to look forward to each day. But today he noticed something unusual. As they rode, Miller observed a spot, almost a perfect square, 20 by 20 feet, in the sparse grass on the hillside. Within the square no grass grew, nor did anything else; the patch looked as if it had been burned. Miller asked Shillem if he knew what it was.

"Yes, the government sent us some bags of fertilizer so we could grow better grass, but all it did was kill it."

"How much did you use here?" asked Miller.

"Only one bag; you can see what happened."

"What size bag was it?"

"About 27 kilos, I think."

"Sixty pounds? You used too much my friend; and a little goes a long way, a few handfuls would have been plenty. Spread it evenly just before the rain falls and the next time you use this range, the grass will be much better. Do you still have the fertilizer?"

"Yes, thank you. We will try again; just before the rain, you say?" Just then Shillem looked up with a jerk and, pointing, he said, "Look!"

"What?" Miller thought he caught a glimpse of something, but there seemed no doubt in Shillem's mind as to what he saw. Spurring the Black Pearl forward, he shouted urgently, "Follow me!" and rode at break-neck speed up a steep hill, pulling up before he reached the summit. The two men continued up the hill on foot to a cluster of large boulders at the top where they heard a clicking noise.

"Shhh.." Shillem placed his finger to his lips and listened intently to the clicking for a moment; then turning to Miller, he whispered, "...we have our spy. Follow me." They made their way through the maze of rocks in the direction of the clicking. Suddenly, they came upon a man busily packing up a heliograph, his back to the searchers. He had used the morning sun to send a message to the northeast. Hearing us, startled, he turned to look.

"You!" Shillem choked in surprise. It was Ahmed Muhari, one of his trusted leaders, who stared down the muzzle of Shillem's pistol.

"Don't shoot!" Miller shouted, fearing Shillem's quick temper might cost them a source of information.

"Fear not, my friend...his death will not be so quick."

Returning to camp, Miller found that Bright had returned by helicopter from Shadri with news. The Sahbi security police had arrested the Oil Minister, Imnah Asani, climaxing an ongoing investigation of many months duration. His assistant, Shabi Asim, is believed to have fled across the border to Tibistan. Asim had not been suspected, but when he panicked and took flight, further investigation revealed he had been schooled in Moscow by an infamous KGB agent, code named KRAIT. Asim is now believed to be a political assassin, which might explain several as yet unsolved murders over the past year. This information was passed by special code to Taft in Tibistan. By this time, tensions had cooled, both sides made aware that the other was not responsible for the massacres. Therefore, it remained for Miller and his crew to eliminate the perpetrators in a manner the Soviets would accept as accidental.

Miller persuaded Shillem that in order to extract the most information from the traitor Muhari, who was paid handsomely for his treachery but had no politics, a promise of banishment would get them all he knew. As expected this loosened Muhari's tongue, and with profuse apologies he heaped information upon them, but the prime item, pertinent to the mission, was hearsay; the only time the entire Soviet team met together in one place was a rendezvous inside but near the Soviet border. Muhari had heard that the spot was an abandoned granary considered too close to the border and too isolated for the Soviet government to permit anyone to live there. The building provided a safe shelter for agents operating south of the border as well as safe storage for weapons, explosives and equipment they might need. Miller reasoned that if Shillem cancelled the planned raid Muhari had signaled his contact about, the Soviet's team, concerned about the lack of action, might call a meeting at the granary to discuss new strategy. Muhari had not been to the rendezvous but was told the granary was due north of a certain spot on the border. Good enough!

Calling a meeting of his team, Miller discussed the situation, seeking a course of action which would eliminate the Soviets without pointing the finger at anyone. It was also known that the agents kept a cache of ammunition and explosives at the granary, but in what quantities nobody could be certain. The key man for this job was John Kellogg. When discussing the method, Kellogg had mentioned he was short of explosives and doubted he had enough to do the job, but smiled wryly when Miller told him he had a 60 pound sack of nitrate fertilizer.

That night, after assuring Shillem he would settle the problem once and for all, Miller, Bright and Kellogg drove to a point near the border where the vehicle could be concealed, then walked the remaining distance to the crossing point, spelling each other carrying their heavy load. Within 30 minutes after crossing that unguarded portion of the isolated Soviet frontier, they located the deserted granary. Posting Bright to watch from a nearby hill, Miller and Kellogg entered the granary to find some unused equipment, weapons and some empty explosive boxes. They quickly set to work digging a shallow hole in the middle of the big room, placing most of the meager explosive charge at the bottom with an electric blasting cap, covering it with the unopened sack of fertilizer. They then covered the sack with a couple inches of earth, restoring the dirt floor to its natural appearance. A separate and still smaller charge of plastic explosive was hidden in the rafters to detonate he nitrate dust by remote control. The three took positions on a nearby hill, from which the building could be observed and the charges detonated. With a clear view of the entrance, they waited and watched.

Sixteen hours into their vigil, the soviet team of killers showed up, eight in number, and went into the granary. Miller decided to wait a few minutes longer, *just in case* of late arrivals. His patience was rewarded when three more Soviets appeared about ten minutes later; one of them, Shabi Asim himself. Miller decided to take all eleven while he had them. The powerful explosion disintegrated the building and everyone in it sending a shock wave so powerful it nearly knocked Miller's group off the hill. The explosion left nothing to tell the tale. Assuring themselves that no evidence remained, the three returned to Shillem's camp.

Held up by other pressing matters, KRAIT had arrived only moments after Millers departure. He stood and surveyed the destruction, but while appreciating his personal good luck, he nevertheless lamented his professional misfortune. Nothing further was heard from the Soviets.

That evening Miller made his final radio contact with Taft, arranging a meeting between Eleazar Shillem and Ramah Ben-habib. The Shiminites and the Zirkas have had no trouble since. In fact, when Shillem showed Ben-habib the proper use of fertilizer to thicken and green the tired grass land, they became fast friends. As an ironic aside, I must mention that the amateur oil explorers on Taft's team actually located and reported a promising area which was developed later and produces oil to this very day in Tibistan.

Operation ARROW II was over, a war with Russia averted and a daring president felt justified in his action because MOPS suffered no casualties and the mission was accomplished. The CIA's hands were clean and the Soviets knew it, chalking up the incident at the granary to an accident involving explosives known to be stored there. Essential to the success of both ARROW I and ARROW II was timely, accurate intelligence and hitting the enemy professionally and quietly before he had something to lose publicly. The Red Army, moved secretly into place for the expected occupation, called off the alert and returned to their bases. Other MOPS actions will continue so long as we have a daring and courageous president who doesn't try to make political hay out of these covert foreign policy victories, and who leaves the execution of these missions to a handful of professionals trained to do or die without drawing attention to themselves or our country. As a Task Team Commander, WILLIAM TELL's future contributions, although unsung, would bring the treacherous KRAIT to closer quarters.

CHAPTER 9

THE REUNION

MAGNOLIA's research library was deserted. Bill tried to study but it was no use. Despite the ideal conditions, he was unable to concentrate or account for his resistance to the pages before him. He rose and walked to the stereo for a few minutes' break. Collapsing into a chair, he slipped on the headset and listened to Gershwin's Concerto in F, followed by a selection of the composer's more popular melodies. Bill's taste in music was fairly broad, but he was particularly drawn to the more dynamic of the classics, with jazz running a close second. Gershwin was the master of both, but Bill had never given his romantic ballads much attention. However, today his mood was unusual, and this music had special appeal as he listened with heightened pleasure to the lyrics which seemed to speak directly to the confirmed bachelor, awakening long suppressed feelings which, though pleasant, disturbed him. When the music stopped he thought perhaps now he could get some work done, but he remained restless and something in his subconscious seemed to be struggling for recognition. Perhaps a fast game of handball would settle him down. He played until he was dripping with perspiration, then showered, dressed and returned to the library, but still the printed word would not hold his attention so he closed his eyes and leaned back in his chair to meditate and relax as he had been taught.

An old refrain played persistently in his head, and he began to hum..."Won't you tell her please to put on some speed, follow my lead, oh *how I need* someone to watch over me." His mind drifted into fantasy, imaging more vividly than ever before. Her raven hair was shoulder length, soft and fragrant. Her lovely dark eyes searched his face, and her full lips smiled an invitation to be touched. Their bodies tingled as they embraced and each tasted the others feverish lips. Engrossed in her loveliness, he almost failed to notice her left eye, bruised—Antonia Lopez! He opened his eyes with a start and stood up, repeating her name, "Antonia!" Without debate, he hurried to the communication room, contacted the U.S. Embassy in Tierra Blanca and secured Antonia's phone number.

An hour later, from his bachelor apartment in town, Bill dialed her number direct.

"Antonia Lopez?"

"Yes"

"This is Bill Bowman. I'm calling from the United States about that invitation."

"Who? What invitation?"

"Bill Bowman. Don't you remember? I *dropped* in on you one night a month ago with some friends. Do you still like to fly?" Bill heard a perceptive gasp, followed by what sounded like a short whispered prayer.

"Bill..."speaking his name for the first time..."so that's your name. I like it. It fits you."

"May I see you again?" asked Bill. She tried to suppress the excitement building inside her, but without much success, and stopped for a moment to catch her breath.

"Antonia?" Bill thought he had been disconnected. She finally responded softly.

"I've been praying you'd call. Of course you can. When?

I have two weeks, beginning tomorrow." Two weeks, she thought. She'd have to cancel an appointment she dreaded and delegate her business plans to a subordinate.

"What a coincidence, I have two weeks starting the moment you step off the plane."

I'll call you from the airport."

"Bill?"

"Yes, Antonia?"

"I can still taste your kiss." Bill recalled their farewell that night, and thought to himself, "*My kiss?*" and replied,

"The sooner I leave the sooner I can return yours."

"I won't leave the phone till you call."

"Till then?"

"Till then." Click.

Calling from the airport, Bill waited as the phone rang only twice and Antonia answered,

"Bill?"

"How many times have you answered the phone that way and it wasn't me?"

"Only once, I heard my mother ask, "Who is Bill?" Laughing Antonia continued, "Listen Bill, my driver is waiting for you in front of the terminal. He'll be holding a sign with your name. He'll bring you to my home."

"I'm on my way."

The hilltop villa was palatial, befitting the family descended from pioneer businessmen of Tierra Blanca. Bill had the feeling he was out of his element as the car rounded the water fountain centered in the wide circular driveway. The villa and its lush garden were walled from the outside world; he was impressed by luxurious privacy. The driveway, garden walkways and veranda were surfaced with burgundy tiles, and the garden required a staff of workers to keep it from becoming overgrown in the tropical climate. As he stepped out of the car, Bill saw Antonia standing on the veranda, a vision in white, nervously shifting from foot to foot, poised excitedly to run to his arms at the slightest sign of welcome. It was as if he was seeing her for the first time; she was radiant, and his heart melted at the sight of this lovely lady so eager to greet him; he opened his arms to receive her, as she flew into his arms.

Bill's mind was whirling, unaccustomed to the intensity of affection displayed by this relative stranger. He'd heard of hot-blooded latin women, but did not understand what appeared to be her complete emotional surrender to him. He uttered a silent prayer, "Lord, if this be your will. Please guide me in word and deed." He pulled away to arm's length, looking at her in a new and nearly blinding light.

"The last time you had a black eye. But now... do your eyes always sparkle like that?"

"Only when I'm excited."

"You expected our reunion to be so?"

"Just looking at you again is exciting. See, I'm trembling like a little girl."

"Antonia, are you always this...direct?"

"We have so little time in this life. I thought I'd never see you again and here you are. You remembered. You called me. I'm not going to let you slip away again without playing all my cards face up. Know something else?"

"No, what?"

"The night we kissed goodbye..." she squeezed his hand. "...I knew that if you did not come back, I'd hunt you down if only for another kiss."

"I'm flattered, but..."

"But what?"

"I don't understand all this. Being a bachelor at my age doesn't mean I'm a swinging single. My romantic experience is very limited. I'm here, but if you ask me why, I'm not sure I could explain."

"My dear, you don't have to. I know why you're here, and nothing more need be said."

They turned, arm in arm, to enter the villa through the big, handsomely-carved double doors followed by the driver carrying Bill's bag who continued upstairs. Antonia said softly, "You will stay here." She took his hand and led to the living room, spacious and airy despite heavy carved wooden beams overhead, where she greeted a distinguished couple.

"Mother, Father, this is Bill Bowman."

"How do you do ma'am, sir?" Senor Lopez spoke first, in cultured English,

"On behalf of our family, I wish to thank you personally for your valuable assistance to our country. We are grateful."

"Thank you, sir. I can only say that your government did a fine job and mine was happy to help."

"Nevertheless, your personal contribution is appreciated, Senor Bowman. You are welcome to call on us anytime."

"Bill, please call me Bill."

Senora Lopez had been looking at Bill while exchanging glances with her daughter. Finally, she said approvingly,

"We want only the best for Tonia, she means the world to us. We are happy she has met someone she can care for again. It has been a long and troubled four years." Looking puzzled Bill said,

"I don't understand…" Interrupting, Antonia quickly added,

"I'll explain Bill; we should talk." Senora Lopez grasped her husband's hand and said considerately,

"We must be on our way. I know you two have much to discuss, and it would be easier without the parents lurking about. I'll call you, Tonia."

"Thanks mama. Goodbye papa."

Returning from seeing her parents out, Bill and Antonia settled down in the living room to talk. He looked at her and asked,

"Do you like to be called Tonia?"

"Until now, only mama and papa used that name. Will you call me…wait a minute, something special just between us. Call me 'Toni', at least until 'darling' becomes appropriate." Bill chuckled and said,

"Toni, I like that. It has a perky sound to it—fits your personality." Looking around him, he offered, "Your folks have some place here."

"I live here alone. This is my home. Also I am sole owner of a portion of the family business."

"Which is?"

"I export the family's crops of sugar, pineapple and bananas. I own the sugar mill here."

"But you're so young."

"Twenty-nine, young? I suppose to an old duffer like you, I seem young enough."

"Thirty-two is not an old duffer." Bill wanted to slow down, regain control of the situation, if he had ever had it. "Toni, things are moving a little fast for me."

"Only a little, then I'll slow down, but I warn you, the direction will be the same."

"What you've just told me makes me realize we know so little about each other."

"Easily fixed. I have been a widow for some four years now, hence, my mother's comment. Until I met you, I was in extended mourning for my husband, Ricardo Montez, who was a flyer in our militia until he was killed in a plane crash. In my depression I became easy prey for some dumb ideas. After he died, for business reasons I reverted to my family name. I thought my life was over and I did some foolish things; then my country, in crisis, asked for my help. Meeting you stirred feelings that made me realize I could love again, and it was time to resume living. In our short time together, I saw qualities in you that I admire. I knew you found me attractive, but you didn't deviate from your duty."

"Toni, I don't understand you. How can a lady like you, well-to-do, genteel and educated, not to mention a knock-out beauty, have designs on me?"

"Designs? You are precious, Bill."

"That doesn't answer my questions."

"Think about it for a minute. I know what it's like to have an intimate relationship with a man I love and trust, and yearn to recapture what God meant marriage to be, a coming together as one, complete physical and emotional surrender to the other. My husband set a pretty high standard in men for me. And, as a business woman, I have learned something about timing. When you are prepared and see the opportunity, it has become second nature not to let the chance slip away. You can call it aggressiveness in business, but in our relationship, I'd hoped you would see it as falling-in-love-with-a-fear-of-losing-you-if-we-don't-come-to-an-understanding-soon. Your mission here required an impersonal evaluation of a situation, a professional detachment in order to do your job properly. But through that veneer, I saw a man, in the true sense of the word, a gentleman, committed to his duty, unselfish and considerate of others. I fell in love with that man, our unnamed benefactor; as much of him as could be seen in that official relationship. I then relied upon my womanly wiles to send a tender message, hoping you'd want to follow up with a personal rendezvous, which would enable me to fall in love with the rest of you, the man you withheld from me. Then I could show you the warmth of affection you can expect for the rest of your life. I prayed each night you would remember my kiss and come back to me. Now, Bill, dearest, tell me you don't understand me."

Until now, Bill had always thought of marriage as the end of his secret service to his country, knowing that day was inevitable, but viewing it as part of the distant future. Now it threatened to pounce upon him before he was ready, or was he? Bill felt he should not encourage Toni, but at this point he didn't want to discourage her either, although somehow he knew that would take some doing.

"Your sincerity is most becoming, ah...businesslike. I understand you better now." That didn't come out right at all, Bill thought looking at a smiling Toni.

"Bill.."

"Wait a minute. Let me finish. My work takes much of my time and I am away a lot, doing hazardous duty; much more dangerous than flying. Could you stand losing another husband? Besides, it wouldn't be fair to our children for me to be away so much." Husband? Children? He couldn't believe he had said the words. Toni lowered her head and looked at the floor saying apologetically,

"Bill, you have to know that I am unable to give you children. I can only give myself, always and forever." Bill didn't want to press the matter of children. He could hardly picture himself as a husband, much less a father; besides if he were in love it wouldn't matter. He continued,

"I can't tell you anything about my work. It's an area of my life I just can't share with anyone. But, on the other hand, trips are usually short and leaves frequent." He paused to organize his thoughts. There was a conflict in his mind he had never come to grips with, and he was at a loss for words.

"Bill, I understand. Considering the briefness of our acquaintance, if you cannot return the strong feelings I have for you at the moment...well, your apprehension is understandable. But, God willing, you shall."

"I hope this trip was...divine will." Bill stopped and began to think about the sensitivity of his work and the suddenness of his involvement with this woman. In just a few minutes, she professed undying love and he'd bought it. Remembering his mission here, he supposed there was time for her to...well, at any rate he was not prepared to rush into anything. It just wasn't in his nature. He needed time to know her better, at an emotional arms-length before giving in to his feelings which, after all, had brought him back in the first place.

Toni continued her autobiography an item at a time,

"I am a graduate of the University of Hawaii, as are both my parents. My biggest market is the United States; I have an office there, in Atlanta. I maintain dual citizenship. Since Ricardo died, I have had time only for business, intimidating or otherwise frightening off would-be suitors." Bill mentally noted the proximity of Atlanta to Washington and offered,

"Except for out-of-country missions, I am always around the capitol."

"I could move to Atlanta and operate my business from there."

"You could?"

"Yes. Only last year a feasibility study recommended we move our headquarters there to be nearer our markets, but I wanted to stay close to my family. Now that move really makes sense."

"Toni, Toni, not so fast..."

"Oh my..." she interrupted, "...it never occurred to me to ask. Is there someone else?"

"Toni, would I be here if there was?" Toni answered with a questioned,

"I don't know, Bill, would you?"

"There has never been anyone else. I married the army 14 years ago and gave it everything. I expected to remain a bachelor until love hit me over the head and got my attention. I just never gave it much thought."

"Well, I hope I didn't give you a concussion. It's such a handsome head. How does having us both continue our separate careers sit with you? You must know you come first with me, but I'm willing to share you with your mistress."

"My what?"

"Your mistress, the army. I'd think of it as your mistress if you were married to me."

"Toni, I'll make a deal with you."

"Yes, Bill." She quickly agreed.

"Wait, you haven't heard my proposition yet."

"Proposition? Oh yes, Bill." She cooed.

"Now stop that! What I mean is, let's not say another word about marriage for at least a week. Agreed?"

"Yes, Bill."

"Let's look at practical matters, like religion. I'm not a Catholic."

"Neither am I; protestant missionaries have been very busy here. I opened my heart to Jesus and was baptized almost a year ago."

"What about a family?' Would you be open to adopting children?"

Thoughtfully she replied, "As our life together progresses, we will both know if children are needed. If they are we can take the necessary steps."

"Good answer." Bill said quietly.

With a flirtatious gleam in her eye, Toni offered, "Bill, ask anything of me and I'll have a good answer for you." She took Bill by the hand and leading him to the stairs, she said softly,

"I'll show you to your room." They stopped at his door and she filled his arms with her body, warm and trembling. Kissing his ear, she whispered,

"Dinner will be served in 45 minutes." She then departed to prepare something special.

Bill breathed a deep sigh as he entered his room. He unpacked, showered and dressed for dinner, all the time wondering about the future. Without being chauvinistic, would having a wife change his attitude toward his work? Would she slow him down, cause him to think twice about his decisions in critical situations. Would spending time with her cause him to neglect study time so important in preparation for assignments? As a married man, could he be as effective, or would he endanger his life and those of his men? No one in MOPS was married and, although he knew of no strict prohibition, only bachelors were recruited. Thinking there was nothing to prevent the marriage, so long as the woman knew the score at the start. Bill wondered what WIZARD's attitude would be. What if he had to make a choice? What if,...what if? He could go on all night. Should he just pack his bag, return to MAGNOLIA and forget he ever knew Antonia Lopez? No, he could never forget, but he *could* go home. Belying the depth of his true feelings, he said to himself, "But not before dinner, I'm hungry."

Starting down the staircase, he saw Toni standing at the bottom, waiting. Her change of clothes took his breath away and he thought, "This is dirty pool, she knew I'd be above her looking down, so she dressed to provide the greatest sex appeal." She was wearing her hair in a casual, natural style to her bare shoulders, and wore a wide skirt flaring from her narrow waist, and a peasant blouse with its low neckline resting on her full bosom. Her beautiful dark eyes did not stray from his. The moment she moved to take his hand, he observed to himself, "Women must not wear bras in this hot climate." The whole thing was grossly unfair: her turf, her rules—the guy was a goner. Still defending his emotions, he decided then and there to let her take the initiative for the rest of the evening. He would go only where invited. That, he reasoned, would be safe. It must be a sin to be so beautiful. She also smelled delicious. Together they walked to a cozy alcove just off the well-equipped and spacious kitchen. There stood a small round table set for two, illuminated by a six candle floor stand and, on the table, a single candle. If all this was calculated to melt his defenses, it was working.

"Sit here." She gestured, as she moved toward the refrigerator just inside the kitchen with a graceful walk that initiated the subtle rhythmic motion of her breasts. He felt like a voyeur, but was unable to pry his eyes from her; she seemed to glow in his appreciation of her charms. Bill could have said something obvious like, "You are very beautiful tonight," but she could see greater eloquence in his eyes, and she loved it. She glided smoothly to his side and, as she poured the wine, she lightly brushed his face. Too soon, his glass was full and she moved away to fill her own. Attempting to damage the mood somewhat, Bill observed,

"University of Hawaii, huh?"

"Uh-huh."

"How many credits do they give for Seduction 101?"

"Not enough for such an important subject. Besides 101 was last month; this is Seduction 225. We have ascended to a higher and more intense level." She returned to the kitchen, adding,

"Enjoy the wine; this'll take a minute." She disappeared from sight, giving Bill eyes a rest, and he could hear some serious activity. She returned, pushing a serving cart, and Bill seemed helpless to control his eyes which were transfixed to the cleavage produced by her pushing the cart.

"I'm heartbroken hearted..." she cooed, "...look at my dinner."

"Sorry, I...ah..."

"Poor darling; hold that thought for later." He admired the food wondering if, in the candle light, his flushed face was as red as it felt. The centerpiece was a very original and artistic pineapple salad with a lobster and steak dinner, the likes of which he could not recall ever having seen.

"Catered?"

"Of course not. I'm trying very hard to make a good impression. Suppose you should ask for this meal again later; then where would I be?"

'Sorry, but ever so grateful." Then, raising his glass, he offered a less-than-spectacular toast,

"To the loveliest chef in the world."

"Thank you, kind sir."

"With a home like this, where is your help?"

"I gave them the week off. There's not another soul in the house. I saw to it" She paused a moment, carefully looking at Bill, and observed, "Bill, you seem defensive. Can I tell you how I feel, right now, a woman's feelings, honestly?"

"Certainly, please do."

"Could you be concerned with my virtue, gentleman Bill?"

"That and more."

"Oh? I think I understand. Darling, we are consenting adults, me a widow and you a man of the world *and* a bachelor. As long as our motivation is love and affection for one another, and not lust, I'm sure we will be forgiven."

"I agree with the motivation, but…"

"Never mind, I understand. Relax and enjoy your meal."

"This is not just a good meal, but a product of real talent, a gift."

"A skill. Before I showed any real business acumen, my parents sent me to Chef Andre's School of Culinary Arts in Paris. Afterward, I ran a successful restaurant in Buena Vista. Later my father brought me into the family business."

"Think of it, Toni, a month ago I didn't know what I was jumping into—and I'm not completely sure yet. You are one surprise after another."

"Ironically, I have the Cubans to thank for sending you to me. But, speaking of surprises, are there any that bother you."

"Yes, but you see I've never been faced with a situation even similar to this so I'm bound to encounter surprises, but the ones that concern me are all on my side and temporary, I hope. You make me feel so free and easy, natural. I have not once tried to give you a wrong impression. What you see is me."

"My dear, I knew that from the beginning, and I liked what I saw. You are strong, and the way you accepted the way I handled things during your mission here told me something else about you, Bill."

"Oh? What's that?"

"You are unselfish. You'd be comfortable allowing me to continue my work without envy or conflict with the so-called male ego. My money won't be a concern for you, nor will you become dependent upon it. You are your own man, committed to your duty, and I like that. Committed to our relationship, our future together will be as secure as Gibraltar." Having her say, Toni decided then and there to release control of this reunion to Bill. She wanted no doubts between them. There it was. He would have to make the next move.

"I believe..." he said, "...that a 50-50 relationship implies a middle ground, a meeting halfway and so forth. I've never been halfway about anything; I look at a relationship as one hundred percent dedication by both partners. Pride is a deadly sin and must never stand in the way of a truly loving relationship."

"And that's commitment; see, I was right about you after all."

They continued to talk for hours, but Bill stuck to his earlier decision to let her take the lead and she was just as resolved that he'd have to make the next move. It was after midnight as they climbed the stairs arm in arm, each wondering what was next, but neither pressing to take the initiative. Their conversation ended with a kiss goodnight at Toni's door.

Bill lay in bed staring at the ceiling, thinking how he had wanted to make love to Toni tonight and wondering what had stopped him. She was ready, wasn't she? But one doesn't visit a lady you've seen in your dreams for weeks, but in person less than 48 hours and climb into bed with her. In the strict sense of the word, that would be *fornication*—a sin. In his present frame of mind wouldn't that be lust, indeed? He had just gotten off the plane.

"Give it a decent interval, Bill." he urged himself. More importantly, his faith dictated he must save sex for marriage. Motivation alone would not be enough—commitment is everything.

Toni wouldn't sleep, even if she had to hold out until dawn. Didn't he realize how much she needed him? Maybe he'd need help. She went to her writing table and took out some paper and pen.

He couldn't sleep, even if he tossed and turned until dawn. The reason for his restlessness was no mystery—he wanted her, and for a lot of reasons, none of which had anything to do with lust. It was the tender affection that intimacy engendered that he yearned for. Maybe some hot chocolate or something would get him through the night. He switched on the lamp and got out of bed to head for the kitchen. Opening his door, he looked down the hall and saw a light under Toni's door—she too was awake. Wait, on her door was a note. He walked softly toward her room and read the note, which said, "Advanced studies, Seduction 424, inside." Bill stopped, he thought a short prayer; he tip-toed away to the kitchen.

She had been up when she sensed his presence at the door. She had prepared herself for Seduction 424 by wearing a negligee so sheer she resembled a nude standing in a mist. She waited for the door to open—and waited. Finally, she thought, "He *does* need help." and rushed to open the door, but no Bill. She looked out and toward Bill's room only to see his back as he descended the stairs. She'd always respected willpower in a person, but now her feelings were a mixture of disappointment and respect for Bill's strong faith. It was at this moment when she acquiesced to Bill's leadership in their relationship, but there would be, she thought, wonderful moments ahead.

The morning sun's rays shined warm on their bodies as they lay by the pool. Toni watched her beloved Bill as he dozed on his stomach. She traced her fingers over the scar on his upper arm, near the shoulder, and noticing a portion of a scar on his hip, she gently pulled away the waistband of his swim trunks and wondered what happened. She examined the scar as if she too could feel the pain of the hot bullet and bent down to kiss the wound.

"For damaged merchandise you look pretty good to me. Bill?"

"Yes dear?"

"What happened last night?"

"Conscience. They say that the most important sexual organ is the mind—mine was in no condition to enjoy the experience no matter how much I wanted you. I hope you know how difficult a decision it was for me to back off and cool down."

"Breakfast in 15 minutes." She knelt and kissed him and left for the kitchen. Bill marveled at his good fortune. The evening had turned out well in spite of temptation. She was intelligent, a fantastic cook and promised to be a passionate lover; the heroine of a man's fantasy. Would the light of the new day show a negative side to this dream? He hoped not. He would learn all that pleased her so he could be successful trying.

Breakfast was set in a splendid manner, out of the hot morning sun. While eating a delicious omelet, they said little to one another, content to enjoy the breakfast in the warm glow of a blossoming love. Afterward Toni took Bill's hand across the table and asked,

"Bill? What are you thinking about?"

"I am so happy that you trust me. I hope you're not too disappointed about last night. I would like to share with you though, why my experience with women is so limited."

"You're sticking to that story are you?" Toni joked.

"I learned early, as a young man, that an affair is a hollow thing without love. Some men love the affair, but not the woman. The idea of being serviced by a whore, or even recreational sex, turned me off. So now you know why I have not sought sex for its own sake. I think it's selfish. I have always thought of sex as beautiful, a means of bringing intense pleasure to the one you love. Toni, it is so important to me that you enjoy what we do, and without your positive feedback, I could not function in that way. You openly anticipated making love and that alone encouraged me. Toni, today I am ready to commit to a love that, frankly, I didn't quite understand yesterday. You have.. Toni...I'm so happy,"

She breathed a quiet, "Wow!" as she rose from her chair and, in tears, came to Bill. They stood together, in each other's arms. After a lingering kiss, Bill asked,

"Toni, will you be my wife?"

"I've answered that question so many times in my prayers. Come." She took his hand and led him into a part of the villa he had not seen, to a door which she had not opened until a year ago, saying, "I'll give you my answer here."

The chapel was a simple small room, an altar, a family bible on a stand, and two chairs. The room was lighted by a candelabra. She lit the candles and following her lead Bill knelt with her at the altar as she prayed aloud.

"Father, forgive me my sin. Thank You for opening my eyes that I may see and for bringing Bill back to me, for answering my prayers." Bill thought she was being a little hard on herself. "Bill has asked me to be his wife, and I will give him my answer before You, Father..." She turned to Bill, the tears flowing freely, and said, half whispering, "...yes, yes dearest, yes." While clinging to Bill, Toni continued her prayer in silence, asking forgiveness for the foolishness and hatred of the past four confusing years which she had come to regret, and promised to atone for her lack of faith.

A few hours later, Bill sat at poolside watching his bikini clad angel standing on the diving board, some ten feet up, and thinking, "She'll probably jump feet first holding her nose." Instead, to his astonishment, she performed a very graceful and athletic backward layout, taking the splash with her on entry. Still under water she recalled her coaches warning not to dive in a bikini—she almost lost her top. She broke the surface to Bill's enthusiastic applause.

"I thank you, and my Rainbows' diving coach thanks you."

"What?" Bill said laughing.

"Want to see my medals? I almost didn't make the team because of my coach. She said I was too shapely."

"Didn't hurt your splash." Bill observed, sailing through the air and swamping her with the biggest splash possible by belly-flopping beside her.

"She also told me never to dive in a bikini. I almost lost my top." Bill imagined briefly what she'd look like without it. Toni swam to the ladder and waited. Quickly he shouted, "Wait!" and swam to her side, gave her a kiss on the forehead and scrambled up the ladder ahead of her, saying,

"This I've got to see."

"You're awful!" she said in mock chastisement. Whereupon she fixed her eyes on his and began to climb the ladder in tantalizingly slow motion. Finally she stood erect before him, her wet body glistening in the sun. Pausing a moment, she then stepped into his arms and said softly as they kissed, "Naughty boy."

Returning to the house, Bill wondered which lit the room brighter, the soft candlelight or the glow of Toni's face. Love was a long time coming to Bill, but he realized now, it was so worth the wait. Love—Bill realized his earlier brushes with it were only the natural development of a young man. He had been raised to respect women, and the natural urges of adolescence had been stifled for the sake of decorum. Norma, his first high school sweetheart, had a body blossomed beyond her years which tormented him, so he broke off the relationship to prevent their heavy petting from going further. Yes, "Gentleman Bill" fit him; he was too embarrassed to tell her why. Now, with love as his motivation, he felt his mind would work with his body to function as it should—worth the wait? Oh yes.

Toni, four years a widow, had so much to give and she had waited for one who met her standard. She had decided immediately that Bill was the one. Any doubt that would change her mind just did not materialize. Surely, this is how it should be; innocent love, free of lust, but liberally sprinkled with spice. Neither doubted their future together.

Still in her bikini, now covered with an apron, Toni looked fetching, to say the least, as she set another fabulous table for Bill. He watched her every move and offered,

"If I were ill, there'd be no prescription more potent than watching you in that getup."

"I find your transparent appreciation to be the most powerful aphrodisiac I can imagine. Hold me, my love."

As Bill held her close, his mind flashed to that part of the marriage ceremony asking if anyone knew of a reason why this couple should not be joined in holy wedlock. "I do!" It was WIZARD, standing in the congregation holding his hand high.

"Toni, dearest?" asked Bill, cutting off his daydream.

"Yes darling?"

"I have to go to the embassy. Don't call or say a word to anyone about our plans until I come back. I shouldn't be long."

"I understand, dear. I'll pray for us."

Bill sent a long coded message from the U.S. Embassy, requesting permission to marry Toni, giving her family background and indicating that they had no plans for a family. In an hour or so, WIZARD's reply refused permission, but recognized that if anyone in MOPS could be granted permission to marry it was he and that Antonia was an ideal candidate, but that such permission for one would open the door to all. He emphasized Bill's vulnerability as a married man in this business. The last line of the message warned: VIOLATION OF THESE INSTRUCTIONS WILL RESULT IN YOUR IMMEDIATE REASSIGNMENT TO CONVENTIONAL DUTIES.

Returning to the villa, Bill stepped from the car and walked slowly toward Toni; taking her in his arms, he silently vowed to convince WIZARD personally to change his mind. In Bill's mind, no obstacle was insurmountable where his love for Toni was concerned. Still, he was upset by the precaution he felt was unjustified in this case. Bill had clipped that portion of the message so Toni could read it. Then he said,

"I'll go to him and change his mind."

"So be it," she said trusting in Bill's ability to win his case, and resigning herself to the exigencies of the service, but she thought it terribly unromantic. She suggested,

"When the time does come, we can be married quietly, here at the villa." She lowered her voice placing her finger to her luscious lips and rolling her flashing eyes at Bill,

"All very hush-hush of course." Bill replied, twisting the corner of his non-existent moustache, in a heavy British accent,

"Sorry, old girl." Toni, playing the game, popped back with, "Can't be helped."

"So when will this historic union take place?" Bill asked.

"Historic?"

"Yes, I'll be the first of my breed to be married." He declared confidently.

"Your breed, fascinating." Toni thought for a moment and suggested they worry about the date after he had sold his boss and the powers-that-be on the idea. Then she added,

"The ceremony will be simple, but there is no good reason why it can't be memorable, is there?" She didn't wait for an answer, "It will be a spectacular ceremony, after dark, poolside, with floating lights."

"Ah yes, under the heavens, attracting only God's attention." Appreciating their situation, Toni leaned her head on Bill's shoulder and said,

"Who else needs to know?"

The next day while Toni was preparing lunch she tasted the the entrée.

"Hmm, it needs something." She stepped into Bill's arms and kissed him softly on his lips and said,

"Ah, that's better." Returning to work, she asked, haltingly, "Bill, sweetheart?"

"Yes darling?"

"I have to tell you something, but I don't want you to get the wrong idea."

"Why would I get the wrong idea?"

"I don't want you to think I'm a nymphomaniac or something, but…" Bill knew instinctively that Toni was about to say something which would only help their relationship, but her way of asking was titillating.

"Yes?"

"Our relationship so far has awakened in me the realization that I love to be touched; I've missed it and I want to be touched, tenderly, as only you can. No, let me alter that; I *need* to be touched, and often. It won't always mean a prelude to making love, but it's nice to know we'd be a kiss or two away. Can you understand that, Bill?"

"Darling, I never knew what loneliness was until it was over. Yes, I understand, and that's a two-way street, my love." Bill moved to a position behind Toni, encircling her waist with his strong arms, and as she tilted her head, he kissed her neck softly as she purred her approval.

"And Bi—ill?" She seemed to "sing" his name in two tones.

"Yes darling?"

Still hoping, she whispered, "Nothing's out of bounds." .

This tender scene was cruelly interrupted by the telephone. As Toni answered, an expression of concern and anxiety came over her lovely face, and she handed the phone to Bill.

"For you." Reflecting Toni's concern, he answered and was told by Colonel Morley, the Military Attache at the American embassy that a message had been received recalling him with immediate effect and requesting the embassy book him on the next available flight home which departed in only two hours. Bill was stunned.

"What is it, dear?" Toni asked, prompted by Bill's expression.

"I've been called home…the plane leaves in two hours."

"No, no!" How could they?"

"This is the first time I've ever been recalled from leave. It must be urgent. It also means there's nobody else available for the mission." Toni was visibly shaken and tearful, but took Bill in her arms and held him close.

"How long? She asked hopefully.

"Not long. Lengthy missions are not in the nature of my business; perhaps a week or two, and I'll be back with permission to make you my soul mate for life." Somewhat relieved, she composed herself and, in a very positive manner, she said,

"I'll be here, darling. Our marriage under the stars is temporarily on hold. It'll give us both something to look forward to. And darling?"

"Yes, Toni?"

"Come back to me safely. I need you, my heart."

Two hours later, Bill was looking out the window of the big 707 jet as it climbed into the azure sky. He was sure he saw the villa atop the hill overlooking Buena Vista, where he had spent three days in paradise with the angel of love who would be his wife. He had conquered the strongest of temptations and kept true to his faith.

The roar of the 707 brought Toni out to the pool and, gazing skyward, she spoke to her beloved, repeating her last words to him, "Come back to me safely, darling. I need you, my heart." Then a dark shadow fell over her face as she realized she no longer had an excuse for missing an appointment she dreaded. She also hadn't much time to prepare herself for an unpleasant and highly dangerous task she had decided must now be undertaken.

CHAPTER 10

THE REVELATION

The neighborhood on the edge of town was poor and squalid and the lengthening shadows heralded nightfall in Buena Vista. A shabby and unshaven man, hands in his pockets, walked in the shadows. His straw hat, frayed at the brim, was tipped back and his expression reflected the smiling contentment of a man under the influence. Weaving his way toward a third class eatery and bar frequented by local farm workers, he stopped short with a momentary expression of concern on his face. Then he turned and urinated against a brick wall, supporting himself against it with one hand. Relieved, he turned away and, tipping his hat to a passerby, continued on his unsteady way.

Arriving at a dirty window, he peered in. The place was deserted except for a man making conversation with a barfly and a bartender, in a grimy T-shirt, rinsing glasses. The coast was clear, so he opened the door and stumbled in, looking back as if some great obstacle had tripped him. Drunk or not, he seemed to know his destination; a secluded booth in the back, in the shadows, where he could be alone. He sat down with a bump and ordered a beer, making a great show of fumbling for change in his pants pocket. Satisfied he had earned the booth with the order, the bartender left him alone. The man then seemed to pull himself together, raising his head and sipping his beer. At least it's cold, he thought as he lit and drew deeply on a cigarette.

He was early. Soon his protégé would be here. He was proud of SWALLOW, his best student—bright, quick, devious and cunning—not unlike himself in many ways. Yes, she was capable and showed initiative; perhaps too much initiative for the rigid disciplined order of the KGB, but in an informed free-wheeling situation SWALLOW was brilliant. This extraordinary trip to Tierra Blanco was occasioned by a lack of progress with SWALLOW's current assignment and KRAIT had to know why. He snuffed out his cigarette and looked around the dingy room. Only the bartender remained when a woman, obviously a prostitute, entered the place to a disrespectful, "What do you want?" from the bartender.

"You mind your own business. I got business with the man in the back booth."

"Then what'll you have?"

"White wine."

"Buena."

SWALLOW had changed sides so now she was meeting the enemy for the first time, an enemy who had been her superior and mentor in the KGB. She would have to be careful with him because now she was compelled to protect the man she loved. KRAIT would be difficult to deceive, but she had readied herself for this moment. She slid into the booth and seated herself opposite KRAIT who hissed,

"What do you have for me?"

"What do you want?"

"You know what I want—more information on Bowman."

Antonia had concluded much from Bill's chance remarks but kept it to herself. "I have nothing new to tell you. If you want meaningful information, you must give me more time. He has been recalled to the states."

"You are telling me that, after spending three days with the man, all you can tell me is his name. Is that right?"

"That's all. I spent that time gaining his confidence. How was I to know he'd be called home early?" I thought I'd have two weeks.

An alarm sounded in KRAIT. He had seen this pattern in women agents before. He wondered if she had learned the truth of his hold on her. Had she discovered that it was he who killed her husband? He recalled the day four years ago when her husband, Montez, discovered information linking the Soviet Embassy personnel with Cuban insurgents operating in his country. To shut him up, KRAIT, disguised as a mechanic, tampered with the oxygen system in his jet fighter resulting in his death. KRAIT then persuaded an embittered Antonia *Montez* to work with him. It started while she was in Paris with little things at first, then before she knew it, she had been "reoriented" and sent to the KGB Academy in Moscow.

"Let me review the situation, comrade. First, you disobey your instructions by not betraying Bowman and his friends when they arrived in country. Second, you were responsible for them killing one of my agents. I accepted your explanation. The story you cooked up and took a beating for gave you instant credibility. I told you then it was a brilliant ploy, but..."

"But what, as a mole, I couldn't openly aid and abet a coup. I fed you information all along which, had the coup been properly managed, guaranteed success. The whole thing was bungled from the start."

KRAIT was uncomfortable with the accusation because it was his operation, in spite of the Cuban's ineptitude. But she was right. He had given them too much credit and failed to check them at every turn. Yes, they had failed, but it was his responsibility and therefore the failure was his. This fact could never be allowed to reach the ears of his superiors at home.

"Your report stated you thought Bowman was a member of a special intelligence unit, perhaps an arm of the CIA. But further investigation could not pinpoint the organization. Since the defection of a top British agent assigned as liaison to the CIA, we have come to know their organization in most minute detail. No, your American, nameless at the time, must have been a minor agent of a Military Intelligence Detachment; one of several in the U.S. Army. Next, your report, rendered immediately following Bowman's phone call from America, revealed only his name, nothing more."

Antonia listened, but all the while entertaining thoughts of joining Bill in whatever organization he belonged. Failing that, she'd be content with marriage and a career. Meanwhile, KRAIT had a gut feeling he had lost control of SWALLOW and her usefulness had come to an end. Besides she was the only one who knew just how badly he had botched the coup attempt.

Antonia spoke, "My value to you as an agent will be increased in time. He has asked me to marry him. I will learn all there is to know about him eventually." As soon as she said it she knew she shouldn't have.

"Are you becoming emotionally involved with Bowman?"

"Of course not, comrade. I want only to get to the bottom of this situation. I can think of no better way to gain his absolute confidence and perhaps penetrate his organization."

"A double agent?"

"No comrade, your agent." KRAIT was convinced, now more than ever, he had lost her. Deciding on the spot what must be done, he asked,

"Do you mind if I smoke?"

Bill was at home in his apartment near the military complex which sheltered MAGNOLIA. He had just phoned his folks and shared the good news. He had told them to be prepared to travel on short notice to attend his wedding. He was preparing to report to Magnolia as directed by the recall message when the phone rang. It was Colonel Morley, the Military Attache in Tierra Blanca.

"Bill?"

"Yes."

Bill, I want you get ahold of yourself. I hate to be the bearer of bad news but..."

"What is it, sir?"

"Antonia—she's dead." Bill knew Colonel Morley's voice and took the news as fact; and therefore the impact was immediate and devastating. Bill felt as if he had been hit in the face with a tremendous blow and his legs could not support him as he struggled to find a chair.

"Bill, are you there? Bill? After a moment Bill responded in barely a whisper, "Yes George, what happened?"

"Bill, did you say something? I can't hear you."

"How'd it happen, George?"

"We suspect foul play, Bill. But we cannot establish the cause of death. As far as the doctors can tell she suffered a cardiac arrest, but she has no history of heart trouble. It was so quick she felt no pain."

"That's a blessing. Have her folks been notified?"

"Yes. Bill, there is something very disturbing about all this. The circumstances were strange, so unlike Antonia. She was a very classy lady."

'What do you mean? What happened?"

"The scene of death was a sleazy greasy spoon bar and grill. You know what a nutrition nut she was?" Bill broke down and sobbed at the thought of Toni in the past tense.

"Bill?"

"Yes sir?"

"You have my deepest condolences."

"Thank you, George. I appreciate that. Can you tell me more?"

'Well yes, if you feel up to it Strangely they found her sitting in a booth in the back of the place in the vulgar clothing of a street walker. I found it hard to recognize her through the cheap make-up and brassy wig. The bartender said she was soliciting business from a farm worker in the booth. I don't know what she was up to, and her government denies any knowledge of her activities since the coup attempt. Whatever she was doing, she was on her own."

"Have they got the farm worker?"

"No, he disappeared, and no one can identify him."

"That's puzzling. What do you make of it?"

"We can only suspect that her unusual behavior is tied into another piece of information we have about her which until now we didn't give much credence to."

"Oh? What's that?"

"When her husband crashed she took the news very hard and took a trip to Europe to recover from shock. Quite naturally, she sought solitude, but she dropped out of sight for nearly six months. When she resurfaced, according to friends, she had been transformed. There was a hardness about her and she became dedicated to her business."

"Thanks George, you have been very considerate. If you learn any more please let me know. You might question her mother; she alluded to some difficulties of the last four years that might be of help.

Bill hung up, buried his face in his hands and quietly grieved for his beloved Toni. He recalled his excited lovely lady so full of life and imagined, or at least hoped, that he must have been a turning point in her life. He couldn't bring himself to believe she would hurt him. Besides, what did she know? If she was a professional, she knew enough to want to interrogate him further. Deep down he had the feeling she knew her life was in danger and he wanted to believe she died protecting him in some way. The thought consoled him somewhat, but the burning questions remained: how was she killed and who did it?

CHAPTER 11

THE BATON PASS

It was mid-November and a controversial presidential election had produced a close winner. The outgoing president was one of the most popular ever, with an 84 percent approval rating, and for the first time the constitutional amendment prohibiting a third term was universally painful to the American people. Thanks in no small measure to his skillful use of MOPS, the president had established a fine reputation in the free world as an expert in foreign relations and for the first time in many years Americans were beginning to feel safe in the world.

The president-elect gave considerable thought to the elements of success the outgoing president enjoyed, particularly in foreign affairs, and wondered how he managed to stabilize the volatile world situation with apparent ease. Considering foreign criticism of the two-term amendment which they felt doomed America to mediocrity, he hoped to keep personnel and policy changes in his administration to a minimum. After all, too many changes would not only be dangerous, it would break faith with the electorate.

Yes, he would have to be very careful when attempting to put his stamp on the new administration. Still, the president-elect was of the same party and prevailing sentiment at this point was to run the former president again in four years, assuming his good health and a propitious political situation. Nonetheless, the president-elect had made it clear he was his own man and, should the next four years bring success, there will be a second term; the fickle voters willing, and if the opposition and media don't try to turn some minor molehill into a mountain. However, party loyalty would cause him to yield the nomination should his political fortunes wane.

But now was the time for the orderly transition of government with all the usual cabinet briefings and intelligence estimates concerning the world situation. The president-elect found this sudden mass of information mind-boggling and struggled to sort out clearly overlapping and conflicting information and differences of opinion among advisors. This so-called orderly transition seemed to take on the proportions of a major flap and was temporarily confusing.

The outgoing chief executive sat alone at his desk looking around the oval office thinking over the past eight years. There were problems which seemed without solution, but somehow the ship of state sailed on as if it had a mind of its own, belying its need for a steady hand at the helm. Good government, after all, was a matter of public confidence. Anything which shook that confidence was to be avoided. While good management of all aspects of the nation's domestic affairs was mostly a matter of proficiency, foreign affairs were subject to all manner of unmanageable outside influences which had been the bane of existence for previous presidents, keeping them on the defensive and swamped in crisis after crisis. Yet he was able to take the offensive while keeping adversaries off-balance, chiefly owing to an idea and the resulting formation of a secret organization the previous president had passed on to him. He thought of the Soviets as waging the cold war, seizing every opportunity to further their goal of world domination spelled out in the Communist Manifesto. Where there was none, they sought to create the opportunity through subversion and manufacturing chaotic conditions. The president thanked God and the former president that he now had the means of actively waging peace in the cold war arena with built-in plausible deniability should something go amiss.

    He tried to place himself in the shoes of the president-elect when he would hear for the first time what had astounded him in that same position eight years earlier. He asked himself some hard questions. How would he react when the nation's best kept secret was revealed to him? Would he be reluctant to use this unorthodox tool, or worse, misuse it and thereby render it useless? Perhaps he would, in righteous indignation, dismantle the organization out of hand. As outgoing chief executive, he must settle him into the idea with briefings on specific past successful operations to provide a feel for the uses to which the tool could be put. Moreover, he would provide the president-elect with a more complete understanding of this secret organization than he was given. No longer a fledgling, it now has a highly successful track record no one could deny. Perhaps this would overcome the natural inclination to delay deploying this important organization because of failure to recognize the opportunity. Also, the president had conceived a special operation of unusually long duration, currently underway, which would probably extend beyond inauguration day, necessitating a full briefing of every detail.

    The next day, the president-elect, his mind buzzing with the farm problems of the mid-west, left the conference room at the Department of Agriculture in his limousine which would take him to his next appointment at the White House with the president. He welcomed the respite from the cramming and anticipated the break. His Secret Service escort was pleased to find him energetic and a fast walker, hurried or not. He seemed to appreciate his election as the world's number one target and wouldn't be easy to hit.

Upon arrival at 1600 Pennsylvania Avenue, he noticed an army helicopter, instead of Marine One, warming up on the White House helipad and wondered who was visiting the president. He hurried inside to find the president waiting to direct him personally to the helicopter. The aircraft lifted off, climbed above the Washington Monument and turned toward the Potomac. They could see the reflecting pool and the Lincoln Memorial below. It looked as if they were going to Andrews Air Force Base, but when they flew wide of the landing pattern the president-elect wondered. Their destination became clear as the big chopper circled to set down with little notice on a Pentagon helipad.

They were greeted quietly, without the usual protocol, and ushered quickly to the office of General Betancourt. The incoming commander-in-chief wondered why they had not been met by the chairman of the joint chiefs instead of a mere Brigadier. Several other questions needed answers and very soon, but for the moment he held his silence and did what he was asked. General Betancourt, turning to his secretary, ordered,

"Hold all calls. The door to my office will be locked and don't expect us out for two hours or so." Looking her in the eyes as if to convey a special emphasis, he asked. "Do you understand, Miss Bishop?"

"Yes sir, two hours at least."

Upon entering the General's office, the president-elect located a seat and began walking toward it, when he was redirected toward the closet door by the president, who said,

"Just follow the General." The president-elect witnessed the entry procedure with fascination as the General opened the heavy soundproof door and announced, in a loud voice,

"Gentlemen, the President of the United States!" All in the room rose to their feet as the president led the way in. One of the president-elect's questions was answered when the Chairman of the Joint Chiefs of the Staff stepped forward to greet the two men. Looking at the incoming Commander in Chief, he said,

"I'm sorry, sir, I didn't meet you at the helicopter because, as you will soon realize, we didn't want to attract attention to this meeting." Then the president said,

"Take seats, gentlemen." Turning the meeting over to the CJCS, he said, "Start the briefing, Admiral." CLIMBER, holding in his hand for all to see, an electronic remote control unit, he stepped to the platform and pressed a button and said,

"I have just activated a special electronic field which renders this room impervious to any known intrusion or eavesdropping device because..." as he spoke, a notice flashed on the screen behind him, stating a briefing security classification of TOP SECRET, "...what we are to discuss here and now, I say to you in deadly seriousness, is the closest held secret since the atomic bomb." Looking directly at the president-elect, "I say *closest* because only those in this room are privy to the information we will reveal in this briefing." The new CINC looked briefly around the conference table expecting to recognize someone he knew. However, the Chairman of the Senate Armed Services Committee, the Secretary of Defense, and the Secretary of the Army were conspicuous by their absence. Instead, only the President (EVEREST), the Chairman of the Joint Chiefs (CLIMBER), a Vice Admiral (WIZARD) and General Betancourt (MULEY) were in attendance. This only intensified his interest as CLIMBER continued.

"Mr. President-elect, you have inherited a legacy from two previous presidents who, beginning eleven years ago, developed a concept which has become an effective tool to thwart Soviet ambitions outside their borders. This concept was passed to the current president, and now by means of this briefing, he is passing the baton to you. Used properly, with courage, it can as in the past, manage serious situations to the very doorstep of Russia herself to prevent them from becoming crises. The skill of this small, tightly-organized force is demonstrated by the fact the Soviets have yet to learn who they are up against if in fact they feel there *is* an unknown force deployed against them. In each situation using this force, Soviet failures have appeared to be accidents or just plain bad luck. We have a track record of 26 successes and only one failure: about two years ago, a mission was aborted and most of the Task Team was recalled safely, but three very brave men died, taking with them the secret of MOPS." As he spoke, the TOP SECRET title flashed on the screen which read,

MILITARY OPERATIVES to PREVENT SUBVERSION

MOPS

"Successful beyond our wildest hopes, MOPS has become the cheapest, most effective means for inhibiting Soviet aggression and combating global terrorism. We have indeed, terrorized the terrorists. Let me emphasize, sir, that this is your tool and operates only at your discretion under mission type orders. It cannot deploy except by your order. If you, as president, choose never to use MOPS, it will simply cease to exist, except on paper which will go into deep freeze to be resurrected and presented as a recommendation to the next president. However, it would be a terrible waste to dismantle this small but magnificent group of highly dedicated professionals, only to find at some point in your administration a dire need for their timely services.

"Utilizing the full resources of our government's information and intelligence agencies, a small group of 43 people have succeeded in reducing the Soviet apparatus for conducting subversive operations to a second class effort by eliminating their most skilled operatives in the field, without their knowing how it was done nor by whom. Except for BLANKET, our covert contact in the CIA even the CIA knows nothing of the help they have received in the field. Because MOPS operatives never permit themselves to come under surveillance, their pinpoint actions of short duration keep the enemy second guessing themselves, and the organization has remained undetected by friend and foe alike."

During the hours that followed, the president-elect was held spellbound by the narrative of successful missions and situations which called for the use of MOPS. Finally, CLIMBER closed the briefing by announcing,

"Mr. President-elect, you and I will tour the home of MOPS, code named MAGNOLIA, after your inauguration and at your convenience. However, you are now sitting in the only MOPS facility outside MAGNOLIA. Obviously, as the safe house of safe houses, MANOLIA is not a showplace. Outside of the tenants, the only people who have seen it are in this room. This briefing room is convenient to all and, hidden away in General Betancourt's office it is not likely to be compromised. Meetings of a policy nature will be held here."

The president-elect was impressed with how much had been accomplished by so few. As it happened, an important plank in his party's platform was the streamlining of government bureaucracy. He had long held the view that fewer people, held accountable, could accomplish more at less cost, and would speed up the slowly turning wheels of government. Moreover, he felt the government of the people, by the people and for the people, had over time become the government of the politicians, by the politicians and for the politicians, serving themselves rather than the nation. As the briefing ended, he assured all present that under his administration, MOPS would continue to function without skipping a beat, and further commented that next to squaring off in a personal duel with the chairman of the communist party, this sounded like the best way to fight a war; keeping thousands or even millions of innocent lives out of it.

Contrary to an optimistic forecast, inauguration day turned bitterly cold as a weather front moved in suddenly and both the

President and his audience were uncomfortable to distraction. The president, rushing the pace of his inaugural address, lost his place several times but, as a practiced orator, he ad-libbed appropriate remarks to cover himself. But he got into serious trouble talking about streamlining the bureaucracy when in an off-the-cuff remark he declared that all departments should be as efficient as MOPS. While apparently the world at large accepted the remark, the privileged few shuddered at the first public utterance of the acronym.

In the city room of the Washington CLARION, the editor, reading the transcript of the inaugural address, spoke as he read the final sentence,
"I don't see it. What's all this fuss about, Charlie?" Sitting in front of him was his ace investigating reporter, Charlie Hall.
"It's not there." said Charlie, "It wasn't written into the speech. It was a throw-away line, an ad-lib, and I think it was a slip, perhaps a breach of security. There's a story here and I want to follow up on it. What made me suspicious is the way it was worded. The president's speech writers are pros and certainly capable of writing in a positive, non-controversial manner. The weather was miserable and the President rushed his speech. That, together with the fact that, as a new president, he had a headful of new information from numerous briefings, it was probably difficult to recall what was classified and what was not. It may be nothing, but my ear lobe is itching and that sets off an alarm in my mind."
"Well, Charlie, I've trusted your ear for news since our early days on the STARS & STRIPES, and most of the time you've been right. I'll give you a couple of days to dig into it, but if you don't find enough to keep you digging, drop it; there's a couple of other tips I need you to follow up."
Over a period of years, Charlie Hall had developed friends and sources in every branch of government and together with

documents available to him through routine sources, there wasn't much he didn't know about official Washington behind the scenes. Usually, what he didn't know didn't take long to find out. Yet, he loved his country, and as a responsible citizen, he wanted to believe what he was told officially. This attitude made his job easier because public officials knew he wasn't malicious nor destructive and so he earned their cooperation, insofar as national security would permit. More than once he had sat on a story until given the go-ahead to publish. Nonetheless, the slightest hint of corruption or malfeasance in office spurred him to action, and once on the scent, this bulldog couldn't release his grip.

Unaccustomed to being lectured the president sat in silence as CLIMBER admonished,

"That was very careless of you Mr. President. With one unguarded remark you almost undid the work of two previous presidents and rendered useless your most effective means of countering Soviet covert moves. You must understand you are no longer a state governor; this is global politics where mistakes can cost lives. Because of your slip there is no telling how many have started snooping, nor from what quarter. We have to be extremely cautious until we are certain this has blown over. I don't think an explanation alone will completely satisfy everybody. So may I suggest, Mr. President that you accelerate your plan to trim the fat in government, even at the risk of political injury, to help sell everyone on your explanation, should you be asked for one. Later, we can back off to a slower pace when all this is forgotten, and hopefully, we will have deceived the bloodhounds." The President responded,

"CLIMBER, you missed your calling; you should have been a politician. OK, you're right."

Moscow's bitter cold and gray winter made Washington feel like a fall day as Moscow suffered through one of the most severe temperatures on record. Having cancelled a trip to the Ukraine because of the weather, Anotoly Kirishnin, head of the KGB, took time to study the translation of the president's radio broadcast. The translated version of the chance remark made no sense to him. Therefore, he called upon his staff linguist who took it to mean the president planned to clean up the bureaucracy, but commented that the word *broom* was more often used in English colloquialism such as, "a new broom sweeps clean" in references to cleaning house, but a wet mop thereafter might finish the job. But the wily old Bolshevik wasn't satisfied, and ordered a review of all U.S. government agencies, thinking the President was using one as an example or had given it the task of cutting unnecessary fat. However, the review showed no such agency on the record; but there could be a covert operation? If anyone knew or could find out it would be Karenski.

Vassily Karenski regarded no one in the Kremlin as his superior. His lust for power was only temporarily under control and, while a setback, he hoped his position as schoolmaster for the KGB was only a stopover on his devious journey to the party chairmanship, an ambition fully understood by his enemies in the Presidium. The paramount reason for his success over the years was the consistent underestimation of the outrageous extremes to which he'd resort to win. This failure to appreciate KRAIT's tactics usually cost his opponents dearly; they just were not around to tell of it. Woe be to the next to tangle with him. One man, probably the only man, who fully appreciated the depths of KRAIT's evil and the most immediate and strongest of his antagonists was the chief of the KGB himself, Anatoly Kirishnin, in front of whose desk KRAIT now stood. The undercurrent of distrust and suspicion between the two men notwithstanding, they spoke as cold professionals with no friendship for one another. Kirishnin spoke first,

"Have you read the President's inaugural address?"

"Yes."

'What do you think of it?"

"The President was not dressed for the weather."
"Is that all?"
"What are you getting at, comrade?"
"I don't know. Here is a reference to something 'as efficient as mops.' Have you ever heard of 'mops'?"
"Of course."
"Have you? What is it?"
"It's something you clean the floor with." KRAIT replied impatiently. "Is this why you called me away from my work? You really should retire, you senile old man; you're seeing things." Having said that, and without waiting to be dismissed, he stormed out of the office muttering to himself, "Stupid old man!" The 'old man' watched in silence, thinking as KRAIT disappeared through the door, "He's the best we have, but someday that monumental ego will be his undoing."

Moscow police were baffled by an ongoing case involving the disappearances of nine women over a period of five years, so when their decayed remains were discovered in a remote area the police knew they were up against a serial killer. Although positive identification was achieved through comparison with dental records, a cause of death could not be determined. With no murder weapon and no cause of death, police questioning of friends and relatives was vigorous, but without result. The investigation was kept quiet, and the location of the dumping ground remained a secret shared only by the police and the killer. The discovery of a fresh body by a policeman, detailed to search the area periodically, encouraged investigators, who now believed they were close to solving the case. Surely, the new body, dead only two days, would yield new clues. But again, an autopsy failed to disclose a cause of death. To make matters worse, the nude victim had been dumped into a shallow, fast running stream which washed the body and hair clean of possible forensic evidence. There was no sign of a struggle, but internal examination revealed evidence of recent sexual activity. The police did not want their mystique of infallibility tarnished, so the case remains unsolved to this day because of their failure to go public and enlist the aid of the state run press. As it turned out, there was more than one person who could have contributed to the emaciated body of evidence, but who did not come forward and therefore were never questioned. It is strange that the international espionage community would come to know the identity of the killer and the Moscow police would not.

Two years earlier and exchange of spies at the Berlin wall and an unrelated defection of a high ranking KGB agent in London provided what were to be critical missing pieces which shed the first dim light on KRAIT. From this, a dossier of his many years of activity was constructed, answering questions western agents had asked for years.

The MOPS operation which would extend into the new president's term had begun. MAGNOLIA was alive with activity. For the first time, all four Task Teams were assembled, summoned to an extraordinary briefing, and this time WIZARD listened along with the rest as CLIMBER explained the concept of the upcoming operation. Pointing to a map of east Africa, he said,

"Gentlemen, this is the country of Equatoria. Since joining the commonwealth as an independent nation, it has been targeted by the Soviets for subversion. It is not the best location for an Indian Ocean Port, but when you haven't got one...they've been stymied everywhere else. However, the Soviets have found Equatoria a tough nut to crack. Most of the country's internal security personnel, highly trained British professionals, chose to stay on in their positions after independence, becoming citizens. The CIA has reported to the president that, in cases like this, where their efforts are frustrated by efficient security, the KGB tends to bring in the varsity, the first string, their best trouble shooter to find the problem and deal with it ruthlessly.

"This mission is unusual for MOPS. Normally, when see an opportunity we go in, do the job and get out. From the Task Team point of view, that won't change. However, we and the British feel we stand a far greater chance of success if we do the hunting with their support; we will now create our opportunity by taking the offensive. Fellas, we're going on a snake hunt, but to catch our viper we'll need more than one hunter, unless we're incredibly lucky. In contrast to previous operations, it will take patience and probably many weeks to bag our snake, but as in previous missions, the individual Task Team will be used only once. If they fail, another will try, keeping with our tactic to prevent prolonged exposure of a team to the enemy and to conduct operations in such a way as to hold secret from all sides our very existence.

"Over the past few years, we have succeeded in doing serious damage to the cream of the Soviet agents in the field, but they are being replaced with high caliber people, well-schooled in subversion, terrorism and intelligence information gathering. As you know, information is not intelligence until it is collated and analyzed by experts to produce a conclusion; this conclusion is then intelligence. Information gathered over a period of 25 years has produced conclusions concerning our snake, code named KRAIT. For those snake-ignorant among you, the Banded Krait is the deadliest of the Southeast Asian vipers, of the genus Bungarus, which strikes without warning. Its venom is neurotoxic and kills quickly. His code name alone should be ample warning of his lethal nature. KRAIT has survived years of exposure to the hazards of his profession, as well as vicious political in-fighting costing the lives of some of his less wary, and, may I say less ruthless contemporaries.

"Currently, he is their best. As Superintendent of the KGB Academy, more than anyone, he is responsible for the high level of agent training. The elimination of KRAIT would be a serious blow to future Soviet covert operations. Every free country on earth would breathe a sigh of relief at the news of his demise.

Bluntly put, our mission is to lure KRAIT out of Moscow into the field and kill him.

"Let us examine carefully his profile dossier to garner what I would characterize as a portrait of evil. There is no doubt what you are about to see and hear represent one in the same man, KRAIT. He is a cold, calculating killer. His first known killing, directed by the party, was his own wife. When as young communist worker, he murdered her because she disagreed with his politics. During the communist party purges of the thirties, he informed on and was designated to eliminate fellow party members whom he personally executed; a task which he grew to enjoy. Because of his party zeal and penchant for intrigue, he was appointed a high ranking agent of the KGB in charge of internal security, where he was turned loose on deviant KGB agents who, one by one, disappeared. His ambition knew no bounds, resorting to first framing and then executing people who stood in the way of his personal timetable for advancement. Years ago, he gave up the use of firearms because they were easily traced and provided ballistic evidence, relying first on the knife and then preferring exotic lethal gadgets. Utterly ruthless and sadistic, he murdered his mistresses by using them first to satisfy his lust and then as guinea pigs on whom he tested newly-developed lethal devices for effectiveness. Since their attendance at the KGB Academy was secret, family and friends provided nothing to implicate KRAIT, who had destroyed their dossiers. Typical of communist ideology, KRAIT is an advocate of the favorite Soviet axiom, 'the end justifies the means' and since in his mind a companion rule was 'the quicker the better,' very often his tyranny was heavy-handed. For years, he worked in the Eastern Europe Section and was responsible for the assassination of key Czech, Pole and Romanian government leaders. His successes here brought him to the attention of the party chairman, and he was promoted to Deputy Commissar of the KGB where he attempted to unseat the commissar. Except for the chairman's intervention, KRAIT would have been exiled to Siberia. Instead, he was made

Superintendent of the KGB Academy, where he instituted sweeping changes to the curriculum and introduced more practical exercises under realistic conditions. We are told he teaches some subjects personally. Most recently, he opposed MOPS in South America and in the Middle East, although, to our knowledge, he was and still is unaware of our existence.

"The CIA, with their worldwide contacts, and the FBI, working through Interpol, are cooperating to identify KRAIT. A cagey and elusive agent all his life, he never knowingly allowed himself to be photographed. Also cooperating in this effort are MI-5, French Intelligence and the West German Intelligence. Together, we hope to gather in one dossier all the pictures which we suspect are him. Combining these with the dates the pictures were taken and what knowledge we have of his operations, we hope to produce a quality picture we can use for identification. We have a composite drawing from a description by a KGB defector, but it is of little use as positive ID. Our defector will be able to single him out from a group of photos of reasonable quality. So the trick is to lure KRAIT out from under his rock and kill him. He may not be caught the first, second, third or even the fourth time, but he must never be aware of the attempt, the close calls. We don't want to spook him, and we don't want to take him alive. Capture would be too risky; he's too dangerous. He has been cornered before but never caught. No one who got close enough to identify him has survived. A conservative estimate shows KRAIT responsible for the loss of more than 40 excellent allied agents. He is a survivor because his superiors are afraid of him and his enemies haven't lived to finger him. This operation has been underway, in the preparation stage, dating back to the previous president and is endorsed by the new president. We call it OPERATION SNARE."

Charlie Hall's day and night efforts, calling in favors and meeting face to face with the most informed sources in Washington, had proven fruitless. Nobody had the slightest notion of what he was talking about, yet his itching ear lobe persisted—there had to be a story here. He thought again about the comment in the speech and the ignorance professed by all his contacts; they couldn't or wouldn't even hazard a guess. There was nothing to do but ask the president himself to clarify his statement. But, to gauge for himself whether or not he had a story, he'd try to catch the president in an unguarded moment, asking him point blank in order to judge his reaction. The inaugural ball would have been the place, but that was yesterday. Wait! The president is presenting decorations to that crew of astronauts today and the press is invited. Charlie jumped from his chair and ran to the editor's office. Addressing his boss,

"Who is covering the presentation to the astronauts at the White House today?"

"Linda Walkins."

"Send me. I need to speak to the president."

"Has she left yet?" Turning around, Charlie saw her at her desk.

"No."

"Good. Send her in. You got it."

In route to the White House, Charlie realized the importance of phrasing the question properly for maximum shock effect. He disliked doing this to the president, but he wanted a reaction, which might tell him more than words alone. The wording should imply prior knowledge of the answer, but saying too much might reveal the truth; he hadn't a clue. He suspected MOPS to be a secret agency, so why not ask directly, "What are the responsibilities of the agency you call MOPS?" Charlie knew also he had an advantage because the president knew him; most recently from the campaign trail where they had talked informally many times while traveling. He felt he had the president's respect and confidence as a responsible journalist, and as such, he would pick a moment to pose the question where they were out of earshot of other reporters. That was the least he could do since he didn't know the content of Pandora box he was attempting to pry open. Charlie felt strongly that he'd leave the White House today with either a story or a new assignment. If nothing came of this last probe his story was dead, but either way he hoped his familiarity with the president would help him read the reaction accurately.

Charlie Hall watched in admiration as the president demonstrated his mastery of occasions of this nature. His easy charm and good humor were evident in his remarks to the astronauts and their families, as he voiced the nation's pride in their accomplishments. Charlie had begged a favor from the president's press secretary to speak to the president immediately following the ceremony, for the purpose of asking one question privately. The president had graciously agreed.

"Hello Charlie. How's my favorite newshound?"

"I'm fine, thank you, Mr. President."

"Tell me something, Charlie; if asked, would you have served as my press secretary?" Charlie was knocked a bit off balance by the question.

"I would have been honored you asked, Mr. President, but no sir, I don't think so. I..."

"I didn't think so either." the president interrupted, "I just couldn't see a great reporter like you in the job. There aren't enough like you around, so I didn't want to take you out of circulation."

"That's nice of you to say that, sir, but your final choice was a wise one. He is respected by the entire media; he'll serve you well."

"Thank you, Charlie. Now, What's on your mind?" Without hesitation Charlie inquired,

"MOPS, Mr. President; what are the responsibilities of the agency you call MOPS?" Charlie watched the president's eyes and looked for the tell-tale body language that would indicate he had struck a nerve. Instead, the president looked puzzled and asked,

"Mops? I don't understand, what do you mean, mops?"

"Your inaugural address sir, you said you wanted other government agencies to be as efficient as MOPS. What does MOPS do?"

Showing no outward signs of discomfort, the president's gut was churning, "Oh, I see. Charlie, we were all freezing our butts out there and I rushed through the speech skipping over whole paragraphs to shorten it, but I wanted to emphasize bureaucratic house cleaning. I guess that comment could have been clearer if the phrase included both brooms and mops."

"Thank you, Mr. President."

"Was that it? Was that your question, Charlie?"

"Yes sir,"

"Well, I'm sorry it wasn't something more earth shaking for you."

"Sir, I'm glad it wasn't. Goodbye, and thanks for seeing me, I know you are busy." As Charlie Hall left the White House he reached up and pulled on his ear lobe—no itch.

So the baton had passed; not smoothly and perhaps with a stumble or two, but the runner was on his way and for the moment striding ahead of the opposition.

CHAPTER 12

THE BITE

Standing before the assembled Task Teams, WIZARD looked grim as he announced that everyone was restricted to the confines of MAGNOLIA for the duration of SNARE. "Gentlemen..." he warned, "...prepare yourselves to look at the face of Satan." A picture flashed onto the screen and WIZARD delighted in announcing success in efforts to obtain a quality ID photo of KRAIT.

"There he is—an anathema. This is an authenticated photograph of KRAIT." He turned away from the screen and winked at his men, "Handsome devil, isn't he? This is a blow-up from a group picture taken three years ago by a hidden camera. At the time no one had any idea he was in the group, but we got lucky when our informant spotted him in the photo. Under the circumstances, we couldn't have asked for a better result. We've learned another interesting fact; he is a chameleon, capable of taking on any look, personality or disguise. We do know he has a tendency toward the humble when assuming a role. Surveillance by several governments over a great number of years have produced only the stills and motion picture clips you are about to see." The first photo flashed on the screen and WIZARD explained,

"In this one, observers were certain they had KRAIT, here in the foreground. He *was* in the picture. This is KRAIT, the janitor pushing the broom in the background. In the second shot, the subject of this stake-out was this well-dressed man, carrying the attache case, getting out of the limousine. But this is our man, the chauffeur. This next film clip was obtained from French Intelligence. Agents had staked out a known message drop. To keep from blowing the stake-out, they had to chase off this rag picker who happened along. See, this agent is telling her to move along." There was some mumbling among the men and WIZARD acknowledged, "You guys are way ahead of me. Yes, *she* turned out to be KRAIT. Later it was discovered that he had picked up the message right under the French agents' noses. Only too late did they realize *she* was KRAIT. Let this be a lesson to you; no one is above suspicion. But, be especially alert to the lowly."

WIZARD returned to the ID photo and left it on as he spoke,

"We know our friend KRAIT has disdained the use of firearms in favor of more sophisticated, silent and deadly devices which render the cause of death very obscure, if not impossible to determine. One such lethal device he is responsible for developing is an innocent looking cigarette lighter which actually light cigarettes with one end, but from the other end projects a fatal dose of concentrated gas up to three feet. Highly directional, it is safe for the operator, but kills instantly. So effective is this odorless, colorless gas that the victim is dead before he or she hits the ground. Once released into the air, the gas mixes with oxygen and is rendered harmless in less than ten seconds, but kills in one to three, giving the appearance of cardiac arrest and leaving no trace even to an experienced pathologist. If KRAIT gets close to you, expect an attack because he has no fear of revealing himself to his victims. There are other devices he might use, all of which have passed his litmus test of committing murder in a crowded room with no one the wiser, but the lighter is his favorite."

The simple addition of two-plus-two hit WILLIAM TELL suddenly and he knew KRAIT was Toni's killer. Deep in his gut, a rage boiled like a cauldron stinking with hate, an intensity of bad feeling he had never known before, even in the face of mortal combat in Korea. He wanted something he had never desired before; something counter to his closely held belief that *Vengeance is mine sayeth the Lord*. He prayed to be the instrument of God's vengeance. For better or worse, the impersonal detachment was gone, but WT would not risk WIZARD taking him off the mission, so he remained silent about what he knew to be true and prepared to make the most of his opportunity when it came. He listened closely as WIZARD continued,

"We have developed a defense against KRAIT's little plaything, but it is not foolproof. First, you must feel in imminent danger of attack; second, you must breathe only through your nose." Holding between his thumb and forefinger a tiny round object, WIZARD explained that it was a nasal implant to be inserted by the user temporarily in each nostril to filter the gas long enough to permit the oxygen to render it harmless, about ten seconds.

"The best defense always has a countermeasure; in this case, it is a swift blow to the stomach to force the victim to gasp through the mouth. There is only one drawback to the filter. Because it restricts normal breathing somewhat, there is a tendency to bypass the filters by breathing through the mouth. Guard against this; there is plenty of filtered air for the body to function normally for up to 15 minutes without undue discomfort. We don't recommend running the 100-meter dash breathing only through the nose. And, of course, the filters won't stay put if you have a cold in the nose, without first a good dose of antihistamine.

"The composition of the individual Task Teams won't be announced until the situation into which you'll be deployed is known, but the sequence of deployment is as follows: first, BUCKAROO, followed in turn, if required, by WILLIAM TELL, VICEROY, and SIDEKICK. No team will be deployed until we are certain KRAIT is in-country. We anticipate each team will enter the country in the manner recommended by our key contact, Chief Inspector Howard of the Equatoria National Police; a night air-drop out in the bush. Your reception committee will be a licensed safari guide, who will transport you into the capitol, Komendabi, just as though you were American tourists on safari. Arriving in the city by Land Rover caravan, you should be free from suspicion.

"Chief Inspector Howard is a dedicated professional, a specialist in internal security to the chagrin of the KGB, with a distinguished war record as a commando in WWII, when he participated in or led raids in Norway and France. He's a tough ally who can appreciate our methods and objectives, and allows him to strike a blow without repercussions from the Soviets. Of course, he knows nothing of our organization."

Anatoly Kirishnin paced the floor of his office, concerned over the botched operation in Equatoria. This brought to mind a lengthy succession of failures in recent years which he had dismissed as a combination of the west's increased alertness and bad luck. He disparately needed a coup, a victory to pacify his superiors, who had started asking the tough questions. If he was to keep his job he needed a master stroke; but for now, even a moment of glory would do. Fully aware of the competence of the opposition in Equatoria, the situation demanded a maximum effort. He needed to step up the pressure to keep the authorities' hands full while his top people got the job done. If he could present Equatoria to the Supreme Soviet, the party chairmanship could be in sight. It was time to call in the best; Karenski and his picked band of cutthroats, to finish the job no one else could. When Karenski was personally in charge, success was only a matter of time because he left nothing to chance and was ruthless enough to smash opposition viciously. Privately, Kirishnin hoped Karenski would someday meet his match and he'd be rid of him forever. For once, he could find solace no matter how the dice turned up, but to win and lose Karenski in the process was too much to hope for.

High in the back row of the amphitheater classroom, Kirishnin sat in the shadows observing Karenski, the teacher. He was a showman and presented his lecture with imagination and drama, no matter the subject. It was a pity such talent was diminished by so twisted a personality. His performance captured the universal admiration of his students, who would shudder if they knew how readily expendable they'd be in an operation led by their mentor. He would sacrifice his own as easily as killing the enemy if it got the job done or aided in his own survival. As the class ended several students, mostly female, came to ask questions because he had with skits and demonstrations taught the art of seduction. It was easy to see why he never lacked for bed partners on whom to test his gadgets. To the ladies, he was quite the dashing figure, an indomitable and superior being in their godless society. If a woman showed promise as an agent, he'd keep his distance, but those of slow wit and mediocre grades became willing objects of his lust. As the group broke up, one young woman dallied behind as the classroom door closed. Still unseen in the shadows, Kirishnin watched as she practiced one aspect of the art of seduction on her instructor until she was urged by Karenski not to be late for her next class. As the door closed behind her, Karenski was startled by his elderly boss who began to applaud from the shadows above.

"Wonderful performance comrade. Your dedication to duty is commendable. Did you really care if she was late to her next class?" His question remained unanswered.

"How long have you been up there?"

"I slipped in through the upper door about 30 minutes ago." the old man said showing himself as he descended the center aisle stairs to the speakers platform.

"I've come to see you because we are in trouble in Equatoria."

"*You* are in trouble, you old reprobate."

"No matter, the trouble is there and we need the best we have to settle it. You are the best and you can hand pick your help."

"You dimwit, I told you a year ago what was needed there but you wouldn't listen. Now it's too late for subtleties; we must improvise to salvage something from your fiasco and hope the new plan will work. This kind of situation is dangerous for us. I don't like it. We have lost so much time."

"Whatever it takes, it's in your hands." The old man handed Karenski a document. "This is for you."

"What is it?"

"You surprise me, you have it in your hands and you ask me what it is? You must be slipping. The original is in the hands of the Politburo and recommends you take my job only if I am promoted or retire, not in the event of my death."

"I see we understand each other."

"Comrade, did you ever think otherwise? So make me look good, and yourself *a Hero of the Soviet Union,* and you could be the next Commissar of the KGB."

The word came when BLANKET announced that KRAIT had arrived in Equatoria. The CIA was alert and the vigil paid off. It was now time to deploy BUCKAROO into a cold situation. With little to go on, it would be catch-as-catch-can, a circumstance which did not promise success beforehand. BUCKAROO and his people were understandably apprehensive.

In the grim and shadowy world of MOPS, an occasional relief of tension was welcome. No one was more alert to the mood of his Task Teams than WIZARD and, when he could, he injected his highly individual brand of humor. The military is very prone to the use of trendy buzzwords which become part of an era. Not really jargon, these words of fashion spread like wildfire throughout the military establishment like an epidemic, eventually dying out and being replaced by synonyms. WIZARD did not subscribe to these trends, convinced that effective communication should rely on words everyone new, simple and direct. He was not above the well-worn cliché if it got the point across clearly. But now and then, to satisfy a need to show he was not a verbal simpleton and to poke fun at those who would spread this "diarrhea of the mouth," he'd say something profuse, but to the point. At BUCKAROO's team briefing, speaking of KRAIT, he jested,

"We must necessarily nullify this nefarious, nihilistic Neanderthal, who remains our nameless nemesis, with a neat and nifty but nasty knock on the noggin, negating the nuisance and relegating the nauseating nincompoop to nostalgia." With this clear and concise mission directive, BUKAROO and three of his team were deployed the next night.

Later, WILLIAM TELL was advised by WIZARD that *Sergeant Major* Caruth, whose promotion was effective with his arrival, was ready for his final training, which would have to wait, however, because all training except classroom and research had been suspended for the duration of SNARE. WT was delighted and asked where he was. WIZARD replied he was due at MAGNOLIA tomorrow and wanted WT's opinion whether to let him report now or put him on leave until after SNARE.

"I want him now. What better introduction to MOPS than to sit in on our preparations for this mission, whether or not he's deployed."

"Did you know he's a licensed pilot?"

"No, he didn't tell me; it wasn't on his service record. But I'm not surprised. He always has had something else going, *just in case.*"

"I know, our background investigation revealed he spent a leave taking flying lessons and soloed. He belonged to the Fort Lewis Flying Club for a year or so until you lured him away. He's a responsible pilot; I checked."

"That must have been one of the 'irons-in-the-fire' he spoke of. Sir, Caruth is a responsible anything. That's why I want him."

"Here's a list of unassigned numbers. What do you think?"

"We first met in Korea, at the 38th Parallel; so why not 38."

"Done! We have him in a parking orbit at the Franklin Hotel in Washington. I'll have him meet you tomorrow at the main gate at 1300, and you can show him the way into MAGNOLIA. After your orientation briefing, he can begin attending the daily SNARE briefings.

The next day the two old friends met at the main gate and drove to the outskirts of the containment area to a thickly wooded spot and released the vehicle. Then they hiked to the dummy water pump station. Caruth now understood why he was permitted no luggage, only a few personal items in one bag. All would be provided him in MAGNOLIA.

"We are now under electronic observation and every word we say, even whisper, is being monitored."

"I don't see anything."

"We had a fence marked RESTRICTED AREA but there were too many questions asked, so we took down the fence and, in these woods, it wasn't hard to conceal security devices."

Soon they arrived at what appeared to be a pump station; a small concrete structure with a large pipe from underground entering the side and reemerging from the opposite wall and into the ground again. WT handed Caruth a peculiar looking key and showed him where to insert it, while he inserted another some seven feet away. Then he directed,

"On the count of three, turn your key counterclockwise while I turn mine clockwise; in other words away from each other. Ready, one, two, three!" The door opened and the two men entered, closing it quickly behind them. Before them a ramp disappeared into an underground passageway which became lighted three seconds after closing the pump house door.

"Follow me." At the end of 120 yards of tunnel they reached a small room, and as the elevator door opened, a voice greeted them in an electronic monotone, "*Welcome. Please state your code identities.*" WT answered for both,

"WILLIAM TELL and 38."

"*Thank you, sir, please step in.*" The two entered and rose to a modestly furnished lobby where they were met by WIZARD. WT spoke first,

"Sir, allow me to introduce Sergeant Major Billy R. Caruth. Sergeant, this is WIZARD, my boss."

"Welcome aboard and welcome to your new home, a combination headquarters, armory, training facility and health club. We've gone to great lengths to make MANOLIA a comfortable home."

"Thank you, sir. I'm impressed already. This is some set up."

"Speaking of arrival, you heard your new ID announced at the elevator. From this moment on your surname will never again be uttered. Your sponsor is code named WILLIAM TELL and you are 38. He will brief you on the organization, mission and the short but proud history of MOPS and show you around the facility."

"MOPS, sir?"

"Yes, 38, we'll get into that at your briefing. For now get settled in and WT will brief you this evening." Departing, WIZARD reminded, "See you at the daily."

Four days later, WIZARD announced, to everyone's surprise, a tentative end to OPERATION SNARE.

"I am happy to announce that Task Team BUCKAROO, posing as hold-up men making an escape from a robbery scene, shot and killed KRAIT and another Soviet agent. The government of Equatoria has apologized to the Soviet Embassy for the unfortunate incident and promised to bring the guilty to quick justice when captured. BUCKAROO and his people are in route home at this moment. Until all current information is confirmed and the final debriefing is concluded, all personnel remain restricted to MAGNOLIA."

WT looked at 38 and said incredulously.

"Hard to believe—too easy. Krait is too smart and too experienced to be nailed by the first attempt." Agreeing, 38 replied,

"Still, BUCKAROO's play was clever and imaginative. I hope it worked."

"I'm not taking a thing away from BUCKAROO or KRAIT. It just seems too easy."

At the next day's briefing, WT's doubts were confirmed when WIZARD explained,

"The CIA confirms we got the wrong man, a Soviet agent yes, but not KRAIT. To BUCKAROO's credit, the man he thought was KRAIT was a double, hand-picked and a dead-ringer. However, because of the nature of the incident, a second attempt can be launched safely without the Soviets being alerted."

After the briefing WT looked at 38 and said apologetically,

"I'm not proud of BUCKAROO's attempt. It wasn't worthy of MOPS. I know we can do better."

"What do you mean? I thought it was a clever set up. If it had worked, everyone would have been in the clear."

"Being the first team deployed BUCKROO had little going for him. His attempt had to be opportunistic but it was hurried, a long shot—too long. KRAIT was too smart to show himself without a decoy until he was sure of the situation."

"How do you see the mission?" asked 38 seeking WT's experience.

"First, I want you to consider this instruction. Any criticism of BUCKAROO is academic and completely without malice; I love the guy, he had only one shot at KRAIT. I'm not trying to second-guess BUCKAROO. To be fair about it, I don't know what he was thinking or how carefully the attempt was thought out, but on the surface it seems a feeble effort. No, it will take an elaborate scheme to finish Krait, with a back-up plan…"

"*Just in case.*" they both said in unison, laughing.

"Do you have any ideas?" asked 38.

"Not quite yet, specifically, but in principle and in baseball jargon: as a lefty, we must hit to the opposite field by first faking a bunt on strike one, and fouling down the first base line on strike two."

"Deception."

"You bet. But, as the pitcher, KRAIT will initiate the action, so we'll have to go with the pitch; let's not forget that."

"Let's hope it won't be too far out of reach." offered 38.

"Preparation is the key." WT answered drifting into thought for a moment. Then added "You know, we do a lot of reading in preparation for a mission, and I remember a bit about Equatoria that might be helpful."

Meanwhile, in one of Komendhabi's cheaper hotels, KRAIT sat in his bathtub seeking relief from the mid-day heat, an electric fan oscillating above his body as he listened to a comrade explaining the unfortunate loss of his two top agents as bad luck.

"I wonder. I use a double, now and then, to test if the enemy expects me. But something like this; who can tell? Bad luck, like good luck, is random. According to the laws of probability, our string of bad luck is much too long."

"It would seem so, comrade, but the police were on the scene and the criminals shot their way out of a trap. It was unfortunate our people happened along."

"Yes, but were there police casualties?" quizzed KRAIT.

"Yes; one killed and one wounded, according to the morning paper."

"Seems legitimate, but if not, how would they know our people would be there? That would take planning—such an elaborate set up."

"I don't know, comrade."

"We certainly won't find out from them, will we?" KRAIT asked rhetorically as he rose from the tub. "Our adversary here is Chief Inspector Howard. I propose to start a reign of terror, beginning with the elimination of Howard and anyone who takes his place, as fast as they do so. Start surveillance on Howard. You have a week. Study his routine; don't miss a thing. We'll set up a series of ambushes of key officials, beginning with Howard, with priority on police and military leadership, to make the populace feel helpless, as if stripped of their government protection. The rest will be easy. They should be especially bloody slaughters for maximum shock affect when the gory pictures are published by the media. We will arrange to put the blame on that renegade from the Kanimba tribe."

During the following week, the Soviets were to find that the only constant appeared to be their quarry's unpredictability. The Inspectors experience and the Kanimba uprising in particular taught him to avoid the routine. He varied his route to work each day; he was a widower with no children at home, so his time was his own. He dined out often, but at a variety of restaurants, using the time to visit with old friends; never sitting with his back to the door. He made a game of the unexpected, claiming it extended the lifespan of a policeman. He did not own a car and rotated the use of police cars and drivers. As a consummate professional, he took his recreation when he could get it, and usually on very short notice, organizing a round of golf or a few sets of tennis. During the week of surveillance, he did neither. His rejection of routine or rhythm forced the Soviets to conclude the only certain time and place for the ambush would be the steps of police headquarters upon his arrival at or about 7 a.m. Moreover, the boldness of this location would serve to heighten public terror.

To avoid capture, it would be necessary to keep their distance, so the long reach of a high-powered rifle was needed. To assure a clear shot, four snipers would be used; one from each of four directions, right, left, left front, and right front. The four positions would need to be within a city block, each with an escape route—two, if possible. KRAIT had developed a breakdown rifle easily hidden on one's person and quickly assembled; it even included a telescopic sight for deadly accuracy. Four of these, one per man were ordered for the job. The snipers were directed to aim at the center of mass with the first shot, and after the target was down, take a second shot at the head to insure a messy killing.

News of the ambush of Chief Inspector Howard outside his own headquarters had the reverse effect on the citizens of Komendhabi. Anger and outrage, not terror, were the predominant sentiments, together, with relief at the news that, while seriously wounded, their much-respected head of police would live. True to his tendency to avoid routine, on this day the inspector chose to bound up the stairs at nearly a dead run. Surprised, his would-be assassins, instead of waiting for another day, jerked off their shots, two missing completely and two striking the inspector in the arm and thigh. Nobody had time for a second shot, as he staggered into the building.

KRAIT was furious and vowed to do the job himself, if he had to kill the man while he was still in his hospital bed. Expecting a second attempt, the Deputy Chief Inspector organized an elaborate scheme to protect his boss and perhaps even capture the assassin. Inspector Howard's hospital room was guarded around the clock by a uniformed policeman and an undercover officer dressed as an orderly. Meanwhile, the Chief Inspector was quietly moved three floors up to a private room in the maternity ward. The room was filled with flowers and he wore a rather charming wig and nail polish of shocking pink. Other security personnel were also dressed as nurses and orderlies. The trap was set.

Upon learning of the attempt on Inspector Howard's life, WILLIAM TELL began shaping a plan. A part of the plan would require the special ability of 38, despite his incomplete training. The scheme was accepted enthusiastically by WIZARD who agreed to allow 38 to participate and ordered the immediate implementation of OPERATION ARROW III, as part of SNARE. WT had a sense of urgency. So much of his plan was keyed to the current situation in Equatoria, that a radical change in the situation would bring them back to square one. His plan had to be implemented now and coordinated with the authorities since it required their help to succeed.

Parachuting his team of four into the country without incident, WT was still working out the details of his plan in his head and asking pertinent questions of his guide as their Rover caravan made its way toward Komendhabi.

"I recall reading somewhere that all licensed safari guides are deputized policemen in order to enable them to do double duty and enforce the country's strict game laws. Is that correct?"

"Right you are, sir…"replied the guide "…and proud of it we are, too!"

"Would it be possible to secure a Rover and provisions for the bush without dealing with a guide?"

"I'm afraid not, sir. Such provisions are available only from guides so we also own our outfitter stores. It's the law, to help prevent outside poachers from operating here. I don't mind telling you, it's tough enough controlling our own illegal slaughter of animals."

"I see. Then have you, as a licensed hunter, been involved in manhunts?"

"Oh, yes, many times."

Arriving at the hospital, WT, together with a police escort in civilian clothes, took the elevator to the third floor where they got off and used the stairs for three more floors to the maternity ward. Inspector Howard was awake and alert as WT entered the room.

"I beg your Pardon Ma'am." He said to the lady in bed.

"Don't be tiresome ol' boy. Do come in."

Expecting help from the U.S., the inspector was given only a name, without rank, so when WT introduced himself as DAVID DENNIS DANIELS, the Inspector said,

"Good show. We've been expecting you." WT looked around the colorful room and then back at the inspector in time to see him pulling off his wig,

"All a very clever ruse…" he said, "…but I must say I feel rather silly in this get-up. These things are beastly hot, like wearing a hat indoors. I couldn't talk business with a straight face wearing it. And please, do try to keep your eyes off my finger nails, if you don't mind, ole boy."

WT smiled at the affable inspector and for a moment concentrated on what he knew of the Inspector's distinguished war record in order to overcome what he was seeing among the bowers of flowers. He composed himself and cleared his throat,

"Sir, has there been a second attempt on your life?"

"No, why do you ask?"

"Has anything out of the ordinary happened since your hospitalization?"

"Since you put it that way, yes, we were all saddened by the passing of Sergeant Cooper while standing guard at my official room downstairs. He collapsed suddenly. Even with medical personnel readily available, efforts to revive him failed; he was dead."

"Did anyone see him stricken?"

"No, he was discovered on the floor outside the room by our undercover man returning from the nurse's station."

'Was anyone else in the room?"

"No, only Rupert."

"Rupert?"

Yes, a mannequin in the bed, taking my place. We named him after dummy parachutists we used on D-day—very realistic."

"Was the cause of death determined?"

'Yes, cardiac arrest."

"Sir, I'm certain his death was a part of a second attempt."

"What make you say that?"

"Our man's favorite weapon is a highly concentrated lethal gas discharged from a cigarette lighter. It leaves no trace and causes cardiac arrest. If in his haste he took Rupert to be you, he might think you are dead also."

"He might have, because, as I recall the investigation, the room was dark with only the light from the doorway, the face of the dummy was turned toward the wall."

"Sir, I have a plan that will need your help. I'm sure it will work."

"Your last plan worked; pity it was the wrong man."

"Tell me sir, did you lose a man or was it just for the papers?"

"Just part of the cover. The only real bullets were discharged by your chaps."

WT paused a moment to gather his thoughts and began to outline his plan,

"We must assume he recognized the dummy for what it was, so we should keep the security arrangements here." He produced the ID photo of KRAIT. "This is our man. We must make it so hot for him here that he'll be forced to flee the country. If we run his picture on the front page of every newspaper and on TV as the man wanted in connection with your shooting and your police dragnet is stepped up to a feverish pitch, we can force his flight. I want to seal off this country; roads, harbors, airports. We'll leave him only one way out—the bush. During the dry season, traveling in the bush can be fatal. A number of disasters could befall him without Soviet suspicion. My team is prepared to follow him into the back country to supervise his *accident* and keep your government clear of any diplomatic entanglements."

"I think we can see to it you have the opportunity. I'll alert all the safari guides."

"We'll need to *doctor* a couple of Land Rovers: they'll need faulty gas gauges showing full when they are only one-third full. We want them to go deep into the bush, but we don't want them getting away. The contents of the extra water and gas cans should be unusable. It's important that all guides, should they be approached, send the business to the guide with the prepared Rovers. Once in our element, we want him on foot. I'll also need a private light aircraft which will be piloted by one of my men."

The next day KRAIT's picture flooded the media nationwide. Police activity was very high profile and foreign passports were being checked carefully. Copies of the photo were distributed to police and customs officials. Safari guides were briefed, given photos and told only to report, but not to attempt apprehension. Checkpoints were established at all streets leading to the Soviet Embassy to prevent his seeking refuge and claiming diplomatic immunity. KRAIT was on his own, where normally he preferred to be. Now it was time for anxious waiting, hoping he would stay within the carefully-composed scenario.

WILLIAM TELL breathed a sigh of relief at the report that two separate occasions KRAIT had narrowly escaped capture by zealous police following up tips from concerned citizens. If the police were told not to attempt capture, KRAIT might spot the hook sticking out of the bait. Two days of intense activity had produced no results, and WT became concerned. Twice a day he visited Inspector Howard for updates. The inspector had turned his hospital room into a command center, receiving hourly reports from all precincts. As WT entered his room for the first time this day, he was handed a report.

"Your scheme worked ole boy; we've forced him into the bush. He's in a spot of bother now—good show! That report says our friend and two of his comrades rented the Rover and provisions and headed into the interior, just as you hoped he would. KRAIT said he didn't need a guide, and knowing the situation, our guide was happy to break the rule and stay behind."

"Yes, be sure to commend your people for all their hard work; our snake has backed into a hole." Immediately he phoned 38 and ordered him into the air. Turning to Inspector Howard he said,

"We are ready to leave immediately."

"Good hunting, whatever your name is. I've rather fancied your company, Yank."

WILLIAM TELL knew better than to underestimate KRAIT so, looking ahead, once they made contact he'd keep his distance and pick his time to strike. Eventually, KRAIT and his comrades would be forced to abandon the Rover and proceed on foot. There was always the chance KRAIT had arranged a pick-up by aircraft, but WT doubted he'd had time to coordinate it. If he was to be picked up, WT's only hope was that KRAIT would run out of gas before he reach the designated point. He expected to find the Rover on the vast plain which, was thinly spotted with single, widely-scattered trees, and would easily accommodate a plane, landing anywhere. There were no paved roads out here and wild animals abounded; lions and lesser cats, antelope, zebra, wildebeest and elephant. As they drove slowly to keep their dust to a minimum, WT was in radio contact with 38, high above. Spread-eagled on the canvas top was 24, an excellent tracker, watching the trail ahead. There had been no rain and little wind, so the tire tracks of the comrade's Rover were still fresh. If the calculated rate of speed was correct, their quarry's dust cloud should soon be visible from higher ground. The first to see it should be 38 now flying directly overhead. As if in perfect sync with WT's thought the transmission from 38 came over loud and clear:

"TALLYHO! DUST CLOUD, COMPASS HEADING 265 DEGREES."

Pulling up to a rugged rock outcropping, WT climbed to the top and searched the horizon with high-powered binoculars, a section at a time, until he spotted the telltale dust plume. They were closing in on KRAIT at long last, and WT could feel an adrenaline rush he'd have to control to keep command of the situation. He pushed on to the next higher ground, a mile or so ahead for a better look. Avoiding a direct over flight of KRAIT, 38 reported they were still on the move in late afternoon, and generally on the same course. WT concluded they were headed for the border to affect their escape from inside Balabi, where insurgents were operating, although with little success, thanks to earlier work by Task Team VICEROY. WT knew KRAIT wouldn't make it, but it was slightly troublesome that he was overdue to run out of gas. The sooner he was on foot the better—it was getting late.

A short time later he saw it: the abandoned Rover. WT again searched ahead through his binoculars until he saw the three men on the march, each with a backpack, a canteen and a side arm. He saw no rifle, but assumed they still had the breakdown rifles in their packs; he could not conceive of anyone travelling in this country without one. At this time of the year, in the intense heat, water holes and streams were scarce and highly contested by predator and prey alike. It would be dangerous to approach them. Progress was slow, but so far, the pursued were not aware of their pursuers, and to keep it that way WT maintained his distance just keeping them in sight.

Nearing dusk, WT closed the range enough to be able to observe them through the starlight scope once it was dark. He wasn't sure they'd chance a fire unless threatened by predators. As the last filtered light from the west faded into darkness, the three began to set up camp for the night. He continued to watch the three eerie green and grainy images though the scope as they built a small fire and ate from their provisions. Then WT switched to binoculars powerful enough to see the color of their eyes.

A stoop-shouldered old man sat staring into the flames as two younger men gathered fuel to keep the fire going. He removed his hat and patted the perspiration from his forehead and the back of his neck; then wiping the sweatband, he put his hat back on. Standing up, he stood hunched over like a question mark and walked toward his bedroll, haltingly, with the aid of a staff.

The second man dropped a heavy load of firewood near the blaze. He was rugged in build and features, with a moustache and beard cropped close around his mouth and chin. By gesture and bearing he had an aristocratic air about him. He appeared to be ordering the third man to tend the fire, at which gesture the man responded instantly, as a soldier responding to an order.

This third man wore a broad rimmed safari hat worn low so as to obscure his features, and appeared to act in an almost subservient manner, downcast and fearful. None of the three resembled the ID photo. A moment of serious concern struck WT when he could not select KRAIT from the three. He handed the glasses to 24 and considered the possibilities. Was this a decoy party? Was KRAIT escaping by a different route? Had he been picked up by aircraft? Had he doubled back alone? Was he still hiding in Komendhabi? If it were none of these, he must have altered his appearance. If he had, which one of the three was he? He snatched the glasses from 24 and looked carefully at each of the three men to determine which might be disguised. Then he deduced that KRAIT, alerted to his trackers when his Rover ran out of fuel, must have realized this was a trap. Since he was positively identified by his provisioner, this was the only plausible explanation. It only remained to determine which man was KRAIT.

After adding more wood to the blaze, the three settled in for the night and WT and 24 spell each other watching the camp. Curiously, after a couple of hours, the old man struggled to his feet and added more wood to the fire. It flared up, illuminating the entire campsite. WT watched in astonishment as the old man moved to his two sleeping comrades and passed his hand close to and over their faces. He then returned to his bedroll and began packing up to continue the trek, but his two companions were still and did not move. WT took the binoculars and watched, by dawn's light, as the old man slowly scanned the horizon full circle with binoculars, and then, satisfied no one was near, brought himself fully erect, cast aside his staff and lit a cigarette. Then, moving to his companions, he removed their lifeless bodies from their bedrolls. KRAIT had taken out survival insurance; extra water, but the premium was high: the lives of his two comrades, gassed as they slept. He slung the three canteens over his shoulder and walked away leaving the bodies to the scavengers.

The pursuers continued to keep their quarry in sight until, in late morning he approached a cluster of trees and thick brush. WT thought for a moment he saw something, but shifted his glasses back to KRAIT who continued to walk close to, but passed the thicket. Then WT saw it, a motionless shadowy form standing in the high brush. KRAIT continued to walk, the great dark form showed itself, emerging to follow KRAIT. Sensing the ground shaking, KRAIT turned to face his most formidable opponent, on whom his gadgets for killing humans were useless. His horror-filled eyes gazed upon a great rogue bull elephant, large ears extended and trunk rising between two enormous tusks as he trumpeted angrily. The huge beast held no fear of KRAIT's reputation, its raw strength able to overpower every living creature in nature. The rogue charged and KRAIT dodged to his left to escape the massive bulk, but was tripped and flipped to the ground by the end of one long tusk. As the giant bull ran by, KRAIT picked himself up and ran in terror toward a nearby tree, stopped when the great rogue stepped on his leg, fracturing it in several places. Scooping the horrified and screaming KRAIT off the ground with its great tusks, the bull whirled its massive head, hurling its victim high into the air, from where he fell into the branches of the very tree in which he had sought refuge. As if obeying a trainer's command, the great elephant approached the tree, rose on its hind legs, secured KRAIT between its trunk and tusks and pulled him off the tree, then turned and once again tossed the screaming wretch into the air. WT watched, as KRAIT hit the ground on top of his fractured leg, seeing the sharply broken bone ends ripping through his trousers in two places as the leg buckled beneath him. Unbelievably, the still-conscious KRAIT attempted to drag himself from the path of the raging bull, but, as if tiring of the game, the great beast stopped short, and with one last trumpet blast fell forward with both front legs falling like pile drivers, crushing KRAIT's hips and rib cage. Its work done, the great beast left the scene with a snort and continued on its solitary way.

Incredibly, KRAIT was still hanging on to life when WT reached him, his mangled body lying in a grotesque position, face up. WT touched the face of evil and found it to be heavy with make-up, the deception, and marveled at the analogy; that evil and deception are brothers under the skin. KRAIT opened his eyes and saw through the haze of death's curtain WILLIAM TELL kneeling over him. Sensing this was the man who had driven him to his fate, he managed to croak through the blood that was strangling him, "Who are you?" WT saw no point in denying the truth to the dying KRAIT and calmly answered,

"I am your misfortune. Bowman's the name."

He searched the body for the "killing lighter," but it was nowhere to be found, probably dropped during the struggle with the rogue bull.

The devil's disciple was dead, pounded into the dust by a force beyond his control. One might think WT was cheated out of his revenge, but the nature of the incident brought to mind once more the words from scripture, familiar even to the agnostic, and he knew that vengeance was not his, but belonged to the Almighty.

* * *

I sat in stunned silence until General Betancourt noticed the flashing of a red light on the table, said,

"Scoop, I hate to leave you hanging again, but I can tell you now, if you haven't guessed already, that most of these interruptions in Bowman's story have been caused by calls from CLIMBER which require me to set up the conference room for a MOPS briefing"

"But how did Bill win his second CMH?" I protested.

"Ah, yes. You must remind me to fill you in on that next time."

"Remind you? You must be pulling my leg. My feeling is you enjoy telling of Bowman's adventures as much as I am listening to them. Remind you, indeed." I pushed my notepad toward the General, which he took for safekeeping, and rising from my chair I elevated my index finger and promised in the immortal words of the General of the Army, Douglas MacArthur, *I shall return.*

"Somehow, Scoop, I know you will. You see, quite aside from your professional curiosity, there are other reasons you'll be back."

"And what are they, Court?"

"First, EVEREST has authorized me to announce to you your appointment as MOPS official historian. We'll have much to talk about in future sessions. You'll have a lot of catching up to do, Scoop, because when the story of MOPS can be told, you will tell it."

"Thanks, Court. You know, as strange as this may sound, I'm going to miss KRAIT."

"You will, huh?'

"Yes, he was the perfect subject for my style of personalized history. Was there another reason I'd be back?"

"Indeed, I have a moment longer to give you a brief glimpse ahead in our story. Sit down for a minute."

CHAPTER 13

THE DECEPTION

KRAIT, ever the master of survival, lay deathly still knowing the searing sun burning his partially stripped body could kill him if he didn't cover himself soon. He dared not move a muscle until his hunters were well clear of the area, but he had no way of knowing where they were. The scavengers were on the wing circling overhead and drawing more company as they did. He heard the heavy beat of wings nearby as, one by one, the vultures landed. With this activity, could the lions be far away? The sound of hyenas calling in the distance sent a chill through his sun-baked body.

Almost hour had elapsed since his trackers passed his campsite following the wrong man. His patience could assure his escape from human predators but the longer he waited, the greater the threat from animal scavengers arriving on the scene in sufficient numbers now to overpower him. He decided to chance it, hoping he wasn't being watched, but changed his mind momentarily as he detected an aircraft in the near vicinity. When the drone of the engine could no longer be heard, he looked to his left; his bearded comrade lay dead and would occupy the jackals and vultures closing in while he made good his escape. He sat up slowly looking around; no one in sight. He got to his feet in a crouch and searched the area with eyes weakened by the ravages of the scorching equatorial sun; much longer and he could have lost his eyesight permanently. Still, he saw no one; he was alone on the plain, except for his unknown pursuers, who had been duped into following a decoy, permitting him to escape the chase.

He reflected with more than a little satisfaction upon how well his trickery had deceived his stalkers. He could only imagine their frustration when they discovered the imposter, and that he, KRAIT, had slipped away once again. He dressed and secured his equipment, thinking all the time how his bit of theater had fooled his trackers, and how his decoy had performed well considering he didn't why he was to pass his hand over their faces in the middle of the night, nor did he know that one of them was already dead, murdered beneath his nose. Yes, his little charade worked to perfection even to the heavy make-up on the face of the decoy which convinced his pursuers they had the right man.

WT inadvertently completed KRAIT's plan by permitting nature to dispose of the bodies so that the entire incident appeared accidental. He and 24 watched from a distance as scavengers made short work of what they were certain was KRAIT's crushed remains, now being torn asunder and carried away in all directions by hyenas and wild dogs.

Nauseated, he directed 24 to drive him back to KRAIT's campsite. As they passed near the scene, the remains of what they thought were too men were obscured by a pride of lions feasting, having driven off the early arrivals. WT was glad OPERATION SNARE had come to a successful end, and radioed his friend, 38, flying cover for the second day: MISSION ACCOMPLISHED—WELL DONE.

Acknowledging instruction to return to Komendhabi, 38 set his course for home, but soon observed a figure on foot below, staggering in the blazing sun. Stalking him, not far behind, were three lions. Banking sharply 38 buzzed the lions which made them scatter. He radioed WILLIAM TELL for permission to let down and lend assistance, which was granted.

A few minutes later WT saw 38 flying in a wide circle. Attempting to raise 38 on the radio, he got no reply—until he heard the microphone key click on, followed by a sinister chuckle and then what sounded like maniacal laughter, on and on, as the plane kept circling. Alarmed, he raced his Rover to the spot where the plane set down. As he approached, he could see 38 lying motionless on the ground. Skidding to a stop he flew from the Rover and ran to the prostrate body of his old friend. Already imagining what happened he looked forlornly at his dead friend and cried,

"Oh Sergeant!" Then in the next moment, WILLIAM TELL looked skyward and gave vent to his rage, shouting at the top of his lungs, startling the predators within earshot,

"KRAAAIT!"

KRAIT continued to circle the area laughing, as if executing a victory roll, when suddenly, the plane disintegrated in a fiery explosion. Taking a simple precaution, 38 had placed a chemical time fuse in a block of plastic explosive and left it under the seat, *just in case.*

"Quite a bang, huh? Ugh, what a headache."

"Billy, I...I thought you'd had it."

"Just a minute, let me get these filters out of my nose. I wore them *just in case,* so when his gadget didn't work I pretended it did and collapsed striking my head on a rock. I guess I was out for a few minutes until I heard you yell. I hope the Chief

Inspector won't mind when we tell him we've misplaced his airplane."

The two knelt in prayer thanking God for their lives and a successful conclusion to OPERATION SNARE—mission accomplished.

In the words of Winston Churchill after the desert victory: "This is not the end, nor the beginning of the end, but it is perhaps, the end of the beginning."

CPSIA information can be obtained at www.ICGtesting.com
Printed in the USA
BVOW071541050313

314770BV00002B/4/P